MUTANT

Then something utterly hateful and cold and deadly quivered silently in the air, like an icicle jaggedly smashing through golden, fragile glass. Burkhalter dropped his napkin and looked up, profoundly shocked. He felt Ethel's thought shrink back, and swiftly reached out to touch and reassure her with mental contact. But across the table the little boy, cheeks still round with the fat of babyhood, sat silent and wary, realizing he had blundered, and seeking safety in complete immobility. His mind was too weak to resist probing, he knew, and he remained perfectly still, waiting, while the echoes of a thought hung poisonously in silence.

*Also by Henry Kuttner
in Hamlyn Paperbacks*
FURY

MUTANT

Henry Kuttner

MUTANT
ISBN 0 600 36320 1

First published in Great Britain
by Weidenfeld & Nicolson Ltd
Hamlyn Paperbacks edition 1979

Copyright © Henry Kuttner 1953

Hamlyn Paperbacks are published by
The Hamlyn Publishing Group Ltd,
Astronaut House,
Feltham,
Middlesex, England

Made and printed in Great Britain by
Hazell Watson & Viney Ltd, Aylesbury, Bucks

This book is sold subject to the condition that it shall
not, by way of trade or otherwise, be lent, re-sold,
hired out, or otherwise circulated without the publisher's prior consent in any form of binding or cover
other than that in which it is published and without
a similar condition including this condition being
imposed on the subsequent purchaser.

CONTENTS

Chapter One
The Piper's Son 1

Chapter Two
Three Blind Mice 33

Chapter Three
The Lion and the Unicorn 73

Chapter Four
Beggars in Velvet 115

Chapter Five
Humpty Dumpty 167

Chapter Six 214

CHAPTER 1

Somehow I had to stay alive until they found me. They would be hunting for the wreck of my plane, and eventually they'd find it, and then they'd find me, too. But it was hard to wait.

Empty blue day stretched over the white peaks; then the blazing night you get at this altitude, and that was empty too. There was no sound or sight of a jet plane or a helicopter. I was completely alone.

That was the real trouble.

A few hundred years ago, when there were no telepaths, men were used to being alone. But I couldn't remember a time when I'd been locked in the bony prison of my skull, utterly and absolutely cut off from all other men. Deafness or blindness wouldn't have mattered as much. They wouldn't have mattered at all, to a telepath.

Since my plane crashed behind the barrier of mountain peaks, I had been amputated from my species. And there is something in the constant communication of minds that keeps a man alive. An amputated limb dies for lack of oxygen. I was dying for lack of . . . there's never been any word to express what it is that makes all telepaths one. But without it, a man is alone, and men do not live long, alone.

I listened, with the part of the mind that listens for the soundless voices of other minds. I heard the hollow wind. I saw snow lifting in feathery, pouring ruffles. I saw the blue shadows deepening. I looked up, and the eastern peak was scarlet. It was sunset, and I was alone.

I reached out, listening, while the sky darkened. A star wavered, glimmered, and stood steadily overhead. Other stars came, while the air grew colder, until the sky blazed with their westward march.

Now it was dark. In the darkness, there were the stars, and there was I. I lay back, not even listening. My people were gone.

I watched the emptiness beyond the stars.

Nothing around me or above me was alive. Why should I be alive, after all? It would be easy, very easy, to sink down into that quiet where there was no loneliness, because there was no life. I reached out around me, and my mind found no other thinking mind. I reached back into my memory, and that was a little better.

A telepath's memories go back a long way. A good long way, far earlier than his birth.

I can see clearly nearly two hundred years into the past, before the sharp, clear telepathically-transmitted memories begin to fray and fade into secondary memories, drawn from books. Books go back to Egypt and Babylon. But they are not the primary memories, complete with sensory overtones, which an old man gives telepathically to a young one, and which are passed on in turn through the generations. Our biographies are not written in books. They are written in our minds and memories, especially the Key Lives which are handed down as fresh as they were once lived by our greatest leaders. . . .

But they are dead, and I am alone.

No. Not quite alone. The memories remain, Burkhalter and Barton, McNey and Linc Cody and Jeff Cody – a long time dead, but still vibrantly alive in my memory. I can summon up every thought, every emotion, the musty smell of grass – where? – the yielding of a rubbery walk beneath hurrying feet – whose?

It would be so easy to relax and die.

No. Wait. Watch. They're alive, Burkhalter and Barton, the Key Lives are still real, though the men who once lived them have died. They are your people. You're not alone.

Burkhalter and Barton, McNey and Linc and Jeff aren't dead. Remember them. You lived their lives telepathically as you learned them, the way they once lived them, and you can live them again. *You are not alone*

So watch. Start the film unreeling. Then you won't be alone at all, you'll be Ed Burkhalter, two hundred years ago, feeling the cool wind blow against your face from the Sierra peaks, smelling the timothy grass, reaching out mentally to glance into the mind of your son . . . *the piper's son* . . .

It began.

I was Ed Burkhalter.

It was two hundred years ago –

THE PIPER'S SON

The Green Man was climbing the glass mountains, and hairy, gnomish faces peered at him from crevices. This was only another step in the Green Man's endless, exciting odyssey. He'd had a great many adventures already – in the Flame Country, among the Dimension Changers, with the City Apes who sneered endlessly while their blunt, clumsy fingers fumbled at death-rays. The trolls, however, were masters of magic, and were trying to stop the Green Man with spells. Little whirlwinds of force spun underfoot, trying to trip the Green Man, a figure of marvellous muscular development, handsome as a god, and hairless from head to foot, glistening pale green. The whirlwinds formed a fascinating pattern. If you could thread a precarious path among them – avoiding the pale yellow ones especially – you could get through.

And the hairy gnomes watched malignantly, jealously, from their crannies in the glass crags.

Al Burkhalter, having recently achieved the mature status of eight full years, lounged under a tree and masticated a grass blade. He was so immersed in his daydreams that his father had to nudge his side gently to bring comprehension into the half-closed eyes. It was a good day for dreaming, anyway

– a hot sun and a cool wind blowing down from the white Sierra peaks to the east. Timothy grass sent its faintly musty fragrance along the channels of air, and Ed Burkhalter was glad that his son was second-generation since the Blow-up. He himself had been born ten years after the last bomb had been dropped, but second-hand memories can be pretty bad too.

'Hello, Al,' he said, and the youth vouchsafed a half-lidded glance of tolerant acceptance.

'Hi, Dad.'

'Want to come downtown with me?'

'Nope,' Al said, relaxing instantly into his stupor.

Burkhalter raised a figurative eyebrow and half turned. On an impulse, then, he did something he rarely did without the tacit permission of the other party; he used his telepathic power to reach into Al's mind. There was, he admitted to himself, a certain hesitancy, a subconscious unwillingness on his part, to do this, even though Al had pretty well out-grown the nasty, inhuman formlessness of mental babyhood. There had been a time when Al's mind had been quite shocking in its alienage. Burkhalter remembered a few abortive experiments he had made before Al's birth; few fathers-to-be could resist the temptation to experiment with embryonic brains, and that had brought back nightmares Burkhalter had not had since his youth. There had been enormous rolling masses, and an appalling vastness, and other things. Pre-natal memories were ticklish, and should be left to qualified mnemonic psychologists.

But now Al was maturing, and daydreaming, as usual, in bright colours. Burkhalter, reassured, felt that he had fulfilled his duty as a monitor and left his son still eating grass and ruminating.

Just the same there was a sudden softness inside of him, and the aching, futile pity he was apt to feel for helpless things that were as yet unqualified for conflict with that extraordinarily complicated business of living. Conflict, competition, had not died out when war abolished itself; the business of adjustment even to one's surroundings was a conflict, and conversation a duel. With Al, too, there was a double problem. Yes, language was in effect a tariff wall, and a Baldy could appreciate that thoroughly, since the wall didn't exist between Baldies.

Walking down the rubbery walk that led to town centre, Burkhalter grinned wryly and ran lean fingers through his well-kept wig. Strangers were very often surprised to know that he was a Baldy, a telepath. They looked at him with wondering eyes, too courteous to ask how it felt to be a freak, but obviously avid. Burkhalter, who knew diplomacy, would be quite willing to lead the conversation.

'My folks lived near Chicago after the Blow-up. That was why.'

'Oh.' Stare. 'I'd heard that was why so many—' Startled pause.

'Freaks or mutations. There were both. I still don't know which class I belong to,' he'd add disarmingly.

'You're no freak!' They did protest too much.

'Well, some mighty queer specimens came out of the radioactive-affected areas around the bomb-targets. Funny things happened to the germ plasm. Most of 'em died out; they couldn't reproduce; but you'll still find a few creatures in sanitoriums – two heads, you know. And so on.'

Nevertheless they were always ill-at-ease. 'You mean you can read my mind – now?'

'I could, but I'm not. It's hard work, except with another telepath. And we Baldies – well, we don't, that's all.' A man with abnormal muscle development wouldn't go around knocking people down. Not unless he wanted to be mobbed. Baldies were always sneakingly conscious of a hidden peril: lynch law. And wise Baldies didn't even imply that they had an . . . extra sense. They just said they were different, and let it go at that.

But one question was always implied, though not always mentioned. 'If I were a telepath, I'd . . . how much do you make a year?'

They were surprised at the answer. A mind-reader certainly could make a fortune, if he wanted to. So why did Ed Burkhalter stay a semantics expert in Modoc Publishing Town, when a trip to one of the science towns would enable him to get hold of secrets that would get him a fortune?

There was a good reason. Self-preservation was a part of it. For which reason Burkhalter, and many like him, wore toupees. Though there were many Baldies who did not.

Modoc was a twin town with Pueblo, across the mountain barrier south of the waste that had been Denver. Pueblo held the presses, photo-linotypes, and the machines that turned scripts into books, after Modoc had delt with them. There was a helicopter distribution fleet at Pueblo, and for the last week Oldfield, the manager, had been demanding the manuscript of 'Psycho-history', turned out by a New Yale man who had got tremendously involved in past emotional problems, to the detriment of literary clarity. The truth was that he distrusted Burkhalter. And Burkhalter, neither a priest nor a psychologist, had to become both without admitting it to the confused author of 'Psycho-history'.

The sprawling buildings of the publishing house lay ahead and below, more like a resort than anything more utilitarian. That had been necessary. Authors were peculiar people, and often it was necessary to induce them to take hydrotherapic treatment before they were in shape to work out their books with the semantic experts. Nobody was going to bite them, but they didn't realize that, and either cowered in corners, terrified, or else blustered their way around, using language few could understand. Jem Quayle, author of 'Psycho-history', fitted into neither group; he was simply baffled by the intensity of his own research. His personal history had qualified him too well for emotional involvements with the past – and that was a serious matter when a thesis of this particular type was in progress.

Dr. Moon, who was on the Board, sat near the south entrance, eating an apple which he peeled carefully with his silver-hilted dagger. Moon was fat, short, and shapeless; he didn't have much hair, but he wasn't a telepath; Baldies were entirely hairless. He gulped and waved at Burkhalter.

'Ed ... *urp* ... want to talk to you.'

'Sure,' Burkhalter said agreeably, coming to a standstill and rocking on his heels. Ingrained habit made him sit down beside the Boardman; Baldies, for obvious reasons, never stood up when non-telepaths were sitting. Their eyes met now on the same level. Burkhalter said, 'What's up?'

'The store got some Shasta apples flown in yesterday. Better tell Ethel to get some before they're sold out. Here.' Moon watched his companion eat a chunk, and nod.

'Good. I'll have her get some. The copter's laid up for today, though; Ethel pulled the wrong gadget.'

'Foolproof,' Moon said bitterly. 'Huron's turning out some sweet models these days; I'm getting my new one from Michigan. Listen, Pueblo called me this morning on Quayle's book.'

'Oldfield?'

'Our boy,' Moon nodded. 'He says can't you send over even a few chapters.'

Burkhalter shook his head. 'I don't think so. There are some abstracts right in the beginning that just have to be clarified, and Quayle is—' He hesitated.

'What?'

Burkhalter thought about the Oedipus complex he'd uncovered in Quayle's mind, but that was sacrosanct, even though it kept Quayle from interpreting Darius with cold logic. 'He's got muddy thinking in there. I can't pass it; I tried it on three readers yesterday, and got different reactions from all of them. So far 'Psycho-history' is all things to all men. The critics would lambaste us if we released the book as is. Can't you string Oldfield along for a while longer?'

'Maybe,' Moon said doubtfully. 'I've got a subjective novella I could rush over. It's light vicarious eroticism, and that's harmless; besides, it's semantically O.K.'d. We've been holding it up for an artist, but I can put Duman on it. I'll do that, yeah. I'll shoot the script over to Pueblo and he can make the plates later. A merry life we lead, Ed.'

'A little too merry sometimes,' Burkhalter said. He got up, nodded, and went in search of Quayle, who was relaxing on one of the sun decks.

Quayle was a thin, tall man with a worried face and the abstract air of an unshelled tortoise. He lay on his flexiglass couch, direct sunlight toasting him from above, while the reflected rays sneaked up on him from below, through the transparent crystal. Burkhalter pulled off his shirt and dropped on a sunner beside Quayle. The author glanced at Burkhalter's hairless chest and half-formed revulsion rose in him: *A Baldy . . . no privacy . . . none of his business . . . fake eyebrows and lashes; he's still a—*

Something ugly, at that point.

Diplomatically Burkhalter touched a button, and on a screen overhead a page of 'Psycho-history' appeared, enlarged and easily readable. Quayle scanned the sheet. It had code notations on it, made by the readers, recognized by Burkhalter as varied reactions to what should have been straightline explanations. If three readers had got three different meanings out of that paragraph – well, what *did* Quayle mean? He reached delicately into the mind, conscious of useless guards erected against intrusion, mud barricades over which his mental eye stole like a searching, quiet wind. No ordinary man could guard his mind against a Baldy. But Baldies could guard their privacy against intrusion by other telepaths – adults, that is. There was a psychic selector band, a—

Here it came. But muddled a bit. *Darius*: that wasn't simply a word; it wasn't a picture, either; it was really a second *life*. But scattered, fragmentary. Scraps of scent and sound, and memories, and emotional reactions. Admiration and hatred. A burning impotence. A black tornado, smelling of pine, roaring across a man of Europe and Asia. Pine scent stronger now, and horrible humiliation, and remembered pain . . . eyes . . . *Get out!*

Burkhalter put down the dictograph mouthpiece and lay looking up through the darkened eye-shells he had donned. 'I got out as soon as you wanted me to,' he said. 'I'm still out.'

Quayle lay there, breathing hard. 'Thanks,' he said. 'Apologies. Why you don't ask a duello—'

'I don't want to duel with you,' Burkhalter said. 'I've never put blood on my dagger in my life. Besides, I can see your side of it. Remember, this is my job, Mr. Quayle, and I've learned a lot of things – that I've forgotten again.'

'It's intrusion, I suppose. I tell myself that it doesn't matter, but my privacy – is important.'

Burkhalter said patiently, 'We can keep trying it from different angles until we find one that isn't too private. Suppose, for example, I asked you if you admired Darius.'

Admiration . . . and pine scent . . . and Burkhalter said quickly, 'I'm out. O.K.?'

'Thanks,' Quayle muttered. He turned on his side, away from the other man. After a moment he said, 'That's silly – turning over, I mean. You don't have to see my face to know what I'm thinking.'

'You have to put out the welcome mat before I walk in,' Burkhalter told him.

'I guess I believe that. I've met some Baldies, though, that were . . . that I didn't like.'

'There's a lot on that order, sure. I know the type. The ones who don't wear wigs.'

Quayle said, 'They'll read your mind and embarrass you just for the fun of it. They ought to be – taught better.'

Burkhalter blinked in the sunlight. 'Well, Mr. Quayle, it's this way. A Baldy's got his problems, too. He's got to orient himself to a world that isn't telepathic; and I suppose a lot of Baldies rather feel that they're letting their specialization go to waste. There *are* jobs a man like me is suited for—'

'*Man!*' He caught the scrap of thought from Quayle. He ignored it, his face as always a mobile mask, and went on.

'Semantics have always been a problem, even in countries speaking only one tongue. A qualified Baldy is a swell interpreter. And, though there aren't any Baldies on the detective forces, they often work with the police. It's rather like being a machine that can do only a few things.'

'A few things more than humans can,' Quayle said.

Sure, Burkhalter thought, if we could compete on equal footing with non-telepathic humanity. But would blind men trust one who could see? Would they play poker with him? A sudden, deep bitterness put an unpleasant taste in Burkhalter's mouth. What was the answer? Reservations for Baldies? Isolation? And would a nation of blind men trust those with vision enough for that? Or would they be dusted off – the sure cure, the check-and-balance system that made war an impossibility.

He remembered when Red Bank had been dusted off, and maybe that had been justified. The town was getting too big for its boots, and personal dignity was a vital factor; you weren't willing to lose face as long as a dagger swung at your belt. Similarly, the thousands upon thousands of little towns that covered America, each with its peculiar speciality – helicopter manufacture for Huron and Michigan, vegetable farming for Conoy and Diego, textiles and education and art and machines – each little town had a wary eye on all the others. The science and research centres were a little larger; nobody objected to that, for technicians never made war except under pressure; but few of the towns held more than a few hundred families. It was check-and-balance in most efficient degree; whenever a town showed signs of wanting to become a city – thence, a capital, thence, an imperialistic empire – it was dusted off. Though that had not happened for a long while. And Red Bank might have been a mistake.

Geopolitically it was a fine set-up; sociologically it was acceptable, but brought necessary changes. There was subconscious swashbuckling. The rights of the individual had become more highly regarded as decentralization took place. And men learned.

They learned a monetary system based primarily upon barter. They learned to fly; nobody drove surface cars. They learned new things, but they did not forget the Blow-up, and in secret places near every town were hidden the bombs that could utterly and fantastically exterminate a town, as such bombs had exterminated the cities during the Blow-up.

And everybody knew how to make those bombs. They were beautifully, terribly simple. You could find the ingredients anywhere and prepare them easily. Then you could take your helicopter over a town, drop an egg overside – and perform an erasure.

Outside of the wilderness malcontents, the maladjusted people found in every race, nobody kicked. And the roaming tribes never raided and never banded together in large groups – for fear of an erasure.

The artisans were maladjusted too, to some degree, but they weren't anti-social, so they lived where they wanted and painted, wrote, composed, and retreated into their own private worlds. The scientists, equally maladjusted in other lines, retreated to their slightly larger towns, banding together in small universes, and turned out remarkable technical achievements.

And the Baldies – found jobs where they could.

No non-telepath would have viewed the world environment quite as Burkhalter did. He was abnormally conscious of the human element, attaching a deeper, more profound significance to those human values, undoubtedly because he saw men in more than the ordinary dimensions. And also, in a way – and inevitably – he looked at humanity from outside.

Yet he was human. The barrier that telepathy had raised made men suspicious of him, more so than if he had had two heads – then they could have pitied. As it was—

As it was, he adjusted the scanner until new pages of the typescript came flickering into view above. 'Say when,' he told Quayle.

Quayle brushed back his grey hair. 'I feel sensitive all over,' he objected. 'After all, I've been under a considerable strain correlating my material.'

'Well, we can always postpone publication.' Burkhalter threw out the suggestion casually, and was pleased when Quayle didn't nibble. He didn't like to fail, either.

'No. No, I want to get the thing done now.'

'Mental catharsis—'

'Well, by a psychologist, perhaps. But not by—'

'—a Baldy. You know that a lot of psychologists have Baldy helpers. They get good results, too.'

Quayle turned on the tobacco smoke, inhaling slowly. 'I suppose . . . I've not had much contact with Baldies. Or too much – without selectivity. I saw some in an asylum once. I'm not being offensive, am I?'

'No,' Burkhalter said. 'Every mutation can run too close

to the line. There were lots of failures. The hard radiations brought about one true mutation: hairless telepaths, but they didn't all hew true to the line. The mind's a queer gadget – you know that. It's a colloid balancing, figuratively, on the point of a pin. If there's any flaw, telepathy's apt to bring it out. So you'll find that the Blow-up caused a hell of a lot of insanity. Not only among Baldies, but among the other mutations that developed then. Except that the Baldies are almost always paranoidal.'

'And dementia praecox,' Quayle said, finding relief from his own embarrassment in turning the spotlight on Burkhalter.

'And d. p. Yeah. When a confused mind acquires the telepathic instinct – a hereditary bollixed mind – it can't handle it all. There's disorientation. The paranoia group retreat into their own private worlds, and the d. p.'s simply don't realize that *this* world exists. There are distinctions, but I think that's a valid basis.'

'In a way,' Quayle said, 'it's frightening. I can't think of any historical parallel.'

'No.'

'What do you think the end of it will be?'

'I don't know,' Burkhalter said thoughtfully. 'I think we'll be assimilated. There hasn't been enough time yet. We're specialized in a certain way, and we're useful in certain jobs.'

'If you're satisfied to stay there. The Baldies who won't wear wigs—'

'They're so bad-tempered I expect they'll all be killed off in duels eventually,' Burkhalter smiled. 'No great loss. The rest of us, we're getting what we want – acceptance. We don't have horns or haloes.'

Quayle shook his head. 'I'm glad, I think, that I'm not a telepath. The mind's mysterious enough anyway, without new doors opening. Thanks for letting me talk. I think I've got part of it talked out, anyway. Shall we try the script again?'

'Sure,' Burkhalter said, and again the procession of pages flickered on the screen above them. Quayle did seem less guarded; his thoughts were more lucid, and Burkhalter was able to get at the true meaning of many of the hitherto muddy statements. They worked easily, the telepath dictating rephrasings into his dictograph, and only twice did they have to hurdle emotional tangles. At noon they knocked off, and Burkhalter, with a friendly nod, took the dropper to his office, where he found some calls listed on the visor. He ran off repeats, and a worried look crept into his blue eyes.

He talked with Dr. Moon in a booth at luncheon. The conversation lasted so long that only the induction cups kept the coffee hot, but Burkhalter had more than one problem to discuss. And he'd known Moon for a long time. The fat man was one of the few who were not, he thought, subconsciously repelled by the fact that Burkhalter was a Baldy.

'I've never fought a duel in my life, Doc. I can't afford to.'

'You can't afford not to. You can't turn down the challenge, Ed. It isn't done.'

'But this fellow Reilly – I don't even know him.'

'I know of him,' Moon said. 'He's got a bad temper. Duelled a lot.'

Burkhalter slammed his hand down on the table. 'It's ridiculous. I won't do it!'

'Well,' Moon said practically, 'your wife can't fight him. And if Ethel's been reading Mrs. Reilly's mind and gossiping, Reilly's got a case.'

'Don't you think we know the dangers of that?' Burkhalter asked in a low voice. 'Ethel doesn't go around reading minds any more than I do. It'd be fatal – for us. And for any other Baldy.'

'Not the hairless ones. The ones who won't wear wigs. They—'

'They're fools. And they're giving all the Baldies a bad name. Point one, Ethel doesn't read minds; she didn't read Mrs. Reilly's. Point two, she doesn't gossip.'

'La Reilly is obviously an hysterical type,' Moon said. 'Word got around about this scandal, whatever it was, and Mrs. Reilly remembered she'd seen Ethel lately. She's the type who needs a scapegoat anyway. I rather imagine she let word drop herself, and had to cover up so her husband wouldn't blame her.'

'I'm not going to accept Reilly's challenge,' Burkhalter said doggedly.

'You'll have to.'

'Listen, Doc, maybe—'

'What?'

'Nothing. An idea. It might work. Forget about that; I think I've got the right answer. It's the only one, anyway. I can't afford a duel and that's flat.'

'You're not a coward.'

'There's one thing Baldies are afraid of,' Burkhalter said, 'and that's public opinion. I happen to know I'd kill Reilly. That's the reason why I've never duelled in my life.'

Moon drank coffee. 'Hm-m-m. I think—'

'Don't. There was something else. I'm wondering if I ought to send Al off to a special school.'

'What's wrong with the kid?'

'He's turning out to be a beautiful delinquent. His teacher called me this morning. The play-back was something to hear. He's talking funny and acting funny. Playing nasty tricks on his friends – if he has any left by now.'

'All kids are cruel.'

'Kids don't know what cruelty means. That's why they're cruel; they lack empathy. But Al's getting—' Burkhalter gestured helplessly. 'He's turning into a young tyrant. He doesn't seem to give a care about anything, according to his teacher.'

'That's not too abnormal, so far.'

'That's not the worst. He's become very egotistical. Too much so. I don't want him to turn into one of the wigless Baldies you were mentioning.' Burkhalter didn't mention the other possibility: paranoia, insanity.

'He must pick things up somewhere. At home? Scarcely, Ed. Where else does he go?'

'The usual places. He's got a normal environment.'

'I should think,' Moon said, 'that a Baldy would have unusual opportunities in training a youngster. The mental *rapport* – eh?'

'Yeah. But – I don't know. The trouble is,' Burkhalter said almost inaudibly, 'I wish to God I wasn't different. We didn't ask to be telepaths. Maybe it's all very wonderful in the long run, but I'm one person, and I've got my own microcosm. People who deal in long-term sociology are apt to forget that. They can figure out the answers, but it's every individual man – or Baldy – who's got to fight his own personal battle while he's alive. And it isn't as clear-cut as a battle. It's worse; it's the necessity of watching yourself every second, of fitting yourself into a world that doesn't want you.'

Moon looked uncomfortable. 'Are you being a little sorry for yourself, Ed?'

Burkhalter shook himself. 'I am, Doc. But I'll work it out.'

'We both will,' Moon said, but Burkhalter didn't really expect much help from him. Moon would be willing, but it was horribly difficult for an ordinary man to conceive that a Baldy was – the same. It was the difference that men looked for, and found.

Anyway, he'd have to settle matters before he saw Ethel again. He could easily conceal the knowledge, but she would recognize a mental barrier and wonder. Their marriage had been the more ideal because of the additional *rapport*, something that compensated for an inevitable, half-sensed estrangement from the rest of the world.

'How's "Psycho-history" going?' Moon asked after a while.

'Better than I expected. I've got a new angle on Quayle. If I talk about myself, that seems to draw him out. It gives him enough confidence to let him open his mind to me. We may have those first chapters ready for Oldfield, in spite of everything.'

'Good. Just the same, he can't rush us. If we've got to shoot out books that fast, we might as well go back to the days of semantic confusion. Which we won't!'

'Well,' Burkhalter said, getting up, 'I'll smoosh along. See you.'

'About Reilly—'

'Let it lay.' Burkhalter went out, heading for the address

his visor had listed. He touched the dagger at his belt. Duelling wouldn't do for Baldies, but—

A greeting thought crept into his mind, and, under the arch that led into the campus, he paused to grin at Sam Shane, a New Orleans area Baldy who affected a wig of flaming red. They didn't bother to talk.

Personal question, involving mental, moral and physical wellbeing.

A satisfied glow. And you, Burkhalter? For an instant Burkhalter half-saw what the symbol of his name meant to Shane.

Shadow of trouble.

A warm, willing anxiousness to help. There was a bond between Baldies.

Burkhalter thought: But everywhere I'd go there'd be the same suspicion. We're freaks.

More so elsewhere, Shane thought. There are a lot of us in Modoc Town. People are invariably more suspicious where they're not in daily contact with – Us.

The boy—

I've trouble too, Shane thought. It's worried me. My two girls—

Delinquency?

Yes.

Common denominators?

Don't know. More than one of Us have had the same trouble with our kids.

Secondary characteristic of the mutation? Second generation emergence?

Doubtful, Shane thought, scowling in his mind, shading his concept with a wavering question. We'll think it over later. Must go.

Burkhalter sighed and went on his way. The houses were strung out around the central industry of Modoc, and he cut through a park toward his destination. It was a sprawling curved building, but it wasn't inhabited, so Burkhalter filed Reilly for future reference, and, with a glance at his timer, angled over a hillside toward the school. As he expected, it was recreation time, and he spotted Al lounging under a tree, some distance from his companions, who were involved in a pleasantly murderous game of Blow-up.

He sent his thought ahead.

The Green Man had almost reached the top of the mountain. The hairy gnomes were pelting on his trail, most unfairly shooting sizzling light-streaks at their quarry, but the Green Man was agile enough to dodge. The rocks were leaning—

'Al.'

—inward, pushed by the gnomes, ready to—

'*Al!*' Burkhalter sent his thought with the word, jolting into the boy's mind, a trick he very seldom employed, since youth was practically defenceless against such invasion.

'Hello, Dad,' Al said, undisturbed. 'What's up?'

'A report from your teacher.'

'I didn't do anything.'

'She told me what it was. Listen kid. Don't start getting any funny ideas in your head.'

'I'm not.'

'Do you think a Baldy is better or worse than a non-Baldy?'

Al moved his feet uncomfortably. He didn't answer.

'Well,' Burkhalter said, 'the answer is both and neither. And here's why. A Baldy can communicate mentally, but he lives in a world where most people can't.'

'They're dumb,' Al opined.

'Not so dumb, if they're better suited to their world than you are. You might as well say a frog's better than a fish because he's an amphibian.' Burkhalter briefly amplified and explained the terms telepathically.

'Well . . . oh, I get it, all right.'

'Maybe,' Burkhalter said slowly, 'what you need is a swift kick in the pants. That thought wasn't so hot. What was it again?'

Al tried to hide it, blanking out. Burkhalter began to lift the barrier, an easy matter for him, but stopped. Al regarded his father in a most unfilial way – in fact, as a sort of boneless fish. That had been clear.

'If you're so egotistical,' Burkhalter pointed out, 'maybe you can see it this way. Do you know why there aren't any Baldies in key positions?'

'Sure I do,' Al said unexpectedly. 'They're afraid.'

'Of what, then?'

'The—' That picture had been very curious, a commingling of something vaguely familiar to Burkhalter. 'The non-Baldies.'

'Well, if we took positions where we could take advantage of our telepathic function, non-Baldies would be plenty envious – especially if we were successes. If a Baldy even invented a better mouse-trap plenty of people would say he'd stolen the idea from some non-Baldy's mind. You get the point?'

'Yes, Dad.' But he hadn't. Burkhalter sighed and looked up. He recognized one of Shane's girls on a near-by hillside, sitting alone against a boulder. There were other isolated figures here and there. Far to the east the snowy rampart of the Rockies made an irregular pattern against blue sky.

'Al,' Burkhalter said, 'I don't want you to get a chip on your shoulder. This is a pretty swell world, and the people in it are, on the whole, nice people. There's a law of averages. It isn't sensible for us to get too much wealth or power, because that'd militate against us – and we don't need it anyway. Nobody's poor. We find our work, we do it, and we're reasonably happy. We have some advantages non-Baldies don't have; in marriage, for example. Mental intimacy is quite as important as physical. But I don't want you to feel that being a Baldy makes you a god. It doesn't. I can still,' he added thoughtfully, 'spank it out of you, in case you care to follow out that concept in your mind at the moment.'

Al gulped and beat a hasty retreat. 'I'm sorry. I won't do it again.'

'And keep your hair on too. Don't take your wig off in class. Use the stickum stuff in the bathroom closet.'

'Yes, but... Mr. Venner doesn't wear a wig.'

'Remind me to do some historical research with you on zoot-suiters,' Burkhalter said. 'Mr. Venner's wiglessness is probably his only virtue, if you consider it one.'

'He makes money.'

'Anybody would, in that general store of his. But people don't buy from him if they can help it, you'll notice. That's what I mean by a chip on your shoulder. He's got one. There are Baldies like Venner, Al, but you might, sometime, ask the guy if he's happy. For your information, I am. More than Venner, anyway. Catch?'

'Yes, Dad.' Al seemed submissive, but it was merely that. Burkhalter, still troubled, nodded and walked away. As he passed near the Shane girl's boulder he caught a scrap: – *at the summit of the Glass Mountains, rolling rocks back at the gnomes until—*

He withdrew; it was an unconscious habit, touching minds that were sensitive, but with children it was definitely unfair. With adult Baldies it was simply the instinctive gesture of tipping your hat; one answered or one didn't. The barrier could be erected; there could be a blank-out; or there could be the direct snub of concentration on a single thought, private and not to be intruded on.

A copter with a string of gliders was coming in from the south: a freighter laden with frozen foods from South America, to judge by the markings. Burkhalter made a note to pick up an Argentine steak. He'd got a new recipe he wanted to try out, a charcoal broil with barbecue sauce, a welcome change from the short-wave cooked meats they'd been having for a week. Tomatoes, chile, mm-m – what else? Oh, yes. The duel with Reilly. Burkhalter absently touched his dagger's hilt and made a small, mocking sound in his throat. Perhaps he was innately a pacifist. It was rather difficult to think of a duel seriously, even though everyone else did, when the details of a barbecue dinner were prosaic in his mind.

So it went. The tides of civilization rolled in century-long waves across the continents, and each particular wave, though conscious of its participation in the tide, nevertheless was more preoccupied with dinner. And, unless you happened to be a thousand feet tall, had the brain of a god and a god's life-span, what was the difference? People missed a lot – people like Venner, who was certainly a crank, not batty enough to qualify for the asylum, but certainly a potential paranoid type. The man's refusal to wear a wig labelled him as an individualist, but as an exhibitionist, too. If he didn't feel ashamed of his hairlessness, why should he bother to flaunt it? Besides, the man had a bad temper, and if people kicked him around, he asked for it by starting the kicking himself.

But as for Al, the kid was heading for something approaching delinquency. It couldn't be the normal development of childhood, Burkhalter thought. He didn't pretend to be an expert, but he was still young enough to remember his own formative years, and he had had more handicaps than Al had now; in those days, Baldies had been very new and very freakish. There'd been more than one movement to isolate, sterilize, or even exterminate the mutations.

Burkhalter sighed. If he had been born before the Blow-up, it might have been different. Impossible to say. One could read history, but one couldn't live it. In the future, perhaps, there might be telepathic libraries in which that would be possible. So many opportunities, in fact – and so few that the world was ready to accept as yet. Eventually Baldies would not be regarded as freaks, and by that time real progress would be possible.

But people don't make history – Burkhalter thought. Peoples do that. Not the individual.

He stopped by Reilly's house, and this time the man answered, a burly, freckled, squint-eyed fellow with immense hands and, Burkhalter noted, fine muscular co-ordination. He rested those hands on the Dutch door and nodded.

'Who're you, mister?'

'My name's Burkhalter.'

Comprehension and wariness leaped into Reilly's eyes. 'Oh, I see. You got my call?'

'I did,' Burkhalter said. 'I want to talk to you about it. May I come in?'

'O.K.' He stepped back, opening the way through a hall and into a spacious living-room, where diffused light filtered through glassy mosaic walls. 'Want to set the time?'

'I want to tell you you're wrong.'

'Now wait a minute,' Reilly said, patting the air. 'My wife's out now, but she gave me the straight of it. I don't like this business of sneaking into a man's mind; it's crooked. You should have told *your* wife to mind her business – or keep her tongue quiet.'

Burkhalter said patiently, 'I give you my word, Reilly, that Ethel didn't read your wife's mind.'

'Does she say so?'

'I . . . well, I haven't asked her.'

'Yeah,' Reilly said with an air of triumph.

'I don't need to. I know her well enough. And . . . well, I'm a Baldy myself.'

'I know you are,' Reilly said. 'For all I know, you may be reading my mind now.' He hesitated. 'Get out of my house. I like my privacy. We'll meet at dawn tomorrow, if that's satisfactory with you. Now get out.' He seemed to have something on his mind, some ancient memory, perhaps, that he didn't wish exposed.

Burkhalter nobly resisted the temptation. 'No Baldy would read—'

'Go on, get out!'

'Listen! You wouldn't have a chance in a duel with me!'

'Do you know how many notches I've got?' Reilly asked. 'Ever duelled a Baldy?'

'I'll cut the notch deeper tomorrow. Get out, d'you hear?'

Burkhalter, biting his lips, said, 'Man, don't you realize that in a duel I could read your mind?'

'I don't care . . . what?'

'I'd be half a jump ahead of you. No matter how instinctive your actions would be, you'd know them a split second ahead of time in your mind. And I'd know all your tricks and weaknesses, too. Your technique would be an open book to me. Whatever you thought of—'

'No.' Reilly shook his head. 'Oh, no. You're smart, but it's a phony set-up.'

Burkhalter hesitated, decided, and swung about, pushing a chair out of the way. 'Take out your dagger,' he said.

'Leave the sheath snapped on; I'll show you what I mean.'

Reilly's eyes widened. 'If you want it now—'

'I don't.' Burkhalter shoved another chair away. He unclipped his dagger, sheath and all, from his belt, and made sure the little safety clip was in place. 'We've room enough here. Come on.'

Scowling, Reilly took out his own dagger, held it awkwardly, baffled by the sheath, and then suddenly feinted forward. But Burkhalter wasn't there; he had anticipated, and his own leather sheath slid up Reilly's belly.

'That,' Burkhalter said, 'would have ended the fight.'

For answer Reilly smashed a hard dagger-blow down, curving at the last moment into a throat-cutting slash. Burkhalter's free hand was already at his throat; his other hand, with the sheathed dagger, tapped Reilly twice over the heart. The freckles stood out boldly against the pallor of the larger man's face. But he was not yet ready to concede. He tried a few more passes, clever, well-trained cuts, and they failed, because Burkhalter had anticipated them. His left hand invariably covered the spot where Reilly had aimed, and which he never struck.

Slowly Reilly let his arm fall. He moistened his lips and swallowed. Burkhalter busied himself reclipping his dagger in place.

'Burkhalter,' Reilly said, 'you're a devil.'

'Far from it. I'm just afraid to take a chance. Do you really think being a Baldy is a snap?'

'But, if you can read minds—'

'How long do you think I'd last if I did any duelling? It would be too much of a set-up. Nobody would stand for it, and I'd end up dead. I can't duel, because it'd be murder, and people would know it was murder. I've taken a lot of cracks, swallowed a lot of insults, for just that reason. Now, if you like, I'll swallow another and apologize. I'll admit anything you say. But I can't duel with you, Reilly.'

'No, I can see that. And – I'm glad you came over.' Reilly was still white. 'I'd have walked right into a set-up.'

'Not my set-up,' Burkhalter said. 'I wouldn't have duelled. Baldies aren't so lucky, you know. They've got handicaps – like this. That's why they can't afford to take chances and antagonize people, and why we never read minds unless we're asked to do so.'

'It makes sense. More or less.' Reilly hesitated. 'Look, I withdraw that challenge. O.K.?'

'Thanks,' Burkhalter said, putting out his hand. It was taken rather reluctantly. 'We'll leave it at that, eh?'

'Right.' But Reilly was still anxious to get his guest out of the house.

Burkhalter walked back to the Publishing Centre and whistled tunelessly. He could tell Ethel now; in fact, he had to, for secrets between them would have broken up the completeness of their telepathic intimacy. It was not that their minds lay bare to each other, it was, rather, that any barrier could be sensed by the other, and the perfect *rapport* wouldn't have been so perfect. Curiously, despite this utter intimacy, husband and wife managed to respect one another's privacy.

Ethel might be somewhat distressed, but the trouble had blown over, and, besides, she was a Baldy too. Not that she looked it, with her wig of fluffy chestnut hair and those long, curving lashes. But her parents had lived east of Seattle during the Blow-up, and afterward too, before the hard radiation's effects had been thoroughly studied.

The snow-wind blew down over Modoc and fled southward along the Utah Valley. Burkhalter wished he was in his copter, alone in the blue emptiness of the sky. There was a quiet, strange peace up there that no Baldy ever quite achieved on the earth's surface, except in the depths of a wilderness. Stray fragments of thoughts were always flying about, subsensory, but like the almost-unheard whisper of a needle on a phonograph record, never ceasing. That, certainly, was why almost all Baldies loved to fly and were expert pilots. The high waste deserts of the air were their blue hermitages.

Still, he was in Modoc now, and overdue for his interview with Quayle. Burkhalter hastened his steps. In the main hall he met Moon, said briefly and cryptically that he'd taken care of the duel, and passed on, leaving the fat man to stare a question after him. The only visor call was from Ethel; the play-back said she was worried about Al, and would Burkhalter check with the school. Well, he had already done so – unless the boy had managed to get into more trouble since then. Burkhalter put in a call and reassured himself. Al was as yet unchanged.

He found Quayle in the same private solarium, and thirsty. Burkhalter ordered a couple of dramzowies sent up, since he had no objection to loosening Quayle's inhibitions. The grey-haired author was immersed in a sectional historical globe-map, illuminating each epochal layer in turn as he searched back through time.

'Watch this,' he said, running his hand along the row of buttons. 'See how the German border fluctuates? And Portugal. Notice its zone of influence? Now—' The zone shrank steadily from 1600 on, while other countries shot out radiating lines and assumed sea power.

Burkhalter sipped his dramzowie. 'Not much of that now.'

'No, since ... what's the matter?'

'How do you mean?'

'You look shot.'

'I didn't know I showed it,' Burkhalter said wryly. 'I just finagled my way out of a duel.'

'That's one custom I never saw much sense to,' Quayle said. 'What happened? Since when can you finagle out?'

Burkhalter explained, and the writer took a drink and snorted. 'What a spot for you. Being a Baldy isn't such an advantage after all, I guess.'

'It has distinct disadvantages at times.' On impulse Burkhalter mentioned his son. 'You see my point, eh? I don't *know*, really, what standards to apply to a young Baldy. He is a mutation, after all. And the telepathic mutation hasn't had time to work out yet. We can't rig up controls, because guinea pigs and rabbits won't breed telepaths. That's been tried, you know. And – well, the child of a Baldy needs very special training so he can cope with his ultimate maturity.'

'You seem to have adjusted well enough.'

'I've – learned. As most sensible Baldies have. That's why I'm not a wealthy man, or in politics. We're really buying safety for our species by foregoing certain individual advantages. Hostages to destiny – and destiny spares us. But we get paid too, in a way. In the coinage of future benefits – negative benefits, really, for we ask only to be spared and accepted – and so we have to deny ourselves a lot of present, positive benefits. An appeasement to fate.'

'Paying the piper,' Quayle nodded.

'We are the pipers. The Baldies as a group, I mean. And our children. So it balances; we're really paying ourselves. If I wanted to take unfair advantage of my telepathic power – my son wouldn't live very long. The Baldies would be wiped out. Al's got to learn that, and he's getting pretty anti-social.'

'All children are anti-social,' Quayle pointed out. 'They're utter individualists. I should think the only reason for worrying would be if the boy's deviation from the norm were connected with his telepathic sense.'

'There's something in that.' Burkhalter reached out left-handedly and probed delicately at Quayle's mind, noting that the antagonism was considerably lessened. He grinned to himself and went on talking about his own troubles. 'Just the same, the boy's father to the man. And an adult Baldy has got to be pretty well adjusted, or he's sunk.'

'Environment is as important as heredity. One complements the other. If a child's reared correctly, he won't have much trouble – unless heredity is involved.'

'As it may be. There's so little known about the telepathic mutation. If baldness is one secondary characteristic, maybe – something else – emerges in the third or fourth generations. I'm wondering if telepathy is really good for the mind.'

Quayle said, 'Humph. Speaking personally, it makes me nervous—'

'Like Reilly.'

'Yes,' Quayle said, but he didn't care much for the comparison. 'Well – anyhow, if a mutation's a failure, it'll die out. It won't breed true.'

'What about hemophilia?'

'How many people have hemophilia?' Quayle asked. 'I'm trying to look at it from the angle of psycho-historian.

If there'd been telepaths in the past, things might have been different.'

'How do you know there weren't?' Burkhalter asked.

Quayle blinked. 'Oh. Well. That's true, too. In medieval times they'd have been called wizards – or saints. The Duke-Rhine experiments – but such accidents would have been abortive. Nature fools around trying to hit the ... ah ... the jackpot, and she doesn't always do it on the first try.'

'She may not have done it now.' That was habit speaking, the ingrained caution of modesty. 'Telepathy may be merely a semi-successful try at something pretty unimaginable. A sort of four-dimensional sensory concept, maybe.'

'That's too abstract for me.' Quayle was interested, and his own hesitancies had almost vanished; by accepting Burkhalter as a telepath, he had tacitly wiped away his objections to telepathy *per se*. 'The old-time Germans always had an idea they were different; so did the Japanese. They knew, very definitely, that they were a superior race because they were directly descended from gods. They were short in stature; heredity made them self-conscious when dealing with larger races. But the Chinese aren't tall, the southern Chinese, and they weren't handicapped in that way.'

'Environment then?'

'Environment, which caused propaganda. The Japanese took Buddhism, and altered it completely into Shinto, to suit their own needs. The samurai, warrior-knights, were the ideals, the code of honour was fascinatingly cock-eyed. The principle of Shinto was to worship your superiors and subjugate your inferiors. Ever seen the Japanese jewel-trees?'

'I don't remember them. What are they?'

'Miniature replicas of espaliered trees, made of jewels, with trinkets hanging on the branches. Including a mirror – always. The first jewel-tree was made to lure the Moon-goddess out of a cave where she was sulking. It seemed the lady was so intrigued by the trinkets and by her face reflected in the mirror that she came out of her hide-out. All the Japanese morals were dressed up in pretty clothes; that was the bait. The old-time Germans did much the same thing. The last German dictator, Hitler, revived the old Siegfried legend. It was racial paranoia. The Germans worshipped the house-tyrant, not the mother, and they had extremely strong family ties. That extended to the state. They symbolized Hitler as their All-Father, and so eventually we got the Blow-up. And, finally, mutations.'

'After the deluge, me,' Burkhalter murmured, finishing his dramzowie. Quayle was staring at nothing.

'Funny,' he said after a while. 'This All-Father business—'

'Yes?'

'I wondered if you know how powerfully it can affect a man?'

Burkhalter didn't say anything. Quayle gave him a sharp glance.

'Yes,' the writer said quietly. 'You're a man, after all. I owe you an apology, you know.'

Burkhalter smiled. 'You can forget that.'

'I'd rather not,' Quayle said. 'I've just realized, pretty suddenly, that the telepathic sense isn't so important. I mean – it doesn't make you *different*. I've been talking to you—'

'Sometimes it takes people years before they realize what you're finding out,' Burkhalter remarked. 'Years of living and working with something they think of as a Baldy.'

'Do you know what I've been concealing in my mind?' Quayle asked.

'No. I don't.'

'You lie like a gentleman. Thanks. Well, here it is, and I'm telling you by choice, because I want to. I don't care if you got the information out of my mind already; I just want to tell you of my own free will. My father . . . I imagine I hated him . . . was a tyrant, and I remember one time, when I was just a kid and we were in the mountains, he beat me and a lot of people were looking on. I've tried to forget that for a long time. Now' – Quayle shrugged – 'it doesn't seem quite so important.'

'I'm not a psychologist,' Burkhalter said. 'If you want my

27

personal reaction, I'll just say that it doesn't matter. You're not a little boy any more, and the guy I'm talking to and working with is the adult Quayle.'

'Hm-m-m. Ye-es. I suppose I knew that all along – how unimportant it was, really. It was simply having my privacy violated... I think I know you better now, Burkhalter. You can – walk in.'

'We'll work better,' Burkhalter said, grinning. 'Especially with Darius.'

Quayle said, 'I'll try not to keep any reservation in my mind. Frankly, I won't mind telling you – the answers. Even when they're personal.'

'Check on that. D'you want to tackle Darius now?'

'O.K.,' Quayle said, and his eyes no longer held suspicious wariness. 'Darius I identify with my father—'

It was smooth and successful. That afternoon they accomplished more than they had during the entire previous fortnight. Warm with satisfaction on more than one point, Burkhalter stopped off to tell Dr. Moon that matters were looking up, and then set out towards home, exchanging thoughts with a couple of Baldies, his co-workers, who were knocking off for the day. The Rockies were bloody with the western light, and the coolness of the wind was pleasant on Burkhalter's cheeks, as he hiked homeward.

It was fine to be accepted. It proved that it could be done. And a Baldy often needed reassurance, in a world peopled by suspicious strangers. Quayle had been a hard nut to crack, but – Burkhalter smiled.

Ethel would be pleased. In a way, she'd had a harder time than he'd ever had. A woman would, naturally. Men were desperately anxious to keep their privacy unviolated by a woman, and as for non-Baldy women – well, it spoke highly for Ethel's glowing personal charm that she had finally been accepted by the clubs and feminine groups of Modoc. Only Burkhalter knew Ethel's desperate hurt at being bald, and not even her husband had ever seen her unwigged.

His thought reached out before him into the low, double-winged house on the hillside, and interlocked with hers in a warm intimacy. It was something more than a kiss. And, as always, there was the exciting sense of expectancy, mounting and mounting till the last door swung open and they touched physically. *This*, he thought, *is why I was born a Baldy; this is worth losing worlds for*.

At dinner that rapport spread out to embrace Al, an intangible, deeply-rooted something that made the food taste better and the water like wine. The word *home*, to telepaths, had a meaning that non-Baldies could not entirely comprehend, for it embraced a bond they could not know. There were small, intangible caresses.

Green Man going down the Great Red Slide; the Shaggy Dwarfs trying to harpoon him as he goes.

'Al,' Ethel said, 'are you still working on your Green Man?'

Then something utterly hateful and cold and deadly quivered silently in the air, like an icicle jaggedly smashing through golden, fragile glass. Burkhalter dropped his napkin and looked up, profoundly shocked. He felt Ethel's thought shrink back, and swiftly reached out to touch and reassure her with mental contact. But across the table the little boy, cheeks still round with the fat of babyhood, sat silent and wary, realizing he had blundered, and seeking safety in complete immobility. His mind was too weak to resist probing, he knew, and he remained perfectly still, waiting, while the echoes of a thought hung poisonously in silence.

Burkhalter said, 'Come on, Al.' He stood up. Ethel started to speak.

'Wait, darling. Put up a barrier. Don't listen in.' He touched her mind gently and tenderly, and then he took Al's hand and drew the boy after him out into the yard. Al watched his father out of wide, alert eyes.

Burkhalter sat on a bench and put Al beside him. He talked audibly at first, for clarity's sake, and for another reason. It was distinctly unpleasant to trick the boy's feeble guards down, but it was necessary.

'That's a very queer way to think of your mother,' he said. 'It's a queer way to think of me.' Obscenity is more obscene, profanity more profane, to a telepathic mind, but this had been neither one. It had been – cold and malignant.

And this is flesh of my flesh, Burkhalter thought, looking at the boy and remembering the eight years of his growth. *Is the mutation to turn into something devilish?*

Al was silent.

Burkhalter reached into the young mind. Al tried to twist free and escape, but his father's strong hands gripped him. Instinct, not reasoning, on the boy's part, for minds can touch over long distances.

He did not like to do this, for increased sensibility had gone with sensitivity, and violations are always violations. But ruthlessness was required. Burkhalter searched. Sometimes he threw key words violently at Al, and surges of memory pulsed up in response.

In the end, sick and nauseated, Burkhalter let Al go and sat alone on the bench, watching the red light die on the snowy peaks. The whiteness was red-stained. But it was not too late. The man was a fool, had been a fool from the beginning, or he would have known the impossibility of attempting such a thing as this.

The conditioning had only begun. Al could be reconditioned. Burkhalter's eyes hardened. And would be. *And would be.* But not yet, not until the immediate furious anger had given place to sympathy and understanding.

Not yet.

He went into the house, spoke briefly to Ethel, and televised the dozen Baldies who worked with him in the Publishing Centre. Not all of them had families, but none was missing when, half an hour later, they met in the back room of the Pagan Tavern downtown. Sam Shane had caught a fragment of Burkhalter's knowledge, and all of them read his emotions. Welded into a sympathetic unit by their telepathic sense, they waited till Burkhalter was ready.

Then he told them. It didn't take long, via thought. He told them about the Japanese jewel-tree with its glittering gadgets, a shining lure. He told them of racial paranoia and propaganda. And that the most effective propaganda was sugar-coated, disguised so that the motive was hidden.

A Green Man, hairless, heroic – symbolic of a Baldy.

And wild, exciting adventures, the lure to catch the young fish whose plastic minds were impressionable enough to be led along the roads of dangerous madness. Adult Baldies could listen, but they did not; young telepaths had a higher threshold of mental receptivity, and adults do not read the books of their children except to reassure themselves that there is nothing harmful in the pages. And no adult would bother to listen to the Green Man mind-cast. Most of them had accepted it as the original daydream of their own children.

'I did,' Shane put in. 'My girls—'

'Trace it back,' Burkhalter said. 'I did.'

The dozen minds reached out on the higher frequency, the children's wavelength, and something jerked away from them, startled and apprehensive.

'He's the one,' Shane nodded.

They did not need to speak. They went out of the Pagan Tavern in a compact, ominous group, and crossed the street to the general store. The door was locked. Two of the men burst it open with their shoulders.

They went through the dark store and into a back room where a man was standing beside an overturned chair. His bald skull gleamed in an overhead light. His mouth worked impotently.

His thought pleaded with them – was driven back by an implacable deadly wall.

Burkhalter took out his dagger. Other slivers of steel glittered for a little while—

And were quenched.

Venner's scream had long since stopped, but his dying thought of agony lingered within Burkhalter's mind as he walked homeward. The wigless Baldy had not been insane, no. But he had been paranoidal.

What he had tried to conceal, at the last, was quite shocking. A tremendous, tyrannical egotism, and a furious hatred of non-telepaths. A feeling of self-justification that was, perhaps, insane. And – *we are the Future! The Baldies! God made us to rule lesser men!*

Burkhalter sucked in his breath, shivering. The mutation had not been entirely successful. One group had adjusted, the Baldies who wore wigs and had become fitted to their environment. One group had been insane, and could be discounted; they were in asylums.

But the middle group were merely paranoid. They were not insane, and they were not sane. They wore no wigs.

Like Venner.

And Venner had sought disciples. His attempt had been fore-doomed to failure, but he had been one man.

One Baldy – paranoid.

There were others, many others.

Ahead, nestled into the dark hillside, was the pale blotch that marked Burkhalter's home. He sent his thought ahead, and it touched Ethel's and paused very briefly to reassure her.

Then it thrust on, and went into the sleeping mind of a little boy who, confused and miserable, had finally cried himself to sleep. There were only dreams in that mind now, a little discoloured, a little stained, but they could be cleansed. And would be.

CHAPTER 2

I must have dozed. I woke up slowly, hearing a deep hollow thunder that pulsed a few times and was gone as I opened stiff eyelids. Then I knew what I had heard. It was a jet plane, perhaps searching for me, now that it was daylight again. Its high-speed camera would be working, recording the landscape below, and as soon as the jet returned to base, the film would be developed and scanned. The wreck of my plane would be spotted – if it showed on the film. But had the jet passed over this narrow canyon between the peaks? I didn't know.

I tried to move. It wasn't easy. I felt cold and sluggish. The silence closed in around me. I got stiffly to my knees and then upright. My breathing was the only sound.

I shouted, just to break the lonely silence.

I started to walk around to get my circulation going. I didn't want to; I wanted to lie down and sleep. My mind kept drifting off into blankness. Once I found that I was standing still, and the cold had crept through me.

I began walking again, and remembering. I couldn't run, but I could walk, and I'd better, or else I'd lie down and die. What had happened after Venner was killed? The next Key Life was Barton's, wasn't it? Barton and the Three Blind Mice. I thought about Barton, and I kept on walking in a circle, getting a little warmer, and then time began spinning backward, until I was Barton in Conestoga, not quite two hundred years ago, and at the same time I was myself, watching Barton.

That was the time when the paranoids first began to band together.

THREE BLIND MICE

Under the helicopter, disturbed by the hurricane downblast, the lake was lashed to white foam. The curving dark shape of a bass leaped and vanished. A sailboat tacked and made toward the farther shore. In Barton's mind there flamed for an instant a ravening madness of hunger and then an intensity of pure ecstasy, as his thought probed down into the depths of the waters and made contact with some form of life in which there was instinct, but no reason – only the raging avidity of life-lust that, after fifteen years, was so familiar to him now.

There had been no need for that purely automatic mental probing. In these calm American waters one found no sharks, no crocodiles, no poisonous sea snakes. It was habit alone, the trained alertness that had helped to make David Barton expert in his field, one of the few vocations available to the minority of telepathic Baldies. And after six months in Africa, what he wanted most of all was not – *contact* – but something to calm his psychic tension. In the jungle a Baldy can find a communion with nature that out-Thoreau's Thoreau, but at a cost. Beneath that pagan spirit of the primeval beats the urgent pulse of strong instinct: self-preservation almost without reason. Only in the paintings of Rousseau that had survived the Blow-up had Barton felt the same vivid, almost insane passion for life.

Where men are weary of green wine,
And sick of crimson seas—

Well, he was back now, not far from his grandfather's birthplace near Chicago, and he could rest for a while.

His hands moved over the complicated controls, sending the copter smoothly up, as though by that action he could escape what was inescapable. You lived, for the most part, on the earth, and if you happened to be a telepath, well, there were of course advantages as well as disadvantages. Nobody lynched Baldies any more, of course. Fairly secure, almost accepted, in their cautious self-effacement – italicized by the wigs they invariably wore – they could find jobs and a pattern for living. Specialized jobs, naturally, which must never involve too much power or profit. Jobs in which you turned your specialized talent to the betterment of the social unit. Barton was a naturalist, a collector of big and little game. And that had been his salvation.

Years ago, he remembered, there had been a conference, his parents, and a few other Baldies, drawn together by the deep, sympathetic friendliness and understanding that always had welded telepaths. He could still vividly recall the troubled patterns of thought that had ebbed and flowed in the room, more clearly than the way their faces had looked. Danger, and a shadow, and a desire to help.

... Outlet of his energy ... no scholar ... misfit unless—
—find the right job—

He could not remember the words, only the absolute meanings, with their significant colorations and shadings of implication, those and the – the name-symbol by which the others thought of him. To them he was not Dave Barton. Their thought-references to him personally, while different to each mind, had always the kernel of individual meaning that belonged to him alone, of all the people in the world. The name that a candle flame might have, secret and unuttered. His alone.

And because of this, and because each Baldy *must* survive and adjust, for the ultimate good of the racial mutation, they had found the answer. It was all right for non-Baldies to be reasonably swashbuckling; everyone wore daggers and duelled nowadays. But the telepaths themselves lived on borrowed time. They existed only because of the goodwill they had created. That goodwill had to be maintained, and it could not be done by arousing antagonism. No one could be jealous of a mild-mannered, studious semantic expert, but a d'Artagnan could be envied – and would be. An outlet, then, for the boy's curiously mixed inheritance, his blood from pioneering, trail-blazing ancestors mixed with the cautious Baldy strain.

So they had found the answer, and Barton did his pioneering in the jungles, matching his keen mind against the brute savagery of tiger and python. Had that solution not been reached, Barton might not have been alive now. For the non-Baldies were still wary, still intolerant.

Yet he was no extrovert; he could not be. Inevitably he grew tired of the ceaseless symphony of thought that rolled like a living tide even in the deserts and the seas. Erecting a mental barrier wasn't enough; behind that protective wall beat the torrents of thought, and they were sensed. Only in the upper air was there escape for a while.

The plane lifted, rocking a little in the wind. Beneath Barton the lake was dime-sized and dime-coloured. Around its borders grew, more thickly than it had fifty years before, the Limberlost forests, a swampy wilderness where the small roving bands of malcontents migrated constantly, unable to adjust to communal life in the hundreds of thousands of villages that dotted America, and afraid to unite. They were anti-social, and probably would simply die out eventually.

The lake became a pin-point and vanished. A freighter copter, with its string of gliders, whipped westward below, laden perhaps with cod from the Great Banks towns, or with wine grapes from the New England vineyards. Names had not changed much as the country changed. The heritage of language was too strong for that. But there were no towns named New York, or Chicago, or San Francisco; there was a psychological taboo there, the familiar fugue that took the form of never naming one of the new, small, semi-specializing villages after the cancerous areas of desolation once called New Orleans or Denver. From American history, thence world history, the names came – Modoc and Lafitte, Lincoln, Roxy, Potomac, Mowhasset, American Gun, and Conestoga. Lafitte, on the Gulf of Mexico, shipped the delicate-fleshed porgie and pompano to Lincoln and

Roxy, in the agricultural belt; American Gun turned out farm equipment, and Conestoga, from which Barton had just come, was in mining land. It also had a temperate-zone zoo, one of the many that Barton serviced from Puget to Florida End.

He closed his eyes. Baldies by necessity were socially conscious, and when the world lay spread out map-like below, it was difficult not to visualize it speckled with the heads of coloured pins; very many black ones, and a very few white ones. Non-Baldies and Baldies. There was something to be said for intelligence, after all. In the jungle, a monkey with red flannel coat would be torn to pieces by its undressed colleagues.

The blue, empty wastes of air were all about Barton now; the torrents of world-thought had lessened to a faint, nearly imperceptible beat. He closed the cabin, turned on air and heat controls, and let the copter rise. He lay back in the cushioned seat, a distant alertness ready to galvanize his hands into action if the copter should go into one of its unpredictable tantrums. Meanwhile he rested, alone, in a complete silence and vacancy.

His mind was washed clean. Pure calm, a sort of Nirvana, soothed him. Far below the turbulent world sent vibrations jangling through sub-etheric levels, but few radiations reached this height, and those did not disturb Barton. His eyes shut, utterly relaxed, he looked like someone who had, for a while, forgotten to live.

It was the panacea for abnormally sensitive minds. At first glance, few took Barton for a Baldy; he wore his brown wig close-cropped, and his years in the jungle had made him almost unhealthily thin. Baldies, naturally self-barred from competitive athletics except among themselves, were apt to grow soft, but Barton was not soft. Out-guessing predators had kept him in good trim. Now he relaxed, high above the earth, as hundreds of other Baldies were resting their taxed minds in the blue calm of the upper air.

Once he opened his eyes and looked up through the transparent ceiling panel. The sky was quite dark, and a few stars were visible. He lay there for a while, simply watching.

Baldies, he thought, *will be the first to develop interplanetary travel. Out there are clean new worlds, and a new race needs a new world.*

But it could wait. It had taken a long time for Barton to realize that his race, not himself, was important. Not until that knowledge came to a Baldy was he really mature. Until then, he was always a possible potential danger. Now, though, Barton was oriented, and had found, like most Baldies, a compromise between self and race. And it involved, chiefly, development of the social instinct, and diplomacy.

Several hours had gone past quickly. Barton found a packet of food concentrate in a compartment, grimaced at the brown capsules, and stuffed them back in their place. No. While he was back in America, he wanted the luxuries of civilization. In Africa he had eaten enough concentrate to blast his taste buds. That was because certain game was psychically repugnant to him, after contact with the animal minds. He was not a vegetarian; he could rationalize most of the feeling away, but – for example – he could certainly never eat monkey.

But he could eat catfish, and anticipated the crisp flakiness of white, firm flesh between his teeth. This was good cat country. There was a restaurant in downtown Conestoga that Barton knew, and he headed the helicopter toward the airfield nearest to it, circling the village itself to avoid raising dust storms by his low altitude.

He felt refreshed, ready to take his place in the world again. There were, as far as he knew, no Baldies living in Conestoga, and it was with surprise – pleasant surprise – that he felt a thought probe into his mind. It held question.

It was a woman's thought, and she did not know him. That he could tell by the superficialities of the identity-queries. It was like the outspread fingers of a hand reaching out gently in search of another hand that would interlock with its grip. But the searcher's cognizance of Barton as a personality was lacking. No, she did not know him. She knew of him, probably through – Denham? Courtney? He seemed to recognize the personality-keys of Denham and Courtney sifted through her query.

He answered her question. *Available. Here. A courteous friendly greeting, implying – you are one of Us; a willing desire to help.*

Her name, Sue Connaught, with its curious shadings of how Sue Connaught realized her own identity – an indescribable key thought that could never afterwards be mistaken. The mental essence of pure ego.

She was a biologist, she lived in Alamo, she was afraid—

Let me help.

Must see you) { (*Vital urgency*
Danger, eyes watching secretly
(*Beasts around – Sue Connaught*

Danger – now?

The complicated thought meshed and interlocked as he increased his pace.

Utterly alone) { ('*I*' *of all the world knowing—*
Most urgent secrecy
(*Beasts* – '*I*' *am in zoo, waiting*

Hurrying to you; my mind is with yours; you are one of Us, therefore never alone. Faster than words, the thoughts raced. Oral or written sentences slow the transmission of mental concepts. Adjectives and adverbs convey shades of meaning. But between telepaths complete ideas move with lightspeed. In pre-human times simple meanings were completely transmitted by grunts. As language developed, gradations were possible. With telepathy, a whole universe can be created and – conveyed.

Even so, common denominators are necessary. The girl was dodging some vital issues, afraid to visualize it.

What? Let me help!

Wariness) { (*Even here, danger of Them*
Pretend utterly all is normal
(*Use oral speech until*—

Her mind closed. Puzzled, Barton automatically raised his own barrier. It is not, of course, ever possible to shut one's mind completely away from the persistent probing of another telepath. At best one can only blur the thought wave by superimposing others upon it, or by submerging the salient ideas deep down in the formlessness of non-thought. But they are resilient things, thoughts. Not even the trained minds of Baldies can keep them submerged very long – the very fact of concentrating to keep them down maintains their wavering shapes cloudily in the background of the mind.

So a barrier can be raised, of wilful obscurity or deliberate confusion – reciting the multiplication tables is one evasion – but not for very long or very efficiently. Only the instinctive politeness which a Baldy learns with his alphabet makes the raising of a barrier the equivalent of blanking. A barrier's efficiency is mostly in the mind of the other man, not one's own – if he be a proper telepath.

Barton, like most Baldies, was. He 'looked' away immediately as Sue Connaught's thoughts veered from contact with him. But he was the more eager to meet her now and read in her face, if he could, what convention forbade him to read in her mind. The gates of the zoo lay open before him.

Barton stepped through them, noticing a small crowd, mostly out-villagers who had helicoptered over to see the new acquisitions he had brought.

But, despite barriers, he could, as always, sense a Baldy here, and he let his instinct guide him to where a girl, slim in slacks and white blouse, was standing by a railed enclosure, held there by some fascination. He sent his thought forward, and it was met by a sudden, desperate warning.

Barrier! Barrier!

He reacted instantly. He stepped up beside her, looking beyond the railing, into the enormous tank where a torpedo body moved lazily. He knew that Sue Connaught had looked into the shark's mind, and had seen something there that held a tremendous significance to her.

'So you don't like it,' he said. There was no danger in

speech; to a telepath, with barrier raised, it was more secret than thought.

'No,' she said. 'I suppose it takes conditioning.'

'But you're a biologist.'

'Rabbits and guinea pigs. Even those make me blush sometimes. But – carnivores.'

'Tackle a weasel sometime,' he suggested. 'It's pure insanity. Come on.' He led her out of the crowd, toward the terrace where canopied tables were scattered. 'Have a cocktail?'

'Thanks.' She glanced back at the shark's tank. Barton nodded; it could be bad, if one wasn't used to it. But he was used to it.

'Shall we go somewhere else?' he asked, pausing in the act of drawing out a chair for her. 'A zoo can be pretty uncomfortable if you aren't—'

'No. It's safer here. We've got to talk, and we can do it pretty freely in a place like this. None of Us would come here for pleasure.' With her mind she 'glanced' round at the encircling madness of beast-thoughts, then blurred the surface of her mind again as a protection and smiled at Barton appealingly.

They had met, as all Baldies do, upon a footing of instant semi-intimacy. Non-telepaths may take weeks of friendship to establish a knowledge of one another's character; Baldies do it automatically at first contact, often before they meet at all. Often, indeed, the knowledge formed in first mental meeting is more accurate than later impressions coloured by the appearance and physical mannerisms of the telepaths. As non-Baldies, these two would have been Miss Connaught and Mr. Barton for a while. But as telepaths they had automatically, unconsciously summed one another up while Barton was still in the air; they knew they were mutually pleasant in a contact of minds. They thought of one another instantly as Sue and Dave. No non-Baldy, eavesdropping on their meeting, would have believed that were not old friends; it would have been artificial had the two behaved otherwise than this, once their minds had accepted each other.

Sue said aloud, 'I'll have a Martini. Do you mind if I talk? It helps.' And she glanced around, physically this time, at the cages. 'I don't see how you stand it, even with your training. I should think you could drive a Baldie perfectly gibbering just by shutting him up in a zoo overnight.'

Barton grinned, and automatically his mind began sorting out the vibrations from all around him: the casual trivialities from the monkeys, broken by a pattern of hysteria as a capuchin caught the scent of jaguar; the primal, implacable vibrations from the panthers and lions, with their undertone of sheer, proud confidence; the gentle, almost funny radiations from the seals. Not that they could be called reasoning thoughts; the brains were those of animals, but basically the same colloid organism existed under fur and scales as existed under the auburn wig of Sue Connaught.

After a while, over Martinis, she asked, 'Have you ever fought a duel?'

Barton instinctively glanced around. He touched the small dagger at his belt. 'I'm a Baldy, Sue.'

'So you haven't.'

'Naturally not.' He didn't trouble to explain; she knew the reason as well as he did. For Baldies could not risk capitalizing on their special ability except in very limited cases. A telepath can always win a duel. If David hadn't killed Goliath, eventually the Philistines would have mobbed the giant out of sheer jealousy. Had Goliath been smart, he would have walked with his knees bent.

Sue said, 'That's all right. I've had to be very careful. This is so confidential I don't know who—' Her barrier was still up strongly.

'I've been in Africa for six months. Maybe I'm not up with current events.' Both of them were feeling the inadequacy of words, and it made them impatient.

'Not current . . . future. Things are . . . help from . . . qualify—' She stopped and forced herself into the slower grammatical form of communication. 'I've got to get help somewhere, and it's got to be one of Us. Not only that, but a very special kind of person. You qualify.'

'How?'

'Because you're a naturalist,' she said. 'I've looked the field over, but you know what sort of work We usually get. Sedentary occupations. Semantics experts, medical and psychiatric internes, biologists like me, police assistants – that came closer, but I need a man who ... who can get the jump on another Baldy.'

Barton stared and frowned. 'A duel?'

'I think so,' she said. 'I can't be sure yet. But it seems the only way. This must be completely secret, Dave, absolutely secret. If a word of it ever got out, it would be ... very bad for Us.'

He knew what she meant, and pursed his lips in a soundless whistle. That shadow always hung over every Baldy.

'What is it?'

She didn't answer directly. 'You're a naturalist. That's fine. What I need is a man who can meet a telepath on slightly more than equal terms. No non-Baldy would do, even if I could talk about this to a non-Baldy. What I've got to get is a man with a fast-moving mind who's also trained his body to respond faster than instantly.'

'Uh-huh.'

'There weren't many,' she said. 'Even when minds move at the same speed, there's always a fractional difference in muscular response. And we're not too well trained. Games of competitive skill—'

'I've thought of that,' Barton said. 'More than once, too. Any game based on war is unsuitable for Us.'

'Any game in which you face your opponent. I like golf, but I can't play tennis.'

'Well,' Barton told her, 'I don't box or wrestle. Or play chess, for that matter. But skip-handball – have you seen that?'

She shook her head.

'The backboard's full of convulsions; you never know which way the ball will bounce. And the board's in sections that keep sliding erratically. You can control the force, but not the direction. That's one way. It's something new, and naturally it isn't advertised, but a friend of mine's got one at his place. A man named Denham.'

'He told me about you.'

'I thought so.'

'Uh-huh. For fifteen years you've been catching everything from tigers to king cobras. That takes good timing, the way you do it. Any man who can outguess a king cobra—'

'Watch your barrier,' Barton said sharply. 'I caught something then. Is it that bad?'

She drew a shaky breath. 'My control's lousy. Let's get out of here.'

Barton led her across the zoo's main area. As they passed the shark's tank he sent a quick glance down, and met the girl's eyes worriedly.

'Like that, eh?'

She nodded. 'Like that. But you can't put Them in cages.'

Over catfish and Shasta white wine she told him—

You can't put Them in cages. Shrewd, dangerous, but very careful now. They were the middle group of the three telepathic assortments. The same mutation, but... *but!*

The hard radiations had been plain dynamite. When you implant a completely new function in the delicate human brain, you upset a beautiful and long-standing balance. So there had been three groups: one was a complete failure, thrust into the mental borderland of insanity, dementia praecox and paranoia. Another group, to which Sue Connaught and Barton belonged – the vast majority – were able to adjust to a non-telepathic world. They wore wigs.

But the middle group was paranoid – and sane.

Among these telepaths were found the maladjusted egotists, the ones who for a long time had refused to wear wigs, and who had bragged of their superiority. They had the cunning and the utter self-justification of the true paranoid type, and were basically anti-social. But they were not mad.

And you can't put Them in cages. For they were telepaths, and how can you cage the mind?

They finished with Brazilian chocolate cake, demi-tasse

and Mississippi liqueur, made by the monks of Swanee monastery. Barton touched his cigarette tip to the igniter paper on the pack. He inhaled smoke.

'It's not a big conspiracy, then?'

'These things start small. A few men – but you see the danger.'

Barton nodded. 'I see it, O.K. It's plenty bad medicine. A few paranoid-type Baldies, working out a crazy sabotage scheme— Tell me a little more first, though. For instance, why me? And why you?'

To a non-telepath the question might have been obscure. Sue raised her brows and said, 'You, because you've got the reflexes I spoke of and because I had the luck to find you before I got desperate enough to look for a substitute. As for me' – she hesitated – 'that's the oddest part. No one could have stumbled on to them except by accident. Because telepathy, of course, isn't tight-beam. It's a broadcast. Any receptive mind can pick it up. The minute enough people band together to make a city, *that's* noticeable. And the minute Baldies get together and form any sort of organization, that's noticeable too. Which is why paranoids never made much trouble, except individually. Banding together would have meant running up a flag – one that could be seen for miles.'

'And so?'

'So they've got this special means of communication. It's secret, absolutely unbreakable code. Only it isn't merely code. Then we could detect and trace down, even if we couldn't break it. This is telepathic communication on an entirely new band, one we can't even touch. I don't know how they do it. It might be partly mechanical, or it might not. Children have a higher perceptive level, but we can catch their thoughts. This is mental ultra-violet. Do you realize the implications?'

Smoke jetted from Barton's nostrils. 'Yeah. It wrecks the balance of power – completely. Up to now, decentralization has kept peace. Nobody dared band together or get too big for their boots. They could be detected. But these bichos are wearing invisible cloaks.' His hand clenched. 'It could become world-wide! The one form of organization we can't fight?'

'It's got to be fought,' she said. 'It's got to be smashed. And fast, before anyone suspects. If non-Baldies ever find out, there'll be a wave of anti-Baldism that could wipe Us out. If that should happen, people wouldn't stop to sort out the social and the anti-social groups. They'd say, "We've been nursing a viper, and it's got fangs. Kill 'em all."'

Outside the window a man on horseback clattered past, hoofbeats making an urgent rhythm in Barton's brain.

'How many are there?'

'I told you it's just beginning. Only a few more. But it can spread. I suppose the immediate difficulty is in their training neophytes in their special trick telepathy. That's why I think it must be psychically self-induced. Gadgets can be detected. And mobility would be necessary; they'd never know when they had to get in touch with each other. You can't pack around a big gadget.'

'You could camouflage it,' Barton said. 'Or it might be pretty small.'

'It might,' she said, 'but there's this little girl – Melissa Carr. She tapped their wave without a gadget. She must be some mutant variant.'

'Melissa Carr?' echoed Barton. 'Where does she come in?'

'Oh, I haven't told you. She's my contact. I've been in touch with her off and on for a week or so, but it was only yesterday that she let slip, very casually, what she'd learned on that special thought band.'

'She isn't one of them, then?'

'I'm sure not. It's very odd. Even the way she reached me first—' Sue had been dressing for a party, and the tentative fingering question had crept into her mind. 'It was like Cinderella, somehow. I could feel the pleasure she took in the dress I was wearing, a Mozambique model, and the Karel bag. She strung along with me mentally all evening. And after that—' After that communication had been established. But it had been days before Melissa spoke of the telepathic signals she had inadvertently tuned in on.

'She guessed what they meant, but she didn't seem much

impressed by the danger. I mean, it didn't strike her that something ought to be done. There's some mystery about Melissa; sometimes I've even thought she might have been a member of the group once, and pulled out. Sometimes she won't answer my signals at all. But now that she's told me about this – Faxe – I think I've convinced her of the danger. Sam Faxe. He's one of the paranoids, and from what I've learned, he's trying to sabotage some experiments in Galileo.'

'Why?'

'That's what I don't know. Apparently the paranoids are so familiar with their basic plan that they don't need even to think about it. Their thoughts deal with immediate action. And always on that special wavelength we can't catch. Only Melissa, as far as I know, can get it, and she must have been born receptive.'

'Some are,' Barton agreed. 'Mutants certainly vary a lot, far more than non-mutants. As for this long-term scheme, you know the paranoid type. They figure Baldies were made to rule the world. They look on ordinary humans as a lower species. And if they're trying to sabotage experiments, that's significant. I wonder what sort of experiment this Galileo business is?'

'I don't know,' Sue said. 'Melissa's very shaky on technology.'

'I can find out through Denham. He lives in Galileo.'

'That's where I met him. But maybe you can get more out of Melissa than I can. It isn't wise to' – she hesitated, substituting a familiar word for the unimaginable mental term – 'telepath her too much, but it's necessary, of course. If you feel any probing, sheer off right away.'

'Has there been any?'

'No. Not yet. But we *must* keep in the dark.'

Sue hadn't asked Barton if he would help; she knew that he would. Preservation of the race had been implanted in every Baldy, though in the paranoid type it had been warped and distorted. Now Sue's mind reached out, searching, questioning, seeking the lock to fit her key. And almost immediately the answer came. It was like one hand drawing two others together, Sue mentally introducing Melissa Carr to Barton. He felt something fumble, shy and almost gauche, and then they – locked. He sent out friendliness and warm assurance. Instantly he was conscious of a strong femininity that amounted almost to sexual attraction. Half clear, half clouded, he sensed what Melissa Carr meant to herself: the tangible consciousness of living ego, different in each individual, and the softness of curling hair – hair? Wig – and the softness of a mouth against fingers drawn gently across them. A demure withdrawal that had in it shades of colour and scent, and then something that was the equivalent of a curtsey, purely mental, and with an oddly old-fashioned flavour. After that, he knew he could never mistake Melissa Carr's mind for that of another Baldy.

This is Dave Barton, Melissa.
Recognition and pleasure-shading. A question: trust? So much danger—
Utter trust, yes – strong affirmative.

Urgency ⎰ *Many – (different) – messages coming strongly*
⎮ *Shadow of menace of Sam Faxe*
⎨ *A growing explosive stain in Galileo*
⎮ *Cannot speak – another symbol for speak – long*
⎱ *Possible personal danger*

And all these gradations of meaning at once, three minds interlocking like a colour wheel, focusing to the central white spot of revelation and truth. There were no barriers, as in oral conversation. Like light the thoughts inter-meshed and wove in question, answer, and statement, and despite the concentration, all three had time for the more intimate shadings that took the place of tonal values. It was the capacity for such rapport that made round-table debates so popular among Baldies; the logical and aesthetic play of minds that could ultimately resolve into an ecstasy of complete common awareness. Physically there was no polygamy among Baldies, but mentally the social group had expanded, lending an additional depth and richness to their lives.

But this was merely a hint of complete rapport. Barton was searching for clues in what Melissa told him. He was no technician either, so he was going at it from another angle; that of the naturalist, trained in probing protective coloration, skilled in unravelling the predator's tangled tracks.

How many?
Three.
No more?
Three – and images of Galileo and other towns, symbols of names and identities. A feeling of shadowy communion, links of hatred—

And suddenly, in her mind, he sensed something curiously, disturbing familiar. He did not know what it was. But momentarily it broke the smooth flow of communication, while he searched.

It was nothing; he concentrated again. *Three?*

$$\text{Symbol} \begin{cases} \text{Known name Sam Faxe} \\ \text{Power-lust} \\ \text{Heavy lethargy} \end{cases}$$

The other symbols, resolving into names: Ed Vargan, mixed with a curious concept of size-difference; and Bertram Smith, where there was sensed a cruelty akin to that of the blood-drinking carnivores. Though with a difference; Barton had reached into the mind of a weasel when it was feasting and the sheer flood of ecstasy had almost frightened him. Smith was intelligent, though he, like the others, had that singular quality of – of what?

Darkness. Distortion. Blindness.

Yes, Sue thought, *they're blind. Blinded by their paranoia, They can't see this world at all – as it's meant to be.*

And Melissa's visualization of the three: vicious small things running through the dark, teeth bared. She identified them, Barton realized, with – what? – with mice; she had a horror of mice, which to her were far more horrible than insects or snakes. Well, he could understand phobias; he himself was abnormally afraid of fire. Most Baldies were phobic in one degree or another, a penalty paid for increased mental sensitivity.

He thought: *'I' must move fast. If they communicate, they may go into hiding. 'I' must kill them at one stroke. Can they read your mind?*

They do not know Melissa Carr exists.
But if one is killed, they will be warned. You must be kept safe. Where are you?
Refusal, definite refusal.
It would be best to tell me, so—
No one can find me as long as I don't think my location. There are no directional finders for telepathy. The concept she expressed meant more than telepathy; it was the symbol for a whole race and its unity.

Can you locate Vargan and Smith?
Certainly; they spoke freely in their private wavelength; Vargan is in Rye; Smith is in Huron.
How is it you can catch their wavelength?
Puzzlement. A helpless mental shrug. Born in me?

Barton thought: *When one of them dies, the others will be warned. Listen carefully. Be sure to relay their plans. They must not escape.*

Melissa thought of the three small, grey, vicious things scuttling across the floor. Barton grinned tightly.

See how they run, he told her. *See where they run to.* His hand touched his dagger. It was not a carving knife, but it would do.

There was not much more. Melissa relayed some of the paranoid thoughts she had caught, and Barton's guess at the menace of the paranoids was confirmed. They were deadly, in the long run, to the whole mutant group. Individual deaths did not matter much, in this era of the duello, but to risk the goodwill of the entire race was mad-dog tactics. Nor did there seem to be any motive. Sheer malice? It was not logical, and paranoids are always logical, though their structure is founded on a false keystone. The single clue that would give the whole a meaning was, so far, lacking.

Nor could Barton find it by turning to his training as a naturalist. Animals do not commit sabotage. Nor do birds foul their own nests.

After Melissa had left them, Sue showed her impatience. 'I want to help,' she said, orally now. 'There must be some way.'

'There isn't. You said yourself that this takes a very special skill. You're a biologist. You don't react instantly, the way I do, and if you were along, my attention would be diverted. I've got to concentrate.'

'You'll kill them, then?'

'Certainly I'll kill them. Luckily there are only three, according to Melissa. She wasn't lying; I could tell that.'

'Oh, she's honest,' Sue agreed. 'But she's certainly hiding something.'

Barton shrugged. 'It doesn't matter. What this calls for is prompt action. I can't do much investigating. If I plant any thoughts or questions in non-Baldy minds, the paranoids will start wondering. I've got to eradicate those bichos before the infection spreads. There are plenty of paranoid Baldies who'd join a movement like that, if they were able to master the secret wavelength.'

'So what'll I do?'

'It doesn't matter,' Barton said, 'now. Your job's finished. It's my meat now.'

They stood up together. Outside, on the village sidewalk, he left her, with a handclasp that held a deep significance. All around them the casual, evening life of the town was moving, brightly lighted and symbolic of the vast, intricate check-and-balance system that held civilization together. The civilization that tolerated Baldies, and, though perhaps a little grudgingly, gave them a chance to work out their own salvation. Both of them were thinking of the same thing: how easily that ordinary throng could be integrated into a blood-hungry mob. It had happened before, when Baldies were still new to the world, and the danger still smouldered.

So Barton went off alone, with the unspoken commission

of his whole race commanding him to do what since birth he had been conditioned to do. The race was important; the individuals were not. His helicopter had already been serviced, and he took off for Galileo, on the Atlantic Seaboard, still thinking about what he had to do. He was so abstracted that only automatic radio signals kept him from colliding with other copters. But, finally, the lights of the technicians' town glowed on the horizon.

Like all the communities devoted to technology, Galileo was larger than most villages. Scientists were peaceful folk, and no tech-town had ever been dusted off. Niagara, with its immense source of power, held more people than Galileo, but the latter had a far larger area. Due to the danger of some of the experiments, the town sprawled out for miles, instead of being the tight, compact village that was the general American pattern.

Because of this there was surface-car transport, an unusual thing. Barton guided himself to Denham's house – there were no apartments, of course, in a highly individualistic though interdependent culture – and by good luck found the man at home. Denham was a mild, round-faced Baldy whose wigs had year by year grown greyer until his present one was shot with white. He greeted Barton warmly, but orally, since there were people on the street, and Baldies were tactful about demonstrating their powers.

'Dave. I didn't know you were back. How was Africa?'

'Hot. I haven't had a game of skip-handball for six months. I think I'm getting soft.'

'You don't look it,' Denham said, with an envious glance. 'Come on in. Drink?'

Over the highball they talked non-essentials, except that they didn't – talk. Barton was feeling his way; he didn't want to tell Denham too much, especially since Sam Faxe was here in Galileo, and he went all around the subject without finding out much. It proved more difficult than he had expected. Eventually they ended in the game-room, stripped to shorts, facing a vertical wall, scooped into innumerable convolutions, divided into segments that jiggled erratically. There they played skip-handball. It was easy to tell in advance how hard Denham would swat the ball, but there was no earthly way of judging the angle of reflection. The two bounced around a good deal, getting plenty of exercise, and carrying on a telepathic conversation as they played.

Denham indicated that his favourite game was still crap shooting. Or roulette, by preference. Either of them he could play with his non-Baldy friends, whereas bridge or poker – *uh!* Who'd play poker with a mind reader?

Games that depended on luck or pure muscle were O.K., Barton agreed, but there weren't many of the latter. Wrestling or boxing involved pre-planned thought. But many Olympic trials were possible: shot-putting, high-jumping, racing. In those you didn't face your opponent. Any war game, like chess, was impossible.

Well, Denham thought, your vocation's a sort of war game.

Game hunting? Barton let his mind skim over the field, settling on a tiger after a heavy feed, lethargic, and with the deep consciousness of power as in a silently humming dynamo. He tied that in, subtly, with a hunger, and with something, vague and unformed, that was similar to the symbol by which Melissa knew Sam Faxe. His thought then paralleled the identity of Faxe as one musical chord parallels its complement. If Denham knew Faxe at all, he'd probably respond.

And he did. A sense of elation mounted in Barton as he caught the stray fragment, filtering out non-essentials, squeezing it dry of the accumulated Denham-detritus. What remained was a fat, less competent interpreter who served as liaison man sometimes between technicians of different language-groups. Barton hastily changed to another subject so that Denham would not attach any importance to this particular mnemonic ideation.

After that, Barton was anxious to leave. He let Denham win the game, and the novelty of this so delighted the winner that he accepted Barton's excuse of an appointment without obvious scepticism. A man just back in America, after six months of jungle life, would be looking for something more exciting than skip-handball. But it was swell of Barton to drop in—

Barton strolled along the streets, park-bordered, smooth-tiled, letting his receptive mind absorb the thoughts that boiled around him. Now that he knew what to look for, it was not difficult, though it took patience. Patchwork scraps of information came to him very occasionally. And Barton did something to which Baldies very seldom resorted, he put leading questions into the minds of non-Baldies.

This had to be done, for Barton could read only what lay above the threshold of conscious awareness. And it took real, straining effort to force even a brief stimulating impulse into a non-receptive mind. The average man is not a telepath, and to communicate mentally with him is like trying to push a needle between closely-fitted tiles. He can, under special circumstances, receive thoughts, but he himself cannot recognize them as impulses from another mind.

Barton was sweating when he had finished. Yet he had managed to pick up considerable information. Moreover, he had done it so subtly that Faxe himself, if he tuned in, would certainly be unsuspicious. A good many people had thought of Faxe tonight, but they were ordinary thoughts – except to Barton, who fitted the jigsaw together. A little here and a little there. And finally he had the picture – an interpreter, altering a shade of meaning as a Tibetan talked to a Bengali, and as both of them turned to a Yankee physiochemist. It was the easier because technicians, immersed in their work, were apt to be insensitive to the finer gradations of human contact, and the result was that here in Galileo a gadget was being built that would eventually cause trouble.

Just how, not even Faxe knew, of course, but his smattering of technical knowledge was sufficient to enable him to smear up the works. A shade of meaning in one man's mind, a slightly different hue in another's, when both should have matched exactly – these, and other things, told Barton that Faxe was a racial traitor.

Moreover, he found out where Faxe lived.

Now, standing outside the man's bungalow, he tried to communicate with Melissa Carr. Almost immediately her thought touched his, in the ordinary radiation level.

Play it careful, he ordered. *Use generalities.* And again he was deeply conscious of her femininity, of the softness of curling hair and the smoothness of a curved, youthful cheek. Through the cool, fresh night air breathed something like a wisp of perfume.

Agreement.
Can you locate the others for me quickly? And exactly?
Yes. In—
Keep tuned in to . . . you know what.

Again agreement, and that delicately feminine demureness, soft and curiously attractive. She was a little afraid, Barton sensed, and he felt a strong impulse to protect her. A picture of Melissa Carr was beginning to form in his mind, though he knew that it was of necessity prejudiced. Mental concepts and visual ones may differ a great deal. But he thought that Melissa had a small, triangular face, fragile and with delicate features, and that that face was framed with glossy, jet-black curls. He seemed to see her features *from inside*, reversing the usual procedure in which an individual's face helps form the concept of what is behind it.

How does she do it? He wondered at the lucky chance as he crossed the street. Out of all the people in the world, only she can tune in on the special wavelength of—

Barrier!

He stood now on the porch, facing a closed panel. Through that grained plywood a doubt and a question fingered out, touched his mind, and recoiled. Instantly the man within the house erected a barrier of his own.

Very good. While the mind was thus walled off, Faxe could probably not utilize his super wavelength to communicate with the other paranoids. Or . . . or could he?

Barton stepped aside to a circular window. He could see nothing through the one-way glass. With a wary look around, he lifted his foot and kicked the glass into splinters. He stepped through the gap cautiously, into a well-furnished room where a fat man stood against the wall, facing him. The masculinity of the decor told him that Faxe probably lived alone; that was natural for the true paranoid type, which required a wife's subjugation. Faxe would not have married a telepath, and no non-Baldy could have lived with him for long.

Twenty years ago Faxe would have been wigless, but this particular type had learned caution since then. The man's wig was a gleaming yellow that went oddly with his heavy, ruddy face.

And suddenly the barrier slipped from Faxe's mind; his brain lay fallow and blank, and Barton felt Melissa's urgent warning thrill through him. *He's warning the others—*

Barton ripped out the dagger from his belt and plunged forward. Instantly Faxe's barrier tightened again, as quickly as his own weapon leaped ready to his fat hand. When duelling with another telepath, it is highly advisable to keep your mind guarded, so your intentions cannot be anticipated. As long as Faxe felt himself seriously menaced, he dared not lower his barrier.

Barton moved in, his eyes calculatingly alert, as he might watch the swaying hood of a cobra. He kept his thumb on the hilt of the dagger and held it at thigh-level. The fat man stepped forward from the wall, balancing on his toes, waiting.

It was, after all, too easy. Telepathy wasn't necessary to forestall the stroke of that clumsy arm. With surgical neatness Barton put his knife in the right place, and made certain that Faxe did not communicate with his colleagues before he died. Then, satisfied, he let himself out of the house by the front door and walked quietly toward the nearest surface-car stop.

That was done. He sent his thought probing in search of Melissa. Somewhere, far away in the hidden dark, she heard and answered.

Did they receive Faxe's call?
No. No, you were too fast, and they didn't expect him to touch them.
Good. Vargan and Smith now, then.

Tonight?
Yes.
Good. I don't think you can reach me tomorrow.
Why not?
Evasion. Vargan – at Rye.
Listen. This is important. If there are only three of them, fine. But if they try to communicate with others, be sure to let me know!

Yes. That was all, but the personality of Melissa lingered with Barton as he drove his helicopter north-west through the night. He was not at all affected by the fact that he had committed murder. He did not regard the act as such; there was, undoubtedly, a tough of fanaticism in the way Baldies regarded betrayal from within. Nor was this ordinary betrayal. The means of communication Faxe and the others had discovered was the deadliest menace to the race that had ever existed – more serious than the lynchings a few decades after the Blow-up.

Barton had fallen into a mental pattern that always was dominant when he hunted. Now his quarry was human, but far more predatory than any jungle carnivore. Animals killed for food. That was simple Darwinism, and a basic law of nature. But the three paranoids had violated another basic entirely: preservation of the species. They menaced it.

In any new culture there must be conflict, Barton thought, watching dim lights flicker past below, the innumerable torches of the towns that dotted America. And certainly the Baldies had a new culture. It was almost embryonic as yet, a mutation heading for an ultimate end that was so far inconceivable. But it was the first true step that mankind had made in a million years. Always before mutations had been very slight, or they had been failures. Now, with hard radiations providing the booster charge, a true mutation had opened a thousand possible doors. And before each door lay blind pitfalls.

For there are dominant and secondary, submerged characteristics. Hairlessness was secondary to Baldies, but there might be other, submerged ones that would emerge in the third or fourth generation. This extraordinary method of sub-telepathic communication – was that natural? In

Melissa's case it seemed to be so, though Faxe and the rest might have developed the trick themselves. If so, the latent potential lay, perhaps, in every Baldy. And that meant danger indeed.

It was in the true meaning of the term a focus of infection. Healthy cells could be contaminated. The secret might be passed on, and Barton visualized a perfectly hidden, underground network of paranoids, communicating in utter secrecy, planning – anything. It wasn't a pleasant idea.

He wondered how many social-type Baldies could fight such a menace. Not many; they were not qualified for war. War, because of the atomic bombs, was impossible, but this was a new sort of battle. The thing that made the bombs successful through fear-propaganda – the necessity of centralization before any group could be organized – was inapplicable. There need be no unification, if paranoids could communicate instantly and secretly. Blind luck had stepped in through Melissa, but one could not depend on luck.

Melissa's thought touched him.

Vargan has signalled Smith; Smith is flying to Rye.

What do they know?

Vargan told Smith to come immediately. No more.

To Rye?

It must be a new rendezvous. He gave directions. She relayed them to Barton.

O.K. Keep listening.

Puzzled and a little worried, Barton advanced the copter's speed. He was swinging northward now, toward Lake Erie, by-passing Conestoga. It wouldn't take long to reach Rye. But – had Faxe got through, after all? A telepathic message takes only an instant. Perhaps Vargan had received the fat man's S.O.S. And if Faxe had passed on to his accomplices the knowledge that a Baldy had killed him, and why – Barton shrugged. They would be waiting for him, anyhow. They would know Faxe was dead. If he had no more than called to them in formless appeal and made contact with their minds, they would know. No mistaking that – shapelessness – as life slips inexorably from the body. When they reached out for him now, they would encounter plain nothingness, a curious sort of hiatus in the ether, as if the void had not yet quite closed over the place where a man had been an hour ago. It was unmistakable; no telepath willingly reached out into that quivering blank. But it would impinge upon any receptive mind near it, and soundlessly through the Baldy population of the town the knowledge would spread. *One of Us has died.* Yes, Vargan and Smith knew by now. But they did not yet know, in all probability, how he had died. It might have been accident, it might have been organic. It might have been – murder. They would act upon the assumption that it was. They would be waiting.

The nearest Rye airfield to his destination was deserted, only the automatic landing lights flicking on as he dropped to earth. Melissa's directions had been clear. He walked half a mile up a road, turned into a narrow lane where moonlight made eerie patterns between flickering leaves, and stopped before an unlighted cottage. As he waited, a thought touched him.

Come in. That was Vargan, the size-difference realization a submerged matrix in his mind, a pattern under moving water. *Come in.* But Vargan did not know Barton; he was radiating blind, conscious only that a Baldy was waiting in the lane outside the cottage.

A light came on. The door opened. A small man, scarcely more than five feet tall, with an abnormally large head, stood on the threshold, a black silhouette.

No traps?

There was a trap, but it was merely the advantage of numbers. Barton felt that his question was answered. Vargan fell back as the taller man advanced, and then Barton was in the room, eyeing his opponent.

Vargan had a pinched, worried face, and protuberant eyes. His mouse-brown wig was untidy. He wore eye lenses that reflected the light with a reptilian glitter, and for a moment his gaze took stock of Barton. Then he smiled.

'All right,' he said audibly. 'Come in and sit down.' The thought of contempt was there. Speaking audibly to another Baldy when caution was unnecessary was insultingly patronizing, but Barton was not surprised. *Paranoid*, he thought, and Vargan's mind responded: *Which means super!*

The kitchen valve opened and Bertram Smith came in, a handsome, blond giant, with pale-blue eyes and an expressionless face. Smith carried a tray with bottles, glasses, and ice. He nodded at Barton.

'Vargan wanted to talk to you,' he said. 'I see no reason, but—'

'What happened to Faxe?' Vargan asked. 'Never mind. Have a drink first.'

Poison?

Sincere denial. We are stronger than you—

Barton accepted a glass and sat down in an uncomfortable table chair; he did not want to be too relaxed. His mind was wary, though he knew the uselessness of putting up guards. Vargan hunched his dwarfish form into a relaxer and gulped the liquor. His eyes were steady.

'Now what about Faxe?'

'I killed him,' Barton said.

'He was the weakest of us all—'

All?

Three of us—

Good. Only two left now.

Vargan grinned. 'You're convinced you can kill us, and we're convinced we can kill you. And since our secret weapons are intangible – self-confidence that can't be measured arbitrarily – we can talk on equal ground. How did you know about our means of communication?'

He could not hide the thought of Melissa. The mind has too much free will at times.

Smith said, 'We'll have to kill her too. And that other woman – Sue Connaught, that he was thinking of.'

No point in keeping up useless concealment. Barton touched Melissa's mind. *They know. Listen. If they use their secret wavelength, tell me instantly.*

'Immediately is pretty fast,' Vargan said.

'Thoughts are fast.'

'All right. You're underestimating us. Faxe was the

newest of our band; he wasn't fast-minded, and he was a push-over for you. Our brains are highly trained and faster than yours.' That was a guess: he couldn't *know*, really. Egotism influenced him.

'Do you think,' Barton said, 'that you can get away with whatever you're trying to do?'

'Yes,' Smith said, in his mind a blazing, fanatical conviction that glared like a shining light. 'We must.'

'All right. What are you trying to do?'

'Preserve the race,' Vargan said. 'But actively, not passively. We non-Baldies' – he still used the term, though he wore a wig – 'aren't willing to bow down before an inferior race, homo sapiens.'

'The old quibble. Who says Baldies are homo superior? They simply have an additional sense.'

'That's all that keeps a man from being a beast. An additional sense. Intelligence. Now there's a new race. It's telepathic. Eventually the next race may have – prescience. I don't know. But I do know that Baldies are the future of the world. God wouldn't have given us our power if He hadn't intended us to use it.'

This was merely duelling, but it was something more as well. Barton was intensely curious, for more than one reason.

'You're trying to convince me?'

'Certainly. The more who join us, the faster we'll grow. If you say no, we'll kill you.' Only on these intangibles was there the possibility of mental secrecy. Semantics could never alter the divergence of absolute opinions.

'What's your plan?'

'Expansion,' Vargan ruffled his untidy brown wig. 'And complete secrecy, of course. The sabotage angle – we're just beginning that. Eventually it'll be a big thing. Right now we're concentrating on what we *can* do—'

'Sabotage – and what can you offer in exchange?'

A wave of tremendous self-confidence thrust out at Barton. 'Ourselves. We are homo superior. When our race is free, no longer enslaved by mere humans, we can – go to the stars if we want!'

'Enslaved. I don't see it that way.'

'You don't. You've been conditioned to accept the pap cowards feed you. It isn't logical. It isn't just or natural. When a new race appears, it's destined to rule.'

Barton said, 'Remember the lynchings in the old days?'

'Certainly,' Vargan nodded. 'Humans have one thing we haven't: numerical superiority. And they're organized. The trick is to destroy that organization. How is it maintained?'

'By communication.'

'Which goes back to technology. The world's a smoothly running machine, with humanity in the driver's seat. If the machine cracks up—'

Barton laughed. 'Are you that good?'

Again the fanatical self-belief flamed in Smith's mind. *A hundred – a thousand mere humans — cannot equal one of us!*

'Well,' Vargan said more sanely, 'ten men could still lynch a Baldy, provided they weren't disorganized and in social chaos. That, of course, is what we're after. Ultimate social chaos. We're aiming at a bust-up. Then we can take over – after humans go to pot.'

'How long will that take? A million years?'

'Perhaps,' Vargan said, 'if we weren't telepaths, and if we didn't have the secret wavelength. That, by the way, takes time to learn, but almost any Baldy can learn it. But we're careful; there'll be no traitors among us. How can there be?'

There couldn't. A thought of hesitancy, of betrayal, could be read. It would be a foolproof organization.

Vargan nodded. 'You see? Thousands of Baldies, working secretly for a bust-up, sabotaging, killing where necessary – and always, always avoiding even a hint of suspicion.'

'You've sense enough for that, anyway,' Barton said. 'Even that hint would be fatal.'

'I know it.' *Anger.* 'Humans tolerate us, and we let them. We let them. It's time we took our rightful place.'

'We're getting it anyway, slowly. After all, we're intruders in a non-Baldy world. Humans have come to accept us. Eventually we'll get their complete trust and tolerance.'

'And – forever – live on tolerance, a helpless minority? Eating the crumbs our lessers are willing to throw us – if we lick their boots?'

'How many Baldies are maladjusted?'

'Plenty.'

'All right. They'd be maladjusted in Heaven. The vast majority adjust. I've got the job I want—'

'Have you? You never feel even a little irritated when people know you're a Baldy, and – look at you?'

'Nobody's ever completely happy. Certainly a Baldy world would be rather more pleasant, but that'll come. There are plenty of worlds that will be available eventually. Venus, for one.'

'So we sit and wait for interplanetary travel,' Vargan mocked. 'And what then? There'll be slogans. Earth for humans. No Baldies on Venus. You're a fool. Has it never occurred to you that Baldies *are* the new race?' He looked at Barton. 'I see it has. Every one of us has thought the same thing. But we've been conditioned to submerge the thought. Listen. What's the best of a dominant new race? It must be able to dominate. And we can; we've a power that no non-Baldy can ever hope to match. We're like gods pretending to be human because it'll please humans.'

'We aren't gods.'

'Compared to humans – we are gods. Do you feel pleased at the thought of rearing your children in fear, training them never to offend their inferiors, forcing them to wear – wigs?' Vargan's hand went up to his head, fingers clawed. 'This is the stigma of our cowardice. The day when we can walk hairless in a hairless world – then we'll have come into our heritage. All right. Ask yourself – can you say that I'm wrong?'

'No,' Barton said. 'You may be right. But we're a small minority; the risk's too great. Since you speak of children, you can add a postscript about lynchings. That isn't pretty. Maybe you could get away with this, but you're certain you won't fail. And that's just crazy. You're refusing to admit arguments that might weaken your plan. If even a whisper of this ever got out, every Baldy in the world, wigless or not, would be destroyed. The – humans – could do nothing less, for their own protection. And I couldn't blame them. I admit you're logical – to some extent. And you're dangerous, because you've got the secret telepathic band. But you're paranoid, and that means you're blind. We are getting what we want, on the whole, and because a few paranoid Baldies are malcontent, you set yourselves up as saviours for the whole race. If your idea should spread—'

'That would mean fertile ground, wouldn't it?'

'There are other maladjusted Baldies,' Barton admitted. 'I might have been one myself, maybe, if I hadn't found my pattern for living.' He wondered for a moment. His jungle work was fascinating, but what would it be like to return from it to a completely Baldy culture? A world in which he belonged, as no telepath could belong, really, in this day and age.

Barton turned from the mirage. And simultaneously Melissa's warning thought struck violently into his mind, faster than a shouted word could be; and with equal speed Barton reacted, spinning to his feet and heaving up his chair as a shield. He had not caught Vargan's command; it had been on the secret wavelength, but Smith's thrown knife clattered against the plastic chair seat and bounced off against one of the walls.

Vargan will attack while Smith recovers his weapon. Melissa was afraid; she shrank from the idea of violence, and the emotions surging unchecked in the room, but her thought struck unwaveringly into Barton's mind. He sprang toward the fallen dagger as Vargan ran at him. Then the two were back on the ordinary telepathic wavelength, but with a difference.

One man Barton could have guarded against. Or two men, acting together. But this had been prearranged. Smith was fighting independently, and so was Vargan. Two thought-patterns struck into Barton's mind. Vargan was concentrating on the duello, left, right, feint, and feint again. Barton was skilled enough to be a match for his single opponent, but now Smith had picked up the fallen chair

and was coming in with it. His mind was confused, too.
Drive the chair forward low – no, high – no—

In a feint, there are two mental patterns; dominant and recessive. One has the ring of truth. But Vargan and Smith were attempting to act completely on impulse, purposely confusing their minds in order to confuse Barton. They were succeeding. And more than once they flashed up to the secret band, so Melissa's thought-warning was added to the confusion.

Smith had his dagger back now. A table went crashing over. Barton had taken it fatally for granted that his enemies would act together, and so a sharp point ripped his sleeve and brought blood from a deep cut. In the jungle, where emotion, tropism, instinct, are stronger than intelligence, Barton had been confused in much the same way, but then his own mental power had been the turning factor. Here his opponents were not mindless beasts; they were highly intelligent predators.

The heavy, choking smell of blood was nauseating in the back of his throat. Cat-footed, wary, Barton kept retreating, not daring to be pinned between his enemies. Abruptly Melissa warned: *A rush!* and both Smith and Vargan came at him, blades gleaming where they were not crimson.

Heart – clavicle – up-stroke – feint—

Confused and chaotic, the furious thoughts caught him in a whirlwind. He spun to face Smith, knew his mistake, and ducked not quite in time. Vargan's dagger ripped his left biceps. And with that blow Barton knew that he had failed; he was no match for the two paranoids.

He ran for the chair, thinking of it as a shield, but at the last moment, before his mind could be read, he sent it hurtling toward the fluorescent. With a tinkle of glass the tube broke. In the dark, Barton dived for the door. They knew what he intended and anticipated him; they knew he would depend on impetus to carry him through. But they could not stop him. He got a knee hard on the point of his jaw, and, dazed, slashed right and left half-mindlessly. Perhaps that saved him.

He broke through, thinking of his copter. Escape and help now. He felt Vargan's thought: *the short cut.*

Thanks he sent back mockingly.

The short cut saved time, and he was long-legged. As yet there were no plans. He did not try to think of any. Escape and help; details later. The paranoids came after him for a short distance.

No use; he'll make it. Get my copter.

Right. We'll trail him.

They went elsewhere. Barton felt their brief questions touching his mind, though, and concentrated on running. He could not easily escape the paranoids, now that they knew him. Nor would they again lose touch with his mind.

The landing field was still vacant, except for his own helicopter. He got in and sent the plane south-west, a vague thought of Sue Connaught guiding him. Melissa could not help; he didn't even know where she was. But Sue was in Conestoga, and between the two of them—

Also, she had to be warned. He reached for her mind across the dark miles.

What's wrong?

He told her. *Get a weapon. Protect yourself. I'm coming in.*

Plan—

Don't try to think of any. They'll know.

And Melissa, frightened, the psychic scent of fear strong in her thought. *How can I help?*

Don't reveal where you are. If we fail, tell the truth to other Baldies. These paranoids must be destroyed.

Sue: *Can I intercept their copter?*

No. Don't try. They're following, but not overtaking.

A grotesque silver shape in the moonlight, the pursuing helicopter raced in Barton's track. He improvised a bandage for his wounded arm. After consideration, he wound many heavy strips of cloth around his left forearm. A shield, if—

He could not plan his tactics; that would be fatal. Telepaths could not play chess or any war game, because they would automatically betray themselves. They could play skip-handball, but that had a variable factor, the movable backboard. If a random factor could be introduced—

Vargan's eager question touched him. *Such as?*

Barton shivered. He must, somehow, manage to act on impulse, without any preconceived plan. Otherwise he would inevitably fail.

He called Melissa. *Are they using the secret band?*

No.

If we fail, it's your job. Vargan and Smith must die. This is more important than merely killing three men. If other paranoids get the idea, if they, too, learn the secret wavelength, this suicidal movement will grow. And non-Baldies will inevitably find out about it, sometime. That will mean the annihilation of every Baldy on earth. For the humans can't afford to take chances. If we fail to check the paranoids – it means the end of our whole race.

The lights of Conestoga glowed. No plan yet. Don't try to think of one.

There must be a way, Vargan urged. *What?*

Sue broke in. *I'm coming up in my copter.*

The zoo was below, dark now, except for the silvering moonlight. Another plane, gleaming bright, lifted into view to intercept them. Sue thought: *I'll ram them—*

Fool, Barton thought. *Don't warn them!* But it was a new idea, thrust suddenly into his own mind, and he reacted instantly. Mechanical controls are not instantaneous. By Vargan's sudden decision to drop to a lower level, where a collision with Sue's plane would not be fatal, he had put himself too close to Barton. And Barton's hands stabbed at the controls.

Vargan read the thought as fast as it was conceived. But his copter could not respond with the speed of thought. The flying vanes meshed and crackled; with a scream of tortured alloys the two ships side-slipped. The automatic safety devices took over – the ones that were not smashed – but only low altitude saved Barton and his enemies from death.

They crashed down in the central zoo area, near the

shark's tank. Vargan read the thought in Barton's mind and telepathed to Smith urgently: *Kill him! Fast!*

Barton scrambled free of the wreckage. He sensed Sue hovering above, ready to land, and told her: *Turn your lights on – the spots. Top illumination. Wake the animals.*

He dodged away from the two figures closing in on him. He ripped the bandage from his arm and let the smell of fresh blood scent the air. And – he yelled.

From Sue's copter beams of light glared down, flaring into cages, dazzling bright.

Kill him, Vargan thought. *Quick!*

The asthmatic cough of a lion sounded. Barton dodged by the tank and tossed his blood-stained bandage over the railing. There was a flurry of water slashed into foam as the great shark woke to life.

And, from cage and tank, from the beasts waked into a turmoil of light and sound and blood-smell – came the variable.

Sue had got her siren working, and its shattering blast bellowed through the night. Patterns of light blazed erratically here and there. Barton saw Smith pause and shake his head. Vargan, teeth bared, ran forward, but he, too, was shaken.

Their thoughts were – confused now. For this wasn't chess any more. It was skip-handball, with a variable gone wild.

For beasts are not intelligent, in the true meaning of the word. They have instinct, tropism, a terrible passion that is primevally powerful. Even non-telepaths find the hunger-roar of a lion disturbing. To a Baldy—

What blasted up from the great tank was worst of all. It shook even Barton. The paranoid minds could not communicate, could scarcely think, against that beast-torrent of mental hunger and fury that poured through the night.

Nor could they – now – read Barton's mind. They were like men caught in the blazing rays of a searchlight. Telepathically, they were blinded.

But Barton, a trained naturalist, had better control. It wasn't pleasant even for him. Yet his familiarity with tiger and shark, wolf and lion, gave him some sort of protection against the predatory thoughts. He sensed Melissa's terrified, panic-stricken withdrawal, and knew that Sue was biting her lips and trying desperately to keep control. But for half a mile around that mental Niagara, telepathic communication was impossible except for a very special type of mind.

Barton had that type of mind.

Because he could read the thoughts of Vargan and Smith, and because they could not read his, the duel ended in his favour. He had to kill the pair before help came. The paranoids' secret had to be hushed up forever.

And, with the sharp blade of his dagger, he finished his job. Smith died silently. From Vargan's waning mind came a desperate, passionate cry: *You fool! To destroy your own race—*

Then silence, as the copter's siren faded and the spotlights, blinked out. Only beast-cries, and the turmoil of water in the enormous tank.

'They'll hush it up,' Barton said. 'I've done that much already, since yesterday. Luckily, we've got a few Baldies high up in the judicial. I didn't tell even them too much, but – they have the general idea. It'll be passed over as a personal quarrel. The duello's legal, anyway.'

Afternoon sunlight glittered on the Ohio. The little sailboat heeled under a gust of wind, and Sue moved the tiller, in response to Barton's thought. The soft susurrus of water whispered under the keel.

'But I can't reach Melissa,' he added.

Sue didn't answer. He looked at her.

'You've been communicating with her today. Why can't I?'

'She's ... its difficult,' Sue said. 'Why not forget it?'

'No.'

'Later on – in a week or so—'

He remembered Melissa's demure, feminine gentleness, and her frightened withdrawal last night. 'I want to be sure she's all right.'

'No—' Sue said, and tried to conceal a thought. She almost succeeded, but not quite. Something, a key, a pattern, showed in her mind.

'An altered matrix?' Barton looked at her. 'How could she—'

'Dave,' Sue said, 'please don't touch her now. She wouldn't want it—'

But with the key at hand, and the locked door ready to open, Barton automatically sent his thought out, probing, questioning. And, very far away, something stirred in response.

Melissa?

Silently Sue watched the tiller. After a long time, Barton shivered. His face was strained; there were new lines around his mouth.

'Did you know?' he asked.

'Not till today,' Sue said. For some reason neither of them wanted to use telepathy at the moment.

'The... the business at the zoo must have done it.'

'It isn't permanent. It must be a cycle.'

'So that's why she was able to tune in on the secret wave length,' Barton said harshly. 'This mutation – it runs very close to the line sometimes.' He looked at his shaking hand. 'Her mind – *that* was her mind!'

'It runs in cycles,' Sue said quietly. 'What I wonder now is – will she talk? Can her thoughts be picked up by—'

'There's no danger,' Barton said. 'I stayed in long enough to make certain of that. Otherwise I – wouldn't have stayed in at all. In this state, she has no memory of what happens when she's – rational.'

Sue moved her lips. 'She doesn't know she's insane. She just senses something wrong. That's why she wouldn't tell us where she was. Oh – Dave! So many of us, so many mutants, gone off the track somewhere! It's a horrible price.'

He nodded slowly, his eyes grave. There was always a price, somehow. And yet, if paying it brought security to the mutants—

But it hadn't, really. For Barton saw clearly now that an era had finally ended in the life of the Baldy race. Till yesterday the path had seemed clear before them. But yesterday an evil had been unveiled in the very heart of their own race, and it was an evil which would menace the peace of the world until one race or the other was wiped wholly off the face of the earth. For what a few telepaths had stumbled upon already, others would discover in the future. Had, perhaps, already discovered. And must not be allowed to retain.

Thou, O son of man, I have set a watchman unto the house of Israel.

We must be on guard now, he thought. Always on guard. And he knew suddenly that his maturation had taken one long forward step in the past few hours. First he had been aimless, open to any possibility that knocked loudest at the doors of his mind. Then he had found the job he was suited for, and in its comfortable adjustment thought himself adult at last. Until yesterday – until today.

It was not enough to hunt animals. His work was laid out before him on a scale so vast he could not see it clearly yet, but its outlines were very clear. He could not do the job alone. It would take many others. It would take constant watchfulness from this hour on, over the whole world. Today, perhaps for the first time in nearly two thousand years, the Crusaders were born again.

Strange, he thought, that it had taken a madwoman to give them their first warning. So that not even the mad were useless in the progress of the race. Strange that the threefold divisions of the mutants had so closely interwoven in the conflict just passed. Mad, sane, sane-paranoid. And typical that even in deadly combat the three lines wove together interdependently.

He looked at Sue. Their minds reached out and touched, and in the deep, warm assurance of meeting was no room for doubt or regret. This, at least, was their heritage. And it was worth any price the future demanded of them – this knowledge of confident unity, through any darkness, across any miles. The fire on the hearth would not burn out until the last Baldy died.

CHAPTER 3

It was snowing.

Now there was nothing at all but snow. The world was entirely shut out by the whirling flakes. Until now, even though I couldn't communicate with my people, I'd had the solid earth around me, and I'd been able to see the barrier peaks overhead. Now I was completely shut off and alone.

There was nothing I could do. I huddled in my blankets and waited. The air was a little warmer, but it wasn't cold that would kill me – it was loneliness.

I began to feel that all my previous life had been a dream, and that nothing really existed except myself.

My thoughts began to whirl. I couldn't stop them. I knew I was nearly at the breaking point. The snow whirled meaninglessly around me, and my thoughts whirled too, and there was nothing to stop them. There were no anchors.

Except in the past.

I went back again, trying to find something solid. This time after Barton, while Barton was still alive. The time of McNey and Lincoln Cody. The one unverified story in the Key Lives, because there was an hour in McNey's life which no other telepath had seen, and which had to be filled in by inference alone. But the telepaths who had known McNey for so long and so intimately were well qualified to fill in the missing details.

It was complete, the story of the Lion and the Unicorn. I reached back into the time and the mind of McNey, forgetting, for a while, the snow and the loneliness, finding what I needed there in the past, when McNey waited for the paranoid Sergei Callahan to enter his house. . . .

THE LION AND THE UNICORN

The best way of keeping a secret is to avoid even the appearance of secrecy. McNey whistled a few bars of Grieg, and the vibrations set delicate machinery in operation. The dull amber of the walls and ceiling changed to a cool transparency. Polaroid crystal did tricks with the red glare of the sunset above the Catskills. The deep, cloudless blue sky hung empty overhead. But Barton's helicopter had already arrived, and soon Callahan would be here, too.

That Callahan would dare to come, and alone, gave a horrible clarity to the danger. Twenty years ago a dagger would have ended the matter. But not permanently. Barton had used steel, and, while he had not completely failed, he had not succeeded either. The menace had grown.

McNey, standing by his desk, brushed a hand across his forehead and looked at his wet palm curiously. Hypertension. The result of this desperate, straining attempt to get in contact with Callahan, and the surprise of finding it far too easy. And now Barton as the catalyst – mongoose and snake.

There must be no clash – not yet. Somehow Barton must be kept from killing Callahan. The hydra had more than a hundred heads, and the Power as well. There lay the chief peril, the tremendous secret weapon of the mad telepaths.

But they weren't mad. They were paranoid types, coldly logical, insane in one regard only, their blind warped hatred for non-telepaths. In twenty years, thirty, forty perhaps, they had – not grown – but organized, until today the cancerous cells were spotted throughout the towns of America, from Modoc and American Gun to Roxy and Florida End.

I'm old, McNey thought. *Forty-two, but I feel old. The bright dream I grew up with – it's fading, blotted out by a nightmare.*

He glanced in a mirror. He was big-boned, large-framed, but soft. His eyes were too gentle, not suited for battle. His hair – the wig all telepathic Baldies wore – was still dark, but he'd buy a greying one soon.

He was tired.

He was on leave of absence from Niagara, one of the science towns; but there were no furloughs from his secret job. That was a job many Baldies held, and one no non-telepaths suspected – a combination of policing and extermination. For paranoid Baldies could not be allowed to survive. That was axiomatic.

Over the ridge lay the town. McNey let his gaze travel downward, across pine and sumax groves, to the pool in the brook where trout hid under shadowed overhangs. He opened part of the wall and let the cool air enter. Absently he whistled the phrase that would start the supersonics and keep mosquitoes at a respectful distance. On the flagged walk below he saw a slim figure, trim in light slacks and blouse, and recognized Alexa, his adopted daughter. The strong family instinct of Baldies had made adoption a commonplace.

The fading sunlight burnished her glossy wig. He sent a thought down.

Thought you were in the village. Marian's at the show.

She caught the hint of disappointment in his mind. *Intrussion, Darryl?*

For an hour or two—

O.K. There's an apple-blossom sequence in the pic, and I can't stand the smell of the stuff. Marian asked me – I'll catch a dance or two at the Garden.

He felt wretched as he watched her go off. In the perfect telepathic world there would be no need for secrecy or evasion. That, indeed, was one of the drawbacks of the paranoid system – the mysterious, untappable wavelength on which they could communicate. The thing called the Power. It was, McNey thought, a secondary characteristic of the mutation itself, like baldness, and yet more strictly limited. It seemed that only the paranoid Baldies could develop the

Power. Which implied two separate and distinct mutations. Considering the delicate balance of the mental machine, that was not improbable.

But true rapport was vital for a complete life. Telepaths were more sensitive than non-telepaths; marriage was more complete; friendship warmer; the race a single living unit. For no thought could be hidden from probing. The average Baldy refrained, from courtesy, when a rapport mind went blurred; yet, ultimately, such blurring should become unnecessary. There need be no secrets.

Both Marian and Alexa knew of McNey's connection with the organization, but it was a tacit understanding. They knew without words when McNey did not want to answer questions. And because of the deep trust that comes from telepathic understanding, they refrained from asking any, even in their thoughts.

Alexa was twenty now. Already she had felt the reaction of being an outsider in a world complete in itself. For Baldies were still intruders, no matter how much rationalization was used. The great majority of humanity was non-telepathic – and fear, distrust, and hatred lay latent in that giant tribunal that daily passed judgment upon the Baldy mutation.

Capital punishment, McNey knew very well, was the sentence contingent upon a thumbs-down verdict. And if the thumbs ever turned down—

If the non-telepaths ever learned what the paranoids were doing—

Barton was coming up the path. He walked with the lithe springiness of youth, though he was over sixty. His wig was iron-grey, and McNey could sense the wary alertness of the hunter's thoughts. Technically Barton was a naturalist, a big-game hunter. His quarry was sometimes human, however.

Upstairs, Dave, McNey thought.
Right. Is it here yet?
Callahan's coming soon.

The thoughts did not mesh. The semantic absolute symbol for Callahan was simpler in McNey's mind; in Barton's it was coloured by associations from a half-lifetime of conflict with a group he hated, by now, almost pathologically. McNey never knew what lay behind the violence of Barton's hatred. Once or twice he had caught fleeting mental images of a girl, dead now, who had once helped Barton, but such thoughts were always as inchoate as reflections in rippling water.

Barton came up in the dropper. He had a seamed, swarthy face, and a trick of smiling lopsidedly so that the grimace was almost a sneer. He sat down in a relaxer, sliding his dagger forward into a more handy position, and thought for a drink. McNey supplied Scotch and soda. The sun had dropped beyond the mountain, and the wind grew colder. Automatic induction began to warm the room.

Lucky you caught me. On my way north. Trouble.
About Us?
Always.
This time what?

Barton's thoughts broadened.

$$\text{Peril to Baldies} \begin{cases} \text{Wigless Baldy with Hedgehound group} \\ \text{Villages being raided} \\ \text{Wigless one untrained telepathically} \end{cases}$$

Wigless? Paranoid?
Know little. Can't establish communication.
But – Hedgehounds?

Barton's sneer was reflected by his thought.

Savages. I'll investigate. Can't let the humans connect Us with raiding Hedgehounds.

McNey was silent, pondering. It had been a long time since the Blow-up, when hard radiations had first created the mutations, and brought about the decentralization of a culture. But those days had seen the beginnings of the Hedgehounds, the malcontents who had refused to join the village unions, who had fled to the woods and the backlands and lived the savage life of nomads – but always in small groups, for fear of the omnipresent atomic bombs. Hedgehounds weren't seen often. From helicopters you might catch glimpses of furtive figures trailing in single file through the Limberlost country, or in the Florida Everglades, or wherever the old forests stood. But by necessity they lived hidden in the backwoods. Occasionally there were quick raiding parties on isolated villages – so few, however, that no one considered the Hedgehounds a menace. They were nuisances at best, and for the most part they stayed away from towns.

To find a Baldy among them was less singular than amazing. Telepaths formed a racial unit, branching out into family groups. As infants grew, they were assimilated. *Might be some sort of paranoid plot. Dunno what sort.*

McNey tipped his drink. *No use killing Callahan, you know* he pointed out.

Tropism, Barton's thought said grimly. *Taxis. When I catch 'em, I kill 'em.*

Not—

Certain methods work on Them. I've used adrenalin. They can't foresee a berserker's actions in a fight, because he can't foresee his own. You can't fight Them as you'd play a chess game, Darryl. You're got to force them to limit their powers. I've killed some by making them fight with machines, which don't react as instantly as the mind. In fact – shadow of bitterness – we dare make no plans ahead. The paranoids can read our minds. Why not kill it?

Because we may have to compromise.

The blasting wave of hot, violent fury made McNey wince. Barton's negative was stunningly emphatic.

McNey turned his glass, watching the moisture condense. *But the paranoids are expanding.*

Find a way of tapping their power, then!

We're trying. There's no way.

Find a secret wavelength for us.

McNey's mind blurred. Barton looked away mentally. But he had caught a scrap of something. He tried not to ask the question burning within him.

McNey said aloud, 'Not yet, Dave. I mustn't even think it; you know that.'

Barton nodded. He, too, realized the danger of working out a plan in advance. There was no effective barrier that could be erected against the paranoids probing.

Don't kill Callahan, McNey pleaded. *Let me lead.*

Unwillingly Barton assented. *It's coming. Now.*

His more disciplined mind, trained to sense the presence of the radiations that meant intelligence, had caught stray fragments from the distance. McNey sighed, put down his glass, and rubbed his forehead.

Barton thought. *That Baldy with the Hedgehounds. May I bring him here if necessary?*

Of course.

Then a new thought came in, confident, strong, calm. Barton moved uneasily. McNey sent out an answer.

After a minute Sergei Callahan stepped out of the dropper and stood waiting, warily eyeing the naturalist. He was a slim, blond, soft-featured man, with hair so long and thick that it was like a mane. Only affectation made paranoids wear wigs of such extreme style – that and their natural maladjustment.

He didn't look dangerous, but McNey felt as though a feral beast had come into the room. What had the medievalists symbolized by the lion? Carnal sin? He couldn't remember. But in Barton's mind he caught the echo of a similar thought: *a carnivore, to be butchered!*

'How d'you do,' Callahan said, and because he spoke aloud, McNey knew that the paranoid had classed his hosts as a lower species, and gave them patronizing contempt. It was characteristic of the paranoids.

McNey rose; Barton didn't. 'Will you sit down?'

'Sure.' Callahan dropped on a relaxer. 'You're McNey. I've heard of Barton.'

'I'm sure you have,' the hunter said softly. McNey hastily poured drinks. Barton left his untasted.

Despite the silence, there was something in the room that had the quality of fourth-dimensional sound. There was no attempt at direct telepathic communication, but a Baldy is never in complete mental silence, except in the stratosphere. Like half-heard, distant music of toccata and fugue the introspective thoughts beat dimly out. Instinctively one man's mental rhythm sought to move in the same pattern as another's, as soldiers automatically keep step. But Callahan was out of step, and the atmosphere seemed to vibrate faintly with discord.

The man had great self-confidence. Paranoids seldom felt the occasional touches of doubt that beset the straight-line Baldies, the nagging, inevitable question telepaths sometimes asked themselves: *Freak or true mutation?* Though several generations had passed since the Blow-up, it was still too early to tell. Biologists had experimented, sadly handicapped by the lack of possible controls, for animals could not develop the telepathic function. Only the specialized colloid of the human brain had that latent power, a faculty that was still a mystery.

By now the situation was beginning to clarify a trifle. In the beginning there had been three distinct types, not recognized until after the post-Blow-up chaos had subsided into decentralization. There were the true, sane Baldies, typified by McNey and Barton. There were the lunatic offshoots from a cosmic womb raging with fecundity, the teratological creatures that had sprung from radiation-battered germ plasm – two-headed fused twins, cyclops, Siamese freaks. It was a hopeful commentary that such monstrous births had almost ceased.

Between the sane Baldies and the insane telepaths lay the mutant-variant of the paranoids, with their crazy fixation of egotism. In the beginning the paranoids refused to wear wigs, and, if the menace had been recognized then, extermination would have been easy. But not now. They were more cunning. There was, for the most part, nothing to distinguish a paranoid from a true Baldy. They were well camouflaged and safe, except for the occasional slips that gave Barton and his hunters a chance to use the daggers that swung at every man's belt.

A war – completely secret, absolutely underground by necessity – in a world unconscious of the deadly strife blazing in the dark. No non-telepath even suspected what was happening. But the Baldies knew.

McNey knew, and felt a sick shrinking from the responsibility involved. One price the Baldies paid for survival was the deification of the race, the identification of self, family, and friends with the whole mutation of telepaths. That did not include the paranoids, who were predators, menacing the safety of all Baldies on earth.

McNey, watching Callahan, wondered if the man ever felt self-doubt. Probably not. The feeling of inferiority in paranoids made them worship the group because of pure egotism; the watchword was *We are supermen! All other species are inferior*.

They were not supermen. But it was a serious mistake to underestimate them. They were ruthless, intelligent, and strong. Not as strong as they thought, though. A lion can easily kill a wild hog, but a herd of hogs can destroy a lion.

'Not if they can't find him,' Callahan said, smiling.

McNey grimaced. 'Even a lion leaves spoor. You can't keep on with your plan indefinitely without the humans suspecting, you know.'

Contempt showed in Callahan's thought. 'They're not telepaths. Even if they were, we have the Power. And you can't tap that.'

'We can read your minds, though,' Barton put in. His eyes were glowing. 'We've spoiled some of your plans that way.'

'Incidents,' Callahan said. He waved his hand. 'They haven't any effect on the long-term programme. Besides, you can read only what's above the conscious threshold of awareness. We think of other things besides the Conquest. And – once we arrange another step – we carry it out as quickly as possible, to minimize the danger of having the details read by one of the traitors.'

'So we're traitors now,' Barton said.

Callahan looked at him. 'You are traitors to the destiny of our race. After the Conquest, we'll deal with you.'

McNey said, 'Meanwhile, what will the humans be doing?'

'Dying,' Callahan said.

McNey rubbed his forehead. 'You're blind. If a Baldy kills one human, and that's known, it'll be unfortunate. It might blow over. If two or three such deaths occur, there'll be questions asked and surmises made. It's been a long while since we had Baldy lynchings, but if one smart human ever guesses what's going on, there'll be a world-wide pogrom that will destroy every Baldy on earth. Don't forget, we can be recognized.' He touched his wig.

'It won't happen.'

'You underestimate humans. You always have.'

'No,' Callahan said, 'that's not true. But you've always underestimated Us. You don't even know your own capabilities.'

'The telepathic function doesn't make supermen.'

'We think it does.'

'All right,' McNey said, 'we can't agree on that. Maybe we can agree on other things.'

Barton made an angry sound. Callahan glanced at him.

'You say you understand our plan. If you do, you know it can't be stopped. The humans you're so afraid of have only two strong points: numbers and technology. If the technology's smashed, We can centralize, and that's all We need. We can't do it now, because of the atomic bombs, of course. The moment we banded together and revealed ourselves – *blam!* So—'

'The Blow-up was the last war,' McNey said. 'It's got to be the last. This planet couldn't survive another.'

'The planet could. And we could. But humanity couldn't.'

Barton said, 'Galileo doesn't have a secret weapon.'

Callahan grinned at him. 'So you traced that propaganda, did you? But a lot of people are beginning to believe Galileo's getting to be a menace. One of these days, Modoc or Sierra's going to lay an egg on Galileo. It won't be our affair. Humans will do the bombing, not Baldies.'

'Who started the rumour?' Barton asked.

'There'll be more, a lot more. We'll spread distrust among the towns – a long-term programme of planned propaganda. It'll culminate in another Blow-up. The fact that humans would fall for such stuff shows their intrinsic unfitness to rule. It couldn't happen in a Baldy world.'

McNey said, 'Another war would mean the development of anti-communication systems. That'd play into your hands. It's the old rule of divide and fall. As long as radio, television, helicopter and fast-plane traffic weld humans together, they're racially centralized.'

'You've got it,' Callahan said. 'When humanity's lowered to a more vulnerable status, we can centralize and step in. There aren't many truly creative technological brains, you know. We're destroying those – carefully. And we can do it, because we can centralize, through the Power, without being vulnerable physically.'

'Except to Us,' Barton said gently.

Callahan shook his head slowly. 'You can't kill us all. If you killed me now, it wouldn't matter. I happen to be a co-ordinator, but I'm not the only one. You can find some of Us, sure, but you can't find Us all, and you can't break Our code. That's where you're failing, and why you'll always fail.'

Barton ground out his cigarette with an angry gesture. 'Yeah. We may fail, at that. But you won't win. You can't. I've seen a pogrom coming for a long while. If it comes, it'll be justified, and I won't be sorry, provided it wipes out all of you. We'll go down too, and you'll have the satisfaction of knowing that you've destroyed the entire species through your crazy egotism.'

'I'm not offended,' Callahan said. 'I've always contended that your group was a failure of the mutation. We are the true supermen – unafraid to take our place in the universe whereas you're content to live on the crumbs the humans drop from their table.'

'Callahan,' McNey said suddenly, 'this is suicidal. We can't—'

Barton sprang out of his chair and stood straddle-legged, glowering furiously. 'Darryl! Don't beg the swine! There's a limit to what I'll stand!'

'Please,' McNey said, feeling very helpless and impotent. 'We've got to remember that we're not supermen, either.'

'No compromise,' Barton snapped. 'There can't be any appeasement with those wolves. Wolves – hyenas!'

'There'll be no compromise,' Callahan said. He rose, his

leonine head a dark silhouette against the purple sky. 'I came to see you, McNey, for just one reason. You know as well as I that the humans mustn't suspect our plan. Leave us alone, and they won't suspect. But if you keep trying to hinder us, you'll just increase the danger of discovery. An underground war can't stay underground for ever.'

'So you see the danger, after all,' McNey said.

'You fool,' Callahan said, almost tolerantly. 'Don't you see we're fighting for you too? Leave us alone. When the humans are wiped out, this will be a Baldy world. You can find your place in it. Don't tell me you've never thought about a Baldy civilization, complete and perfect.'

'I've thought about it,' McNey assented. 'But it won't come about through your methods. Gradual assimilation is the answer.'

'So we'll be assimilated back into the human strain? So our children will be degraded into hairy men? No, McNey. You don't recognize your strength, but you don't seem to recognize your weakness, either. Leave us alone. If you don't, you'll be responsible for any pogrom that may come.'

McNey looked at Barton. His shoulders slumped. He sank lower in his relaxer.

'You're right, after all, Dave,' he whispered. 'There can't be any compromise. They're paranoids.'

Barton's sneer deepened. 'Get out,' he said. 'I won't kill you now. But I know who you are. Keep thinking about that. You won't live long – my word on it.'

'You may die first,' Callahan said softly.

'Get out.'

The paranoid turned and stepped into the dropper. Presently his figure could be seen below, striding along the path. Barton poured a stiff shot and drank it straight.

'I feel dirty,' he said. 'Maybe this'll take the taste out of my mouth.'

In his relaxer McNey didn't move. Barton looked at the shadowy form sharply.

He thought: *What's eating you?*

I wish . . . I wish we had a Baldy world now. It wouldn't have to be on earth. Venus or even Mars. Callisto — Anywhere. A place where we could have peace. Telepaths aren't made for war, Dave.

Maybe it's good for them, though.

You think I'm soft. Well, I am. I'm no hero. No crusader. It's the microcosm that's important, after all. How much loyalty can we have for the race if the family unit, the individual, has to sacrifice all that means home to him?

The vermin must be destroyed. Our children will live in a better world.

Our fathers said that. Where are we?

Not yet lynched, at any rate. Barton laid his hand on McNey's shoulder. *Keep working. Find the answer. The paranoid code must be cracked. Then I can wipe them out — all of them!*

McNey's thought darkened. *I feel there will be a pogrom. I don't know when. But our race hasn't faced its greatest crisis yet. It will come. It will come.*

An answer will come too, Barton thought. *I'm going now. I've got to locate that Baldy with the Hedgehounds.*

Good-bye, Dave.

He watched Barton disappear. The path lay empty thereafter. He waited, now, for Marian and Alexa to return from the town, and for the first time in his life he was not certain that they would return.

They were among enemies now, potential enemies who at a word might turn to noose and fire. The security the Baldies had fought for peacefully for generations was slipping away from underfoot. Before long Baldies might find themselves as homeless and friendless as Hedgehounds—

A too-elastic civilization leads to anarchy, while a too-rigid one will fall before the hurricane winds of change. The human norm is arbitrary; so there are arbitrary lines of demarcation. In the decentralized culture, the social animal was better able to find his rightful place than he had been in thousands of years. The monetary system was founded on barter, which in turn was founded on skill, genius, and man-hours. One individual enjoyed the casual life of a fisherman on the California coast; his catch could bring him a televisor set designed by a Galileo man who enjoyed electronics – and who also liked fish.

It was an elastic culture, but it had its rigidities. There were misfits. After the Blow-up, those anti-socials had fled the growing pattern of towns spreading over America and taken to the woods, where individualism could be indulged. Many types gathered. There were bindle stiffs and hobos, Cajuns and crackers, paisanos and Bowery bums – malcontents, anti-socials and those who simply could not be assimilated by any sort of urban life, not even the semi-rural conditions of the towns. Some had ridden the rods, some had walked the highways of a world that still depended on surface travel, and some were trappers and hunters – for even at the time of the Blow-up there had been vast forest tracts on the North American continent.

They took to the woods. Those who had originally been woodsmen knew well enough how to survive, how to set bird-snares and lay traps for deer and rabbit. They knew what berries to pick and what roots to dig. The others—

In the end they learned, or they died. But at first they sought what they thought to be an easier way. They became brigands, swooping down in raids on the unifying towns and carrying off booty – food, liquor and women. They mistook the rebirth of civilization for its collapse. They grouped together in bands, and the atomic bombs found targets, and they died.

After a while there were no large groups of Hedgehounds. Unity became unsafe. A few score at most might integrate, following the seasons in the north temperate zones, staying in the backland country in more tropical areas.

Their life became a combination of the American pioneer's and the American Indian's. They migrated constantly. They re-learned the use of bow and javelin, for they kept no contact with the towns, and could not easily secure firearms. They drifted in the shallows of the stream of progress, hardy, brown woodmen and their squaws, proud of their independence and their ability to wrest a living from the wild.

They wrote little. But they talked much, and by night, around campfires, they sang old songs – 'Barbara Allen', 'The Twa Corbies', 'Oh Susanna', and the folk ballads that last longer than Senates and Parliaments. Had they ridden horseback, they would have known the songs based on the rhythm-patterns of equine gait; as it was, they walked, and knew marching songs.

Jesse James Hartwell, leader of his little band of Hedgehounds, was superintending the cooking of bear steaks over the campfire, and his bass voice rolled out now, muffled and softened by the pines that screened camp from brook. His squaw, Mary, was singing too, and presently others joined in, hunters and their wives – for squaw no longer carried the derogatory shade of meaning it once had. The attitude the Hedgehounds had towards their wives was a more realistic version of the attitudes of medieval chivalry.

> 'Bring the good old bugle, boys, we'll
> sing another song—'

It was dark by the stream. They had been late in finding a camping place tonight; the hunt for the bear had delayed them, and after that it had been difficult to find fresh water. As always when the tribe was irritable, there had been half-serious raillery at Lincoln Cody's expense. It was, perhaps, natural for any group to sense the mental difference – or superiority – of a Baldy, and compensate by jeering at his obvious physical difference.

Yet they had never connected Linc with the town Baldies. For generations now telepaths had worn wigs. And not even Linc himself knew that he was a telepath. He knew that he was different, that was all. He had no memory of the helicopter wreck from which his infant body had been taken by Jesse James Hartwell's mother; adopted into the tribe, he had grown up as a Hedgehound, and had been accepted as one. But though they considered him one of theirs, they were too ready to call him 'skinhead' – not quite in jest.

> 'Sing it as we used to sing it, fifty thousand strong,
> While we were marching through Georgia...'

There were twenty-three in Hartwell's band. A good many generations ago, one of his ancestors had fought with the

Grand Army of the Republic, and had been with Sherman on his march. And a contemporary of that soldier, whose blood also ran in Hartwell's veins had worn Confederate grey and died on the Potomac. Now twenty-three outcast Hedgehounds, discards of civilization, huddled about the fire and cooked the bear they had killed with spear and arrow.

> 'Hurrah! Hurrah! We bring the jubilee,
> Hurrah! Hurrah! The flag that makes men free,
> So we sang the chorus from Atlanta to the sea
> While we were marching through Georgia.'

There was a grey scar of desolation where Atlanta had been. The bright, clean new towns dotted Georgia, and helicopters hummed to the sea and back again now. The great War between the States was a memory, shadowed by the greater conflicts that had followed. Yet in that still northern forest, vigorous voices woke the past again.

Linc rubbed his shoulders against the rough bark of the tree and yawned. He was chewing the bit of a battered pipe and grateful for the momentary solitude. But he could sense – feel – understand stray fragments of thoughts that came to him from around the campfire. He did not know they were thoughts, since, for all he knew, Hartwell and the others might feel exactly the same reactions. Yet, as always, the rapport made him faintly unhappy, and he was grateful for the – something – that told him Cassie was coming.

She walked softly out of the shadow and dropped beside him, a slim, pretty girl a year younger than his seventeen years. They had been married less than a year; Linc was still amazed that Cassie could have loved him in spite of his bald, gleaming cranium. He ran his fingers through Cassie's glossy, black hair, delighting in the sensuous feel of it, and the way it ran rippling across his palm.

'Tired, hon?'

'Nope. You feeling bad, Linc?'

'It's nothing,' he said.

'You been acting funny ever since we raided that town,'

Cassie murmured, taking his brown hand and tracing a pattern with her forefinger across the calloused palm. 'You figure that wasn't on the beam for us to do, maybe.'

'I dunno, Cassie,' he sighed, his arm circling her waist. 'It's the third raid this year—'

'You ain't questioning Jesse James Hartwell?'

'S'pose I am?'

'Well, then,' Cassie said demurely, 'you better start considering a quick drift for the two of us. Jesse don't like no arguments.'

'No more do I,' Linc said. 'Maybe there won't be no more raids now we're southering.'

'We got full bellies, anyhow, and that's more than we had across the Canada line. I never saw a winter like this, Linc.'

'It's been cold,' he acknowledged. 'We can make out. Only thing is—'

'What?'

'I kinda wish you'd been along on the raids. I can't talk to nobody else about it. I felt funny. There was voices inside my head, like.'

'That's crazy. Or else conjure.'

'I'm no hex man. You know that, Cassie.'

'And you ain't been smoking crazy weed.' She meant the marijuana that grew wild in the backlands. Her gaze sought his. 'Tell me what it's like, Linc. Bad?'

'It ain't bad and it ain't good. It's mixed up, that's all. It's sort of like a dream, only I'm awake. I see pictures.'

'What pictures, Linc?'

'I don't know,' he said, looking into the darkness where the brook chuckled and splashed. 'Because half the time it ain't me when that happens. I get hot and cold inside. Sometimes it's like a music in my head. But when we raided that town it was plain bad, Cassie hon.' He seized a bit of wood and tossed it away. 'I was like that chip tossed around in the water. Everything was pulling at me every which way.'

Cassie kissed him gently. 'Don't pay no mind to it. Everybody gets mixed up once in a while. Once we get more south, and the hunting's good, you'll forget your vapours.'

'I can forget 'em now. You make me feel better, just being with you. I love the smell of your hair, sweet.' Linc pressed his face against the cool, cloudy darkness of the girl's braids.

'Well, I won't cut it, then.'

'You better not. You got to have enough hair for both of us.'

'You think that matters to me, Linc? Boone Curzon's bald, and he's plenty handsome.'

'Boone's old, near forty. That's why. He had hair when he was young.'

Cassie pulled up some moss and patted it into shape on Linc's head. She smiled at him half-mockingly. 'How's that? Ain't nobody anywhere that's got green hair. Feel better now?'

He wiped his scalp clean, pulled Cassie closer and kissed her. 'Wish I never had to leave you. I ain't troubled when you're around. Only these raids stir me up.'

'Won't be no more of 'em, I guess.'

Linc looked into the dimness. His young face, seamed and bronzed by his rugged life, was suddenly gloomy. Abruptly he stood up.

'I got a hunch Jesse James Hartwell's planning another.'

'Hunch?' She watched him, troubled. 'Maybe it ain't so.'

'Maybe,' Linc said doubtfully. 'Only my hunches work pretty good most times.' He glanced towards the fire. His shoulders squared.

'Linc?'

'He's figgering on it, Cassie. Sitting there thinking about the chow we got at that last town. It's his belly working on him. I ain't going to string along with him.'

'You better not start nothing.'

'I'm gonna . . . talk to him,' Linc said almost inaudibly, and moved into the gloom of the trees. From the circle of firelight a man sent out a questioning challenge; the eerie hoot of an owl, mournful and sobbing. Linc understood the inflection and answered with the caw of a raincrow. Hedgehounds had a language of their own that they used in dangerous territory, for there was no unity among the tribes, and some Hedgehounds were scalpers. There were a few cannibal groups, too, but these degenerates were hated and killed by the rest whenever opportunity offered.

Linc walked into camp. He was a big, sturdy, muscular figure, his strong chest arched under the fringed buckskin shirt he wore, his baldness concealed now by a squirrel-hide cap. Temporary shelters had been rigged up, lean-tos, thatched with heavy leaves, gave a minimum of privacy, and several squaws were busily sewing. At the cookpot Bethsheba Hartwell was passing out bear steaks. Jesse James Hartwell, an ox-like giant with a hook nose and a scarred cheek that had whitened half of his beard, ate meat and biscuits with relish, washing them down with green turtle soup – part of the raid's loot. On an immaculate white cloth before him was spread caviar, sardines, snails, chow chow, antipasto, and other dainties that he sampled with a tiny silver fork that was lost in his big, hairy hand.

'C'mon and eat, skinhead,' Hartwell rumbled. 'Where's your squaw? She'll get mighty hungry.'

'She's coming,' Linc said. He didn't know that Cassie was crouching in the underbrush, a bared throwing-knife in her hand. His thoughts were focused on the chief, and he could still sense what he had called his hunch, and which was actually undeveloped telepathy. Yes, Hartwell was thinking about another raid.

Linc took a steak from Bethsheba. It didn't burn his calloused hands. He squatted near Hartwell and bit into the juicy, succulent meat. His eyes never left the bearded man's face.

'We're out of Canada now,' he said at last. 'It's warming up some. We still heading south?'

Hartwell nodded. 'You bet. I don't figure on losing another toe with frostbite. It's too cold even here.'

'There'll be hunting, then. And the wild corn's due soon. We'll have a-plenty to eat.'

'Pass the biscuits, Bethsheba. *Urp*. More we eat, Linc, the fatter we'll get for next winter.'

Linc pointed to the white cloth. 'Them don't fatten you up none.'

91

'They're good anyhow. Try some of these here fish eggs.'

'Yeah – *pfui*. Where's the water?'

Hartwell laughed. Linc said, 'We going north come summer?'

'We ain't voted on it yet. I'd say no. Me, I'd rather head south.'

'More towns. It ain't safe to go on raiding, Jesse.'

'Nobody can't find us once we get back in the woods.'

'They got gun.'

'You scared?'

'I ain't scared of nothing,' Linc said. 'Only I sort of know you're thinking about another raid. And I'm telling you to count me out.'

Hartwell's heavy shoulders hunched. He reached for a sardine, ate it slowly, and then turned his head toward the boy. His lids were half-lowered.

'Yaller?' But he made it a question, so a fight wasn't obligatory.

'You seen me fight a grizzly with a knife.'

'I know,' Hartwell said, rubbing the white streak in his beard. 'A guy can turn yaller, though. I ain't saying that's it, understand. Just the same, nobody else is trying to back out.'

'On that first raid we was starving. The second – well, that might pass too. But I don't see no percentage in raiding just so you can eat fish eggs and worms.'

'That ain't all of it, Linc. We got blankets, too. Things like that we needed. Once we lay our hands on a few guns—'

'Getting too lazy to pull a bow?'

'If you're spoiling for a fight,' Hartwell said slowly, 'I can oblige you. Otherwise shut up.'

Linc said, 'O.K. But I'm serving notice to count me out on any more raids.'

In the shadows Cassie's hand tightened on the dagger's hilt. But Hartwell suddenly laughed and threw his steak bone at Linc's head. The boy ducked and glowered.

'Come the day your belt starts pinching, you'll change your mind,' Hartwell said. 'Forget about it now. Git that squaw of yours and make her eat; she's too skinny.' He swung toward the woods. '*Cassie!* C'mon and have some of this fish soup.'

Linc had turned away, readjusting his cap. His face was less sombre now, though it was still thoughtful. Cassie holstered her knife and came out into the firelight. Hartwell beckoned to her.

'Come and get it,' he said.

The air was peaceful again. No more friction developed, though Linc, Cassie knew, was in a quarrelsome mood. But Hartwell's good humour was proof against any but direct insults. He passed around the whisky bottle he had looted – a rare treat, since the tribe could distil smoke only when they settled for a while, which wasn't often. Linc didn't drink much. Long after the fire had been smothered and snores came from the lean-tos around him, he lay awake, troubled and tense.

Something – someone – was calling him.

It was like one of his hunches. It was like what he had felt during the raids. It was like Cassie's nearness, and yet there was a queer, exciting difference. There was a friendliness to that strange call that he had never felt before.

Dim and indefinable, a dweller hidden deep in his mind woke and responded to that call of a kindred being.

After a while he rose on one elbow and looked down at Cassie. Her face was partly veiled by the deeper blackness of her hair. He touched its soft, living warmth gently. Then he slipped noiselessly out of the shelter and stood up, staring around.

There was a rustling of leaves, and the chuckling of the brooklet. Nothing else. Moonlight dappled the ground here and there. A woodrat rustled softly through the wild grasses. The air was very cold and crisp, with a freshness that stung Linc's cheeks and eyes.

And suddenly he was frightened. Old folktales troubled him. He remembered his foster mother's stories of men who could turn to wolves, of the Wendigo that swept like a vast wind above the lonely forests, of a Black Man who bought souls – the formless, dark fears of childhood rose up in nightmare reality. He had killed a grizzly with his knife, but he had never stood alone at night in the woods, while a Call murmured in his mind – silently – and made his blood leap up in fiery response.

He was afraid, but the bait was too strong. He turned south, and walked out of the camp. Instinctive training made his progress noiseless. He crossed the brook, his sandals inaudible on the stones, and mounted a slope. And there, sitting on a stump waiting for him, was a man.

His back was toward Linc, and nothing could be seen but the hunched torso and the bald, gleaming head. Linc had a momentary horrible fear that when the man turned, he might see his own face. He touched his knife. The confused stirring in his brain grew chaotic.

'Hello, Linc,' a low voice said.

Linc had made no sound, and he knew it. But, somehow, that dark figure had sensed his approach. The Black Man—?

'Do I look black?' the voice asked. The man stood up, turning. He was sneering – no, smiling – and his face was dark and seamed. He wore town clothes.

But he wasn't the Black Man. He didn't have a cloven hoof. And the warm, sincere friendliness subtly radiating from his presence was reassuring to Linc in spite of his suspicions.

'You called me,' Linc said. 'I'm trying to figure it out.' His eyes dwelt on the bald cranium.

'My name's Barton,' the man said. 'Dave Barton.' He lifted something grey – a scalp? – and fitted it carefully on his head. The sneer indicated amusement.

'I feel naked without my wig. But I had to show you I was a . . . a—' He sought for the word that would fit the telepathic symbol. 'That you were one of us,' he finished.

'I ain't—'

'You're a Baldy,' Barton said, 'but you don't know it. I can read that from your mind.'

'Read my mind?' Linc took a backward step.

'You know what Baldies are? Telepaths?'

'Sure,' Linc said doubtfully. 'I heard stories. We don't know much about town life. Listen,' he said with fresh suspicion, 'how'd you come to be out here? How'd—'

'I came looking for you.'

'Me? Why?'

Barton said patiently, 'Because you're one of Us. I can see I've got to explain a lot. From the beginning, maybe. So—'

He talked. It might have been more difficult had they not been Baldies. Though Linc was telepathically untrained, he could nevertheless receive enough mental confirmation to clarify the questions in his mind. And Barton spoke of the Blow-up, of the hard radiations – so much Greek to Linc, until Barton used telepathic symbolism – and, mostly, of the incredible fact that Linc wasn't merely a hairless freak in his tribe. There were other Baldies, a lot of them.

That was important. For Linc caught the implications. He sensed something of the warm, deep understanding between telepaths, the close unity of the race, the feeling of *belonging* that he had never had. Just now, alone in the woods with Barton, he was conscious of more genuine intimacy than he had ever felt before.

He was quick to understand. He asked questions. And, after a while, so did Barton.

'Jesse James Hartwell's behind the raids. Yeah, I was in on 'em. You mean you all wear them wigs?'

'Naturally. It's a big civilization, and we belong to it. We're part of the whole set-up.'

'And . . . and nobody laughs at you for being bald?'

'Do I look bald?' Barton asked. 'There are drawbacks, sure. But there are plenty of advantages.'

'I'll say!' Linc breathed deeply. 'People . . . the same sort . . . your own sort—' He was inarticulate.

'The non-Baldies didn't always give us an even break. They were afraid of us, a little. We're trained from childhood never to take advantage of our telepathic powers with humans.'

'Yeah. I can see that. It makes sense.'

'Then you know why I came, don't you?'

'I can sort of understand it,' Linc said slowly. 'These raids ... people might start thinking a Baldy's involved — *I'm* a Baldy!'

Barton nodded. 'Hedgehounds don't matter. A few raids — we can take care of them. But to have one of Us involved is bad medicine.'

'I told Jesse James Hartwell tonight I was having no part in any more raiding,' Linc said. 'He won't push me.'

'Yes— That helps. Listen, Linc. Why don't you come home with me?'

Years of training made Linc pause. 'Me? Go into a town? We don't do that.'

'*You?*'

'The ... Hedgehounds. I ain't a Hedgehound, am I? Gosh, this is—' He rubbed his jaw. 'I'm all mixed up, Barton.'

'Tell you what. Come with me now and see how you like our sort of life. You never were trained to use your telepathic function, so you're like a half-blind man. Take a look at the set-up, and then decide what you want to do.'

On the verge of mentioning Cassie, Linc paused. He was half afraid that if he spoke of her, Barton might withdraw his offer. And, after all, it wasn't as if he intended to leave Cassie permanently. It'd be just for a week or two, and then he could come back to the tribe.

Unless he took Cassie with him now—

No. Somehow he'd feel shamed in admitting that he, a Baldy, had married a Hedgehound. Though he was proud of Cassie herself, all right. He'd never give her up. It was only—

He was lonely. He was horribly, sickening lonely, and what he had glimpsed in Barton's mind and Barton's words drew him with overpowering force. A world where he belonged, where no one called him skinhead, where he'd never feel inferior to the bearded men of the tribe. A wig of his own.

Just for a few weeks. He couldn't miss this chance. He

couldn't! Cassie would be waiting for him when he came back.

'I'll go with you,' he said. 'I'm ready right now. O.K.?'

But Barton, who had read Linc's mind, hesitated before he answered.

'O.K.,' he said at last. 'Let's go.'

Three weeks later Barton sat in McNey's solarium and shaded his eyes wearily with one hand. 'Linc's married, you know,' he said, 'to a Hedgehound girl. He doesn't know we know it.'

'Does it matter?' McNey asked. He was looking very tired and troubled.

'I suppose not. But I thought I'd better mention it, because of Alexa.'

'She knows her own mind. And she must know about Linc being married, too, by this time. She's been giving him telepathic coaching for weeks.'

'I noticed that when I came in.'

'Yeah,' McNey said, rubbing his forehead. 'That's why we're being oral. Telepathic conversations distract Linc when there's more than one; he's still learning selectivity.'

'How do you like the boy?'

'I like him. He's not . . . quite what I'd expected, though.'

'He grew up with the Hedgehounds.'

'He's one of Us,' McNey said with finality.

'No symptoms of paranoid tendencies?'

'Definitely not. Alexa agrees.'

'Good,' Barton said. 'That relieves me. It was the one thing I was afraid of. As for the Hedgehound girl, she's not one of Us, and we can't afford to weaken the race by intermarriage with humans. That's been an axiom almost since the Blow-up. My own feeling is that if Linc marries Alexa or any other one of Us, it's all to the good, and we can forget about previous entanglements.'

'It's up to her,' McNey said. 'Any more Hedgehound raids?'

'No. But they're the least of my troubles. Sergei Callahan's gone underground. I can't locate him, and I want to.'

'Just to kill him?'

'No. He must know other key paranoids. I want to drag that information out of him. He can blur his mind permanently – and once I get him where I want, he'll have few secrets left.'

'We're fighting a losing battle.'

'Are we?'

'I can't talk yet,' McNey said, with subdued violence. 'I can't even let myself think about the problem. I . . . it works out this way. There's crux, a single equation, that must be solved. But not yet. Because the moment I solve it, my mind can be read. I've got to work out all the minor details first. Then—'

'Yes?'

McNey's smile was bitter. 'I don't know. I'll find an answer. I haven't been idle.'

'If we could crack the Power,' Barton said. 'If we could only tap the paranoid's code—'

'Or,' McNey said, 'if we had a code of our own—'

'Unbreakable.'

'Which is impossible, by any mechanical means. No scrambler could work, because we'd have to know the key, and our minds could be read by paranoids. I don't want to think about it any more for a while, Dave. The details, yes, But not the problem itself. I . . . might solve it before I'm ready.'

'The paranoids are plenty busy,' Barton said. 'Their propaganda's spreading. That talk about Galileo's secret weapon is still going around.'

'Haven't the Galileans made any denials?'

'It isn't that tangible. You can't buck a whispering campaign. That, Darryl, is what's apt to cause a bust-up. You can fight a person or a thing, but you can't fight a wind. A wind that whispers.'

'But the atomic bombs! After all—'

'I know. Just the same, some hothead is going to get scared enough to take action one of these days. He'll say, "Galileo's got a secret weapon. We're not safe. They're going to attack us." So he'll jump the gun. After that, there'll be other incidents.'

'With Us in the middle. We can't stay neutral. I think there'll be a pogrom, Dave, sooner or later.'

'We'll survive it.'

'You think so? With every non-Baldy's hand ready to strike down telepaths – man, woman or child? There'll be no quarter given. We need another world, a new world—'

'That'll have to wait till we get interstellar ships.'

'And meanwhile we live on borrowed time. It might be best if we let the human race reassimilate us.'

'Retrogression?'

'Suppose it is? We're in the position of a unicorn in a herd of horses. We daren't use our horn to defend ourselves. We've got to pretend to be horses.'

'The lion and the unicorn,' Barton said, 'were fighting for the crown. Well, Callahan and his paranoids are the lion, all right. But the crown?'

'Inevitably,' McNey said, 'it must be rule. Two dominant species can't exist on the same planet or even in the same system. Humans and telepaths can't evenly divide rule. We're knuckling under now. Eventually, we'll arrive, by a different path, at Callahan's goal. But not by degrading or enslaving humans! Natural selection is our weapon. Biology's on our side. If we can only live in peace with humans, until —'

'—and drummed them out of town,' Barton said.

'So the humans mustn't suspect the lion and the unicorn are fighting. Or what they're fighting for. Because if they do, we won't survive the pogrom. There will be no refuge. Our race is soft, through environment and adaptation.'

'I'm worried about Callahan,' Barton said suddenly. 'I don't know what he's planning. By the time I find out, it may be too late. If he sets something in operation that can't be stopped—'

'I'll keep working,' McNey promised. 'I may be able to give you something soon.'

'I hope so. Well, I'm flying to St. Nick tonight. Ostensibly to check the zoo there. Actually, I've other motives. Maybe I can pick up Callahan's trail.'

'I'll walk you down to the village.' McNey went with Barton into the dropper. They stepped outside into the warm, spring air, glancing through the transparent wall at the televisor where Alexa sat with Linc. Barton said, 'They don't seem worried, anyhow.'

McNey laughed. 'She's sending in her column to the *Recorder*. Alexa's a specialist on heart problems. I hope she never has any of her own to solve!'

'—if you love him,' Alexa said into the mike, marry him. And if he loves you, he'll have no objections to running psycherating tests and comparing *id* balance sheets. You're considering a lifetime partnership, and both of you should read the contracts before signing them.' She managed to look like a cat with cream on its whiskers. 'But always remember that love is the most important thing in the world. If you find that, it will always be springtime in your hearts. Good luck, Wondering!'

She pressed a switch. 'Thirty, Linc. My job's done for the day. That's one sort of job a Baldy can find – heart problem editor on a telepaper. Think you'd like it?'

'No,' Linc said. 'It ain't ... it's not up my alley.'

He was wearing a silken blue shirt and darker blue shorts, and a cropped brown wig covered his skull. He wasn't used to it yet, and kept touching it uneasily.

'Ain't as good as isn't,' Alexa said. 'I know what you mean, and that's more important than grammatical construction. More lessons?'

'Not for a while yet. I get tired easy. Talking's still more natural, somehow.'

'Eventually you'll be finding it cumbersome. Personal endings – you speak, he speaks, *parlons, parlez, purlent* – telepathically you don't use those vestiges.'

'Vestiges?'

'Sure,' Alexa said. 'From the Latin. The Romans didn't use pronouns. Just *amo, amas, amant*,' she clarified mentally, 'and the endings gave you the right pronoun. *Nous, vous*, and *ils* are used now instead, we, you plural, and they. So the endings are unnecessary. If you're communicating with a Swiss telepath, though you might find yourself wondering why he kept thinking of a girl as *it*. But you'd know what *it* meant to him, and you couldn't if you were being oral only.'

'It's plenty hard,' Linc said. 'I'm getting the angles, though. That round-robin business we had last night was—' he groped for a word, but Alexa caught the meaning from his mind.

'I know. There's an intimacy that's pretty wonderful. You know, I've never felt badly about being adopted. I *knew* just where I fitted into Marian's life and Darryl's, and how they felt about me. I knew I belonged.'

'It must be a nice feeling,' Linc said. 'I'm sort of getting it, though.'

'Of course. You're one of Us. After you've mastered the telepathic function, you won't have any doubts at all.'

Linc watched the play of sunlight on Alexa's bronze curls. 'I guess I do belong with your kind of folks.'

'Glad you came with Dave?'

He looked at his hands. 'I can't tell you, Alexa. I can't tell you how wonderful it **is**. I'd been shut out in the dark all my life, thinking I was a freak, never feeling right sure about myself. Then all this—' He indicated the televisor. 'Magical miracles, that's what. And all the rest.'

Alexa understood what was in his mind. Through him she felt the heady excitement of an exile returning to his own kind. Even the visor, familiar symbol of her job, assumed a new glamour, though it was the standard double-screen model, the upper for news flashes, the lower for the twenty-four-hour newspaper that was received, recorded on wire-film, and thereafter available for reference. Push-buttons selected the publications, and the dial made it possible to focus down on the pages, on either the action pictures or the printed matter. Format, of course, was quite as important as news value. The big concealed wall-screen at one end of the room was used for plays, concerts, movies, and Disneys. But for the added sensual attractions of smell, taste, and touch,

101

one had to go to the theatres; such special equipment was still too expensive for the average home.

'Yes,' Alexa said, 'you're one of Us. And you've got to remember that the future of the race is important. If you stay, you must never do anything to hurt it.'

'I remember what you've been telling me about the p-paranoids,' Linc nodded. 'Guess they're sort of like the cannibal tribes 'mong the Hedgehounds. They're fair quarry for anybody.' He felt his wig, stepped to a mirror-unit, and adjusted the headpiece.

Alexa said, 'There's Marian outside. I want to see her. Wait for me, Linc; I'll be back.'

She went out. Lincoln, awkwardly testing his newly-realized powers, felt her thought fingering subtly toward the plump, pretty woman who was moving among the flowers, armed with gloves and spray.

He wandered to the clavilux, and, one-fingered, picked out a tune. He hummed:

'All in the merry month of May,
  When the green buds they were swellin',
Young Jemmy Grove on his death-bed lay
  For love of Barb'ry Allen.'

Memories of Cassie rose up. He forced them back into the shadows, along with the Hedgehounds and the nomad life he had known. That wasn't his life any more. Cassie – she'd get along all right. He'd go after her, one of these days, and bring her to live with him among the Baldies. Only – only she wasn't a Baldy. She wasn't like Alexa, for instance. She was quite as pretty, sure; yet there was all this talk about the future of the race. If, now he married a Baldy and had Baldy sons and daughters—

But, he was already married. What was the good of thinking so? A Hedgehound marriage might not amount to a hill of beans among the townsfolk, of course, and, anyway, all this mental round-robin stuff was sort of polygamy.

Well, he'd climb that hill when he came to it. First he had to get the trick of this telepathy business. It was coming, but slowly, for he'd not been conditioned since infancy, as other Baldies were. The latent power had to be wakened and directed – not as a child could be taught, but allowing for Linc's maturity, and his ability to grasp and understand the goal.

Marian came in with Alexa. The older woman stripped off her cloth gloves and brushed beads of perspiration from her ruddy cheeks. "Lo, Linc,' she said. 'How's it going?'

'Fairish, Marian. You should have asked me to help out there.'

'I need the exercise. I gained three pounds this morning arguing with that turnip-bleeder Gatson, down at the store. Know what he wants for fresh breadfruit?'

'What's that?'

'Catch this.' Marian formed mental concepts involving sight, touch and taste. Alexa chimed in with the smell of breadfruit. Linc had his own arbitrary standards for comparisons, and within a second had assimilated the absolute meaning; he would recognize a breadfruit from now on. Marian threw a quick mental question. Linc answered.

To town (Darryl McNey) by window (ten minutes past).

'A bit confused,' Marian said, 'but I get the idea. He ought to be back soon. I'm in the mood for a swim. Suppose I fix some sandwiches?'

'Swell,' Alexa said. 'I'll help. Linc knows more about catching trout than anybody I've ever seen, except he doesn't know what a dry fly is.'

'I just aim to catch fish,' Linc said. 'Enough to eat. Many a time I had to fish through holes in the ice to keep from being hungry.'

Later, stretching his brown, hard body on the sandy bank of the pool upstream, he luxuriated in the warm sunlight and watched Alexa. Slim and attractive in white shorts and bathing cap, she inexpertly practised casting, while McNey, pipe in his mouth, worked a likely-looking spot under an overhang of branches that brushed the water. Marian placidly ate sandwiches and watched the activities of a community of ants with considerable interest. The deep, unspoken comradeship of the family and the race was intangibly in the air, a bond that reached out, touched Linc, and drew him into its friendly centre. *This is it*, he thought. *I belong here*. And Alexa's mind answered him with quiet confidence: *You are one of Us*.

The months passed very quickly for Linc, broken by occasional visits from Dave Barton, whose manner grew increasingly more troubled, and by the green that covered tree and brush, ground and vine, as spring gave place to summer, and summer drew toward a not-distant autumn. He seldom thought of the Hedgehounds now. There was a sort of tacit acceptance of the situation among the little group; he felt, without actually bringing the realization consciously to mind, that Alexa knew a great deal about his past, and that she would not bring up the matter of Cassie unless he did. That she was beginning to love him he did not doubt. Nor did he doubt much that he loved her. After all, Alexa was his kind, as Cassie never had been.

But he dreamed of Cassie, nevertheless. Sometimes he felt loneliness, even among his own people. At such times he was anxious to finish his telepathic training and join Barton's fight against the paranoids. Barton was eager to enlist Linc, but he warned against the danger of moving too soon. 'The paranoids aren't fools, Linc,' he said. 'We mustn't underestimate them. I've lived this long simply because I'm a trained big-game hunter. My reactions are just a bit faster than theirs, and I always try to manœuvre them in a position where telepathy can't help them. If a paranoid's at the bottom of a well, he may read your intention of dropping a load of bricks on his head – but he can't do a lot about it.'

'Any news about Callahan?' McNey asked.

'No word for months. There's some plan – maybe a big push in the propaganda field, maybe assassinations of key technologists. I don't know what. I've read no minds that knew the right answers. But I think something's going to break soon; I've found out that much. We've got to be ready for it. We've got to break their code – or get one of our own. The same tune, Darryl.'

'I know,' McNey said. He stared out at the empty blue

sky. 'There isn't much I can say now, or even think. The same tune, all right.'

'But you haven't failed? In a few weeks you're due back at Niagara.'

Linc said, 'Look, about this code. I was thinking, the Hedgehounds have got a sort of code. Like this.' He imitated a few bird and animal calls. 'We know what they mean but nobody else knows.'

'Hedgehounds aren't telepaths. If they were, your code wouldn't stay a secret long.'

'Guess you're right. I'd like to take a crack at the paranoids, though.'

'You'll have your chance,' Barton said. 'But, meanwhile, it's Darryl's job to find us a new weapon.'

McNey said wearily, 'I know all about that. No more pep talks, Dave, please.'

Barton stood up, scowling. 'I've a job to do down south. I'll see you when I get back, Darryl. Meanwhile, take care of yourself. If this business – whatever it is – should break soon, don't run any risks. You're vital to Us, much more so than I am.'

With a nod to Linc he went out. McNey stared at nothing. Linc hesitated, sent out a query thought, and met abstracted rebuff. He went downstairs.

He couldn't find Alexa. Finally he went out into the gardens, working his way toward the brook. A flash of colour caught his eye, and he headed for it.

Alexa was sitting on a rock, her flimsy playsuit unzipped to let the slight breeze cool her. The heat was so intense that she had removed her wig, and her bald head was shiny and incongruous, incompatible with her artificial lashes and eyebrows. It was the first time Linc had ever seen her wigless.

Instantly, at his thought, she swung about and began to replace her wig. But her arm stopped in arrested motion. She looked at him, half questionably, and then with pain and growing understanding in her eyes.

'Put it on, Alexa,' Linc said.

She watched him steadily. 'What for – now?'

'I ... it doesn't—'

Alexa shrugged and slipped the headpiece into place. 'That was . . . strange,' she said, deliberately speaking aloud as if she did not want to let her mind slip back into the channels of telepathic intimacy where hurt can strike so unerringly. 'I'm so used myself to Baldies being – bald. I never thought before the sight could be—' She did not finish aloud. After a moment she said, 'You must have been very unhappy among the Hedgehounds, Linc. Even more unhappy than you realize. If you've been conditioned against the sight of baldness to . . . to *that* extent—'

'It wasn't,' Linc denied futilely. 'I didn't . . . you shouldn't think—'

'It's all right. You can't help reactions as deeply rooted as that. Some day standards of beauty will change. Hairlessness will be lovely. Today it isn't, certainly not to a man with your psychological background. You must have been made to feel very keenly that you were inferior because of your baldness—'

Linc stood there awkwardly, unable to deny the thought that had sprung so vividly into his mind, burning with shame and dismay at the knowledge that she had seen as clearly as himself the ugly picture of her baldness in his thought. As if he had held up a distorting mirror to her face and said aloud, 'This is the way you look to me.' As if he had slapped her gratuitously across the cheek with the taunt of her – abnormality.

'Never mind,' Alexa said, a little shakily, smiling. 'You can't help it if baldness disg . . . distresses you. Forget it. It isn't as if we were m-married or . . . anything.'

They looked at each other in silence. Their minds touched and sprang apart and then touched again, tentatively, with light thoughts that leaped from point to point as gingerly as if the ideas were ice-floes that might sink beneath the full weight of conscious focus.

I thought I loved you . . . perhaps I did . . . yes, I too . . . but now there can't be . . . (sudden, rebellious denial) . . . no, it's true, there can't ever be rightness between us . . . not as if we were ordinary people . . . we'd always remember that picture, how I looked (abrupt sheering off from the memory) . . . (agonized repudiation of it) . . . no, couldn't help that ... always between us ... rooted too deeply ... and anyhow, Cas – (sudden closing off of both minds at once, before even the thought-image had time to form).

Alexa stood up. 'I'm going into town,' she said. 'Marian's at the hairdresser's. I ... I'll get a wave or something.'

He looked at her helplessly, half reluctant to let her go, though he knew as well as she how much had been discussed and weighed and discarded in the past moment of voiceless speech.

'Good-bye, Alexa,' he said.
'Good-bye, Linc.'

Linc stood for a long time watching the path, even after she had gone. He would have to leave. He didn't belong here. Even if nearness to Alexa were possible after this, he knew he could not stay. They were – abnormal. He would be seeing the baldness, the contemptible, laughable baldness he had hated in himself, more clearly now than the wigs they wore. Somehow until this moment he had never fully realized—

Well, he couldn't go without telling Darryl. Slowly, dragging his feet a little, he turned back toward the house. When he came to the side lawn he sent out an inexpert, querying thought.

Something answered him from the cellar-laboratory, a queer, strange, disturbing vibration that clung briefly to his mind and then pulled away. It wasn't McNey. It was – an intruder.

Linc went down the cellar steps. At the bottom he paused, trying to sort the tangled confusion in his mind as he thrust out exploratory mental fingers. The door was open. McNey was lying on the floor, his mind blanked, blood seeping from a red stain on his side.

The intruder?
Who—
Sergei Callahan.
Where—
Hidden. And armed.
So am I, Linc thought, his dagger springing into his hand.
Telepathically you are untrained. In a fight you can't win.

That was probably true. Telepathy took the place of prescience with the Baldies. Any Baldy could outguess and conquer a non-Baldy, and Linc was not yet thoroughly trained in the use of the telepathic function.

He probed awkwardly. And, suddenly, he knew where Callahan was.

Behind the door. Where he could strike Linc in the back when the boy entered the laboratory. He had not expected the untrained Baldy to discover the ambush until too late, and even as Linc realized the situation, Callahan made a move to spring out.

All Linc's weight smashed against the panel, slamming the door back against the wall. Callahan was caught. Pressed helplessly between the two metal planes – door and wall – he tried to brace himself, to wriggle free. His hand, gripping a dagger, snaked out. Linc dropped his own weapon, put his back against the door, and planted his feet more firmly. The door frame gave him good purchase. Veins stood out on his forehead as he ground, crushed, drove the door back with all his strength.

What had Dave Barton said once? 'Kill them with machines—'

This was a machine – one of the oldest. The lever.

Suddenly Callahan began to scream. His agonized thought begged for mercy. In a moment his strength would fail, he pleaded. 'Don't – *don't crush me!*'

His strength failed.

Linc's heavy shoulders surged. There was one frightful mental scream from Callahan, more agonizing than the audible sound he made, and Linc let the door swing slowly away from the wall. A body collapsed with its movement. Linc picked up his dagger, used it efficiently, and then turned to McNey.

There was a puddle of blood on the floor, but McNey still lived. Callahan had not had time to finish his task.

Linc became busy administering first aid.

That was it.

It was past midnight. In the cellar laboratory, McNey

leaned back in his chair, wincing as he felt the pressure of the bandages about his ribs. He blinked at the fluorescents, sighed, and rubbed his forehead.

His hand hovered over the note-pad. An equation was lacking. He wasn't quite ready to think of it just yet.

But the job was almost finished. It would give the Baldies a weapon, at last, against the paranoids. They couldn't tap the paranoid's secret wave-length, but they could—

Not yet. Don't think of it yet.

Even Linc had helped, unknowingly, by one suggestion he had made. Mimicry. Yes, that was one answer. The paranoids would not even suspect—

Not yet.

Well, Linc had gone back to his Hedgehound tribe and his Hedgehound squaw. In the end, the psychological fixation implanted in the boy's mind had proved stronger than the strong bonds of race. Too bad, because Linc had had something that few Baldies possessed – an innate hardness, a resourceful strength that might prove useful in the dark days that were coming.

The dark days that might yet be postponed, for a while, if—

Marian was asleep. McNey forced this thought from her. After years of marriage, they were so closely attuned that even that casual thought might waken her. And not until she had fallen asleep had he dared to bring his mind to bear on this ultimate problem. There could be no secrets between Baldies.

But this would be a secret – the one that would give Dave Barton a weapon against the paranoids. It was the unbreakable code that McNey had searched for for two years now.

It was a secret method of communication for Baldies.

Now. Work fast. *Work fast!*

McNey's stylus moved rapidly. He made a few adjustments in the machine before him, sealed its fastenings thoroughly, and watched power-flow develop. After a while, something came out of a small opening at one end of the device, a fine mesh of wire, with a few flatly curved attachments. McNey took off his wig, fitted the wire cap to his head, and donned the wig again. After a glance at a mirror, he nodded, satisfied.

The machine was permanently set now to construct these communicator caps when raw materials were fed into it. The matrix, the blueprint, had been built into the device, and the end result was a communicator gadget, easily hidden under a wig, which every non-paranoid Baldy probably would eventually wear. As for the nature of the gadget—

The problem had been to find a secret means of communication, akin to the paranoids' untappable wave-band. And telepathy itself is simply a three-phase oscillation of electro-magneto-gravitic energy, emanating from the specialized colloid of the human brain. But telepathy, *per se*, can be received by any sensitive mind en rapport with the sender.

And so the trick had been – find a method of artificial transmission. The brain, when properly stimulated by electric energy, will give out electromagneto-gravitic energy, undetectable except to telepaths because there are no instruments sensitive to this output. But when the paranoids would receive such radiations, without the unscrambling assistance of one of McNey's little caps, they wouldn't suspect a code.

Because they'd be hearing – sensing – only static.

It was a matter of camouflage. The waves masqueraded. They masqueraded on a wave-band that nobody used, for that particular band was too close to that of the radio communicators used in thousands of private helicopters. For these radios, five thousand megacycles was normal; fifteen thousand manifested itself as a harmless harmonic static, and McNey's device simply added more squirts of static to that harmonic interference.

True, direction-finders could receive the signals and locate them – but helicopters, like Baldies, were scattered all over the country, and the race travelled a good deal, both by necessity and by choice. The paranoids could locate the source of the fifteen thousand megacycles emanating from the wire caps – but why should they think to?

It was an adaptation of the Hedgehounds' code of imitating bird and animal calls. A tenderfoot in the woods wouldn't look for a language in the cry of an owl – and the paranoids wouldn't be seeking secret messages in what was apparently only static.

So, in these light, easily disguised mesh helmets, the problem was solved, finally. The power source would be an automatic tapping of free energy, an imperceptible drain on any nearby electrical generator, and the master machine itself, which made the communicators, was permanently sealed. No one except McNey himself, knew even the principles of the new communication system. And, since the machine would be guarded well, the paranoids would never know, any more than Barton himself would know, what made the gadget tick. Barton would realize its effectiveness, and that was all. The list of raw materials needed was engraved on the feeder-hopper of the machine; nothing else was necessary. So Barton would possess no secrets to betray inadvertently to the paranoids, for the secrets were all sealed in the machine, and in one other place.

McNey took off the wire cap and laid it on the table. He turned off the machine. Then, working quickly, he destroyed the formulas and any traces of notes or raw materials. He wrote a brief note to Barton, explaining what was necessary.

There was no more time left after that. McNey sank back in his chair, his tired, ordinary face without expression. He didn't look like a hero. And, just then, he wasn't thinking about the future of the Baldy race, or the fact that the other place where the secret was sealed was in his brain.

As his hands loosened the bandage about his ribs, he was thinking of Marian. And as his life began to flow out with the blood from his reopened wound, he thought: *I wish I could say good-bye to you, Marian. But I mustn't touch you, not even with my mind. We're too close. You'd wake up and—*

I hope you won't be too lonely, my dear—

He was going back. The Hedgehounds weren't his people, but Cassie was his wife. And so he had betrayed his own race, betrayed the future itself, perhaps, and followed the wandering tribe across three states until now, with the autumn winds blowing coldly through bare leaves, he had come to the end of his search. She was there, waiting. She was there, just beyond that ridge. He could feel it, sense it, and his heart stirred to the homecoming.

Betrayal, then. One man could not matter in the life of a race. There would be a few Baldy children less than if he had married Alexa. The Baldies would have to work out their own salvation—

But he wasn't thinking about that as he leaped the last hurdle and ran to where Cassie was sitting near the fire. He was thinking about Cassie, and the glossy darkness of her hair, and the soft curve of her cheek. He called her name, again and again.

She didn't believe it at first. He saw doubt in her eyes and in her mind. But that doubt faded when he dropped beside her, a strange figure in his exotic town clothing, and took her in his arms.

'Linc,' she said, 'you've come back.'

He managed to say, 'I've come back,' and stopped talking and thinking for a while. It was a long time before Cassie thought to show him something in which he might be expected to evince interest.

He did. His eyes widened until Cassie laughed and said that it wasn't the first baby in the world.

'I...us...you mean—'

'Sure. Us. This is Linc Junior. How'd you like him? He takes after his dad, too.'

'What?'

'Hold him.' As Cassie put the baby into his arms, Linc saw what she meant. The small head was entirely hairless, and there was no sign of lashes or eyebrows.

'But...you ain't bald, Cassie. How—'

'You sure are, though, Linc. That's why.'

Linc put his free arm around her and drew her close. He couldn't see the future; he couldn't realize the implications of this first attempt at mixing races. He only knew a profound and inarticulate relief that his child was like himself. It went deeper than the normal human desire to perpetuate one's own kind. This was reprieve. He had not, after all, wholly failed his race. Alexa would never bear his children, but his children need not be of alien stock in spite of it.

That deep warping which the Hedgehounds had wrought upon himself must not happen to the child. *I'll train him*, he thought. *He'll know from the start – he'll learn to be proud he's a Baldy. And then if they ever need him . . . no, if We ever need him . . . he'll be ready where I failed.*

The race would go on. It was good and satisfying and right that the union of Baldy and human could result in Baldy children. The line need not come to dead end because a man married outside his own kind. A man must follow his instinct, as Linc had done. It was good to belong to a race that allowed even that much treason to its tradition, and exacted no lasting penalty. The line was too strong to break. The dominant strain would go on.

Perhaps McNey's invention could postpone the day of the pogrom. Perhaps it could not. But if the day came, still the Baldies would go on. Underground, hidden, persecuted, still they must go on. And perhaps it would be among the Hedgehounds that the safest refuge could be found. For they had an emissary there, now—

Maybe this was right, Linc thought, his arm around Cassie and the child. *Once I belonged here. Now I don't. I'll never be happy for good in the old life. I know too much— But here I'm a link between the public and the secret life of the refugees. Maybe some day they'll need that link.* 'Linc,' he mused, and grinned.

Off in the distance a growl of song began to lift. The tribesmen, coming back from the day's hunting. He was surprised, a little, to realize he felt no more of the old, deep, bewildered distrust of them. He understood now. He knew them as they could never know themselves, and he had learned enough in the past months to evaluate that knowledge. Hedgehounds were no longer the malcontents and misfits of civilization. Generations of weeding-out had distilled them. Americans had always been a distillation in themselves of the pioneer, the adventurous drawn from the old world. The buried strain came out again in their descendants. The Hedgehounds were nomads now, yes; they were woodsmen, yes; they were fighters, always. So were the first Americans. The same hardy stock that might, some day, give refuge again to the oppressed and the hunted.

The song grew louder through the trees, Jesse James Hartwell's roaring bass leading all the others.

> 'Hurrah, hurrah, we bring the jubilee!
> Hurrah, hurrah, the flag that makes men free—'

CHAPTER 4

Night had fallen again. I lay looking up at the coldly sparkling stars and felt my mind toppling into that endless void of infinity.

I felt very clear-headed.

I had been lying here for a long time without moving, looking up at the stars. The snow had stopped some while ago, and the starlight glittered on its blue-shadowed mounds.

There was no use waiting any longer. I reached into my belt and took out my knife. I laid its blade across my left wrist and considered. That might take too long. There were quicker ways, in places where the body was more vulnerable.

But I was too tired to move. In a moment I would draw the blade back, with a heavy, pressing motion. Then it would be over, for there was no use waiting for rescue now, and I was blind and deaf and mute here behind the mountain barrier. Life had gone out of the world completely. The little sparks of glowing warmth which even insects possess, the strange, pulsing beat of life that flows like a tidal current through the universe, perhaps emanating from the microscopic organisms which exist everywhere – the light and warmth had gone out. It seemed as though the soul had been drained from everything.

Unconsciously I must have sent out a thought asking for help, because I heard a response within my mind. I almost shouted before I realized that the response had come from my own mind, some memory summoned up by associations.

You're one of us, the thought had said.

Why should I remember that? It reminded me of . . . Hobson. Hobson and the Beggars in Velvet. For McNey had not solved the ultimate problem.

The next battle in the war had been fought in Sequoia. Should I remember?

The blade of the knife lay wire-cold across my wrist. It would be very easy to die. Much easier than to keep on living, blind and deaf and alone.

You're one of us, my thought said again.

And my mind went back to a bright morning in a town near the old Canadian border, and the smell of cold, pine-sharp air, and the rhythmic beat of a man's footsteps along Redwood Street – a hundred years ago.

BEGGARS IN VELVET

It was like stepping on a snake. The thing, concealed in fresh, green grass, squirmed underfoot and turned and struck venomously. But the thought was not that of reptile or beast, only man was capable of the malignance that was, really, a perversion of intellect.

Burkhalter's dark face did not change; his easy stride did not alter. But his mind had instantly drawn back from that blind malevolence, alert and ready, while all through the villages Baldies paused imperceptibly in their work or conversation as their minds touched Burkhalter's.

No human noticed.

Under bright morning sunlight Redwood Street curved cheerful and friendly before Burkhalter. But a breath of uneasiness slipped along it, the same cool dangerous wind that had been blowing for days through the thoughts of every telepath in Sequoia. Ahead were a few early shoppers, some children on their way to school, a group gathered outside the barber shop, one of the doctors from the hospital.

Where is he?

The answer came swiftly. *Can't locate him. Near you, though—*

Someone – a woman, the overtones of her thoughts showed – sent a message tinged with emotional confusion, almost hysterical. *One of the patients from the hospital—*

Instantly the thoughts of the other closed reassuringly around her, warm with friendliness and comfort. Even Burkhalter took time to send a clear thought of unity. He recognized among the others the cool, competent personality of Duke Heath, the Baldy priest-medic, with its subtle psychological shading, that only another telepath could sense.

It's Selfridge, Heath told the woman, while the other Baldies listened. *He's just drunk. I think I'm nearest, Burkhalter, I'm coming.*

A helicopter curved overhead, its freight-gliders swinging behind it, stabilized by their gyroscopes. It swept over the western ridge and was gone toward the Pacific. As its humming died, Burkhalter could hear the muffled roar of the cataract up the valley. He was vividly conscious of the waterfall's feathery whiteness plunging down the cliff, of the slopes of pine and fir and redwood around Sequoia, of the distant noise of the cellulose mills. He focused on these clean, familiar things to shut out the sickly foulness that blew from Selfridge's mind to his own. Sensibility and sensitivity had gone hand in hand with the Baldies, and Burkhalter had wondered more than once how Duke Heath managed to maintain his balance in view of the man's work among the psychiatric patients at the hospital. The race of Baldies had come too soon; they were not aggressive; but race-survival depended on competition.

He's in the tavern, a woman's thought said. Burkhalter automatically jerked away from the message; he knew the mind from which it came. Logic told him instantly that the source didn't matter – in this instance. Barbara Pell was a paranoid; therefore an enemy. But both paranoids and Baldies were desperately anxious to avoid any open break. Though their ultimate goals lay worlds apart, yet their paths sometimes paralleled.

But already it was too late. Fred Selfridge came out of the tavern, blinked against the sunlight, and saw Burkhalter. The trader's thin, hollow-cheeked face twisted into a sour grin.

The blurred malignance of his thought drove before him as he walked toward Burkhalter, and one hand kept making little darts toward the misericordia swung at his belt.

He stopped before Burkhalter, blocking the Baldy's progress. His grin broadened.

Burkhalter had paused. A dry panic tightened his throat. He was afraid, not for himself, but for his race, and every Baldy in Sequoia knew that – and watched.

He said: 'Morning, Fred.'

Selfridge hadn't shaved that morning. Now he rubbed his stubbled chin and let his eyelids droop. 'Mr. Burkhalter,' he said. '*Consul* Burkhalter. Good thing you remembered to wear a cap this morning. Skinheads catch cold pretty easy.'

Play for time, Duke Heath ordered. *I'm coming. I'll fix it.*

'I didn't pull any wires to get this job, Fred,' Burkhalter said. 'The Towns made me consul. Why blame me for it?'

'You pulled wires, all right,' Selfridge said. 'I know graft when I see it. You were a schoolteacher from Modoc or some hick town. What the devil do you know about Hedgehounds?'

'Not as much as you do,' Burkhalter admitted. 'You've had the experience.'

'Sure. Sure I have. So they take a half-baked teacher and make him consul to the Hedgehounds. A greenhorn who doesn't even know those bichos have got cannibal tribes. I traded with the woodsmen for thirty years, and I know how to handle 'em. Are you going to read 'em pretty little stories out of books?'

'I'll do what I'm told. I'm not the boss.'

'No. But maybe your friends are. Connections! If I'd had the same connections you've got, I'd be sitting on my tail like you, pulling in credits for the same work. Only I'd do that work better – a lot better.'

'I'm not interfering with your business,' Burkhalter said. 'You're still trading, aren't you? I'm minding my own affairs.'

'Are you? How do I know what you tell the Hedgehounds?'

'My records are open to anybody.'

'Yeah?'

'Sure. My job's just to promote peaceful relations with the Hedgehounds. Not to do any trading, except what *they* want – and then I refer 'em to you.'

'It sounds fine,' Selfridge said. 'Except for one thing. You can read my mind and tell the Hedgehounds all about my private business.'

Burkhalter's guard slipped; he couldn't have helped it. He had stood the man's mental nearness as long as he could, though it was like breathing foul air. 'Afraid of what?' he asked, and regretted the words instantly. The voices in his mind cried: *Careful!*

Selfridge flushed. 'So you do it after all, eh? All that fine talk about you skinheads respecting people's privacy – sure! No wonder you got the consulate! Reading minds—'

'Hold on,' Burkhalter said. 'I've never read a non-Baldy's mind in my life. That's the truth.'

'Is it?' the trader sneered. 'How the devil do I know if you're lying? But you can look inside my head and see if *I'm* telling the truth. What you Baldies need is to be taught your place, and for two coins, I'd—'

Burkhalter's mouth felt stiff. 'I don't duel,' he said, with an effort. 'I won't duel.'

'Yellow,' Selfridge said, and waited, his hand hovering over the misericordia's hilt.

And there was the usual quandary. No telepath could possibly lose a duel with a non-Baldy, unless he wanted to commit suicide. But he dared not win, either. The Baldies baked their own humble pie; a minority that lives on sufferance must not reveal its superiority, or it won't survive. One such incident might have breached the dyke the telepaths had painfully erected against the rising tide of intolerance.

For the dyke was too long. It embraced all of mankind. And it was impossible to watch every inch of that incredible levee of custom, orientation and propaganda, though the basic tenets were instilled in each Baldy from infancy. Some day the dyke would collapse, but each hour of postponement meant the gathering of a little more strength—

Duke Heath's voice said, 'A guy like you, Selfridge, would be better off dead.'

Sudden shock touched Burkhalter. He shifted his gaze to the priest-medic, remembering the subtle tension he had recently sensed under Heath's deep calm, and wondering if this was the blow-off. Then he caught the thought in Heath's mind and relaxed, though warily.

Beside the Baldy was Ralph Selfridge, a smaller, slighter edition of Fred. He was smiling rather sheepishly.

Fred Selfridge showed his teeth. 'Listen, Heath,' he snapped. 'Don't try to stand on your position. You haven't got one. You're a surrogate. No skinhead can be a real priest *or* a medic.'

'Sure they can,' Heath said. 'But they don't.' His round, youthful face twisted into a scowl. 'Listen to me—'

'I'm not listening to—'

'*Shut up!*'

Selfridge gasped in surprise. He was caught flat-footed, undecided whether to use his misericordia or his fists, and while he hesitated, Heath went on angrily.

'I said you'd be better off dead and I meant it! This kid brother of yours thinks you're such a hot-shot he imitates everything you do. Now look at him! If the epidemic hits Sequoia, he won't have enough resistance to work up antibodies, and the young idiot won't let me give him preventive shots. I suppose he thinks he can live on whisky like you!'

Fred Selfridge frowned at Heath, stared at his younger brother, and looked back at the priest-medic. He shook his head, trying to clear it.

'Leave Ralph alone. He's all right.'

'Well, start saving for his funeral expenses,' Heath said callously. 'As a surrogate medic, I'll make a prognosis right now – *rigor mortis*.'

Selfridge licked his lips. 'Wait a minute. The kid isn't sick, is he?'

'There's an epidemic down toward Columbia Crossing,' Heath said. 'One of the new virus mutations. If it hits us here, there'll be trouble. It's a bit like tetanus, but avertin's no good. Once the nerve centres are hit, nothing can be done.

Preventive shots will help a lot, especially when a man's got the susceptible blood-type – as Ralph has.'

Burkhalter caught a command from Heath's mind.

'You could use some shots yourself, Fred,' the priest-medic went on. 'Still, your blood type is B, isn't it? And you're tough enough to throw off an infection. This virus is something new, a mutation of the old flu bug—'

He went on. Across the street someone called Burkhalter's name and the consul slipped away, unnoticed except for a parting glare from Selfridge.

A slim, red-haired girl was waiting under a tree at the corner. Burkhalter grimaced inwardly as he saw he could not avoid her. He was never quite able to control the turmoil of feeling which the very sight or thought of Barbara Pell stirred up within him. He met her bright narrow eyes, full of pinpoints of light. He saw her round slimness that looked so soft and would, he thought, be as hard to the touch as her mind was hard to the thought's touch. Her bright red wig, almost too luxuriant, spilled heavy curls down about the square, alert face to move like red Medusa-locks upon her shoulders when she turned her head, Curiously, she had a red-head's typical face, high-cheek bones, dangerously alive. There is a quality of the red-haired that goes deeper than the hair, for Barbara Pell had, of course been born as hairless as any Baldy.

'You're a fool,' she said softly as he came up beside her. 'Why don't you get rid of Selfridge?'

Burkhalter shook his head. 'No. And don't you try anything.'

'I tipped you off that he was in the tavern. And I got here before anybody else, except Heath. If we could work together—'

'We can't.'

'Dozens of times we've saved you traitors,' the woman said bitterly. 'Will you wait until the humans stamp out your lives—'

Burkhalter walked past her and turned toward the pathway that climbed the steep ascent leading out of Sequoia.

He was vividly aware of Barbara Pell looking after him. He could see her as clearly as if he had eyes in the back of his head, her bright, dangerous face, her beautiful body, her bright, beautiful, insane thoughts—

For behind all their hatefulness, the paranoids' vision was as beautiful and tempting as the beauty of Barbara Pell. Perilously tempting. A free world, where Baldies could walk and live and think in safety, no longer bending the scope of their minds into artificial, cramping limits as once men bent their backs in subservience to their masters. A bent back is a humiliating thing, but even a serf's mind is free to range. To cramp the mind is to cramp the soul, and no humiliation could surpass the humiliation of that.

But there was no such world as the paranoids dreamed of. The price would be too high. What shall it profit a man, thought Burkhalter wryly, if he gain the whole world and lose his own soul? The words might first have been spoken in this connection and no other, so perfectly did they apply to it. The price must be murder, and whoever paid that price would automatically sully the world he bought with it until, if he were a normal creature, he could never enjoy what he had paid so high to earn. Burkhalter called up a bit of verse into his mind and savoured again the bitter melancholy of the poet who wrote it, perhaps more completely than the poet himself ever dreamed.

> *I see the country, far away,*
> *Where I shall never stand.*
> *The heart goes where no footstep may,*
> *Into the promised land.*

Barbara Pell's mind shot after him an angry, evil shaft of scorn and hatred. 'You're a fool, you're all fools, you don't deserve telepathy if you degrade it. If you'd only join us in—' The thought ceased to be articulate and ran suddenly, gloatingly red with spilled blood, reeking saltily of it, as if her whole mind bathed deliciously in the blood of all humans.

Burkhalter jerked his thoughts away from contact with

hers, sickened. It isn't the end of free living they want any more, he told himself in sudden realization – it's the means they're lusting after now. They've lost sight of a free world. All they want is killing.

'Fool, fool, fool!' Barbara Pell's thoughts screamed after him. 'Wait and see! Wait until – one times two is two, two times two is four, three times two—'

Burkhalter thought grimly, 'They're up to something,' and sent his mind probing gingerly past the sudden artifical barrier with which she had sought to blank out a thought even she realized was indiscreet. She fought the probing viciously. He sensed only vague, bloody visions stirring behind the barrier. Then she laughed without a sound and hurled a clear, terrible, paranoid thought at him, a picture of sickening clarity that all but splashed in his face with its overrunning redness.

He drew his mind back with swiftness that was pure reflex. As safe to touch fire as thoughts like hers. It was one way any paranoid could shut out the inquisitive thoughts of a non-paranoid when need arose. And of course, normally no Baldy would dream of probing uninvited into another mind. Burkhalter shuddered.

They were up to something, certainly. He must pass the episode on to those whose business it was to know about the paranoids. Barbara Pell's mind was not, in any case, likely to yield much information on secret plans. She was an executioner, not a planner. He withdrew his thoughts from her, fastidiously, shaking off the contamination as a cat shakes water from its feet.

He climbed the steep slope that led out of Sequoia to his home, deliberately shutting his mind from all things behind him. Fifteen minutes' walk brought him to the rustic log-and-plastic house built near the shadow of the West Canadian Forest. This was his consulate, and only the cabin of the Selfridge brothers lay farther out in the wilderness that stretched north to the Beaufort Sea that mingles with the Arctic Ocean.

By his desk a glowing red light indicated a message in the terminal of the pneumatic that stretched for six miles into the forest. He read it carefully. A delegation of Hedgehounds would arrive soon, representatives from three tribal groups. Well—

He checked supplies, televised the general store, and sat down behind his desk to wait. Heath would be along soon. Meanwhile he closed his eyes and concentrated on the fresh smell of pine that blew through the open windows. But the fresh, clean scent was sullied by vagrant thought currents that tainted the air.

Burkhalter shivered.

II

Sequoia lay near the border of old Canada, now an immense wilderness that the forest had largely reclaimed. Cellulose by-products were its industry, and there was an immense psychiatric hospital, which accounted for the high percentage of Baldies in the village. Otherwise Sequoia was distinguished from the hundreds of thousands of other towns that dotted America by the recent establishment of a diplomatic station there, the consulate that would be a means of official contact with the wandering tribes that retreated into the forests as civilization encroached. It was a valley town, bordered by steep slopes, with their enormous conifers and the white-water cataracts racing down from snowy summits. Not far westward, beyond the Strait of Georgia and Vancouver Island, lay the Pacific. But there were few highways; transport was aerial. And communication was chiefly by tele-radio.

Four hundred people, more or less, lived in Sequoia, a tight little semi-independent settlement, bartering its specialized products for shrimps and pompano from Lafitte; books from Modoc; beryllium-steel daggers and motor-ploughs from American Gun; clothing from Dempsey and Gee Eye. The Boston textile mills were gone with Boston; that smoking, grey desolation had not changed since the year of the Blow-up. But there was still plenty of room in

America, no matter how much the population might increase; war had thinned the population. And as technology advanced so did improvements in reclamation of arid and unfertile land, and the harder strains of the kudzu plant had already opened vast new tracts for farming. But agriculture was not the only industry. The towns specialized, never expanding into cities, but sending out spores that would grow into new villages – or, rather, reaching out like raspberry canes, to take root whenever they touched earth.

Burkhalter was deliberately not thinking of the red-haired woman when Duke Heath came in. The priest-medic caught the strained, negative mental picture, and nodded.

'Barbara Pell,' he said. 'I saw her.' Both men blurred the surface of their minds. That couldn't mask their thoughts, but if any other brain began probing, there would be an instant's warning, during which they could take precautions. Necessarily, however, the conversation stayed oral rather than telepathic.

'They can smell trouble coming,' Burkhalter said. 'They've been infiltrating Sequoia lately, haven't they?'

'Yes. The minute you copped this consulate, they started to come in.' Heath nibbled his knuckles. 'In forty years the paranoids have built up quite an organization.'

'Sixty years,' Burkhalter said. 'My grandfather saw it coming back in '82. There was a paranoid in Modoc – a lone wolf at the time, but it was one of the first symptoms. And since then—'

'Well, they've grown qualitatively, not quantitatively. There are more true grown Baldies now than paranoids. Psychologically they're handicapped. They hate to intermarry with non-Baldies. Whereas *we* do, and the dominant strain goes on – spreads out.'

'For a while,' Burkhalter said.

Heath frowned. 'There's no epidemic at Columbia Crossing. I had to get Selfridge off your neck somehow, and he's got a strongly paternal instinct towards his brother. That did it – but not permanently. With that so-and-so, the part equals the whole. You got the consulate; he had a nice little racket gypping the Hedgehounds; he hates you – so he jumps on your most vulnerable point. Also, he rationalizes. He tells himself that if you didn't have the unfair advantage of being a Baldy, you'd never have landed the consulate.'

'It was unfair.'

'We had to do it,' Heath said. 'Non-Baldies mustn't find out what we're building up among the Hedgehounds. Some day the woods folk may be our only safety. If a non-Baldy had got the consulate—'

'I'm working in the dark,' Burkhalter said. 'All I know is that I've got to do what the Mutes tell me.'

'I don't know any more than you do. The paranoids have their Power – that secret band of communication we can't tap – and only the Mutes have a method of fighting that weapon. Don't forget that, while we can't read a Mute's mind, the paranoids can't either. If you knew their secrets, your mind would be an open book – any telepath could read it.'

Burkhalter didn't answer. Heath sighed and watched pine needles glittering in the sunlight outside the windows.

'It's not easy for me either,' he said. 'To be a surrogate. No non-Baldy has to be a priest as well as a medic. But I have to. The doctors up at the hospital feel more strongly about it than I do. They know how many psychotic cases have been cured because we can read minds. Meanwhile—' He shrugged.

Burkhalter was staring northward. 'A new land is what we need,' he said.

'We need a new world. Some day we'll get it.'

A shadow fell across the door. Both men turned. A small figure was standing there, a fat little man with close-curling hair and mild blue eyes. The misericordia at his belt seemed incongruous, as though those pudgy fingers would fumble ludicrously with the hilt.

No Baldy will purposely read a non-telepath's mind, but there is an instinctive recognition between Baldies. So Burkhalter and Heath knew instantly that the stranger was a telepath – and then, on the heels of that thought, came sudden, startled recognition of the emptiness where thought should be. It was like stepping on clear ice and finding it clear water instead. Only a few men could guard their minds completely thus. They were the Mutes.

'Hello,' said the stranger, coming in and perching himself on the desk's edge. 'I see you know me. We'll stay oral, if you don't mind. I can read your thoughts, but you can't read mine.' He grinned. 'No use wondering why, Burkhalter. If *you* knew, the paranoids would find out too. Now. My name's Ben Hobson.' He paused. 'Trouble, eh? Well, we'll kick that around later. First let me get this off my chest.'

Burkhalter sent a swift glance at Heath. 'There are paranoids in town. Don't tell me too much, unless—'

'Don't worry. I won't,' Hobson chuckled. 'What do you know about the Hedgehounds?'

'Descendants of the nomad tribes that didn't join the villages after the Blow-up. Gypsies. Woods folk. Friendly enough.'

'That's right,' Hobson said. 'Now what I'm telling you is common knowledge, even among the paranoids. You should know it. We've spotted a few cells among the Hedgehounds — Baldies. It started by accident, forty years ago, when a Baldy named Linc Cody was adopted by Hedgehounds and reared without knowing his heritage. Later he found out. He's still living with the Hedgehounds, and so are his sons.'

'Cody?' Burkhalter said slowly. 'I've heard stories of the Cody—'

'Psychological propaganda. The Hedgehounds are barbarians. But we want 'em friendly and we want to clear the way, for joining them, if that ever becomes necessary. Twenty years ago we started building up a figurehead in the forests, a living symbol who'd be overtly a shaman and really a delegate for us. We used mumbo-jumbo. Linc Cody dressed up in a trick suit, we gave him gadgets, and the Hedgehounds finally developed the legend of the Cody – a sort of benevolent woods spirit who acts as supernatural monitor. They like him, they obey him, and they're afraid of him. Especially since he can appear in four places at the same time.'

'Eh?' Burkhalter said.

'Cody had three sons,' Hobson smiled. 'It's one of them you'll see today. Your friend Selfridge has fixed up a little plot. You're due to be murdered by one of the Hedgehound chiefs when that delegation gets here. I can't interfere personally, but the Cody will. It's necessary for you to play along. Don't give any sign that you expect trouble. When the Cody steps in, the chiefs will be plenty impressed.'

Heath said, 'Wouldn't it have been better not to tell Burkhalter what to expect?'

'No. For two reasons. He can read the Hedgehounds' minds – I give him carte blanche on that – and he must string along with the Cody. O.K., Burkhalter?'

'O.K.' the consul nodded.

'Then I'll push off.' Hobson stood up, still smiling. 'Good luck.'

'Wait a minute,' Heath said. 'What about Selfridge?'

'Don't kill him. Either of you. You know no Baldy must ever duel with a non-Baldy.'

Burkhalter was scarcely listening. He knew he must mention the thought he had surprised in Barbara Pell's mind, and he had been putting off the moment when he must speak her hateful name, open the gates of his thoughts wide enough to let her image slip back in, beautiful image, beautiful slender body, bright and dangerous and insane mind—

'I saw one of the paranoids in town a while ago,' he said. 'Barbara Pell. A nasty job, that woman. She let slip something about their plans. Covered up too fast for me to get much, but you might think about it. They're up to something planned for fairly soon, I gathered.'

Hobson smiled at him. 'Thanks. We're watching them. We'll keep an eye on the woman too. All right, then. Good luck.'

He went out. Burkhalter and Heath looked at one another.

The Mute walked slowly down the path toward the village. His mouth was pursed as he whistled; his plump cheeks vibrated. As he passed a tall pine he abruptly unsheathed his dagger and sprang around the tree. The man lurking there was caught by surprise. Steel found its mark unerringly. The paranoid had time for only one desperate mental cry before he died.

Hobson wiped his dagger and resumed his journey. Under the close-cropped brown wig a mechanism, shaped like a skull-cap, began functioning. Neither Baldy nor telepath could receive the signals Hobson was sending and receiving now.

'They know I'm here.'

'Sometimes they do,' a soundless voice came back. 'They can't catch modulated frequencies the helmets use, but they can notice the shields. Still, as long as none of 'em know why—'

'I just killed one.'

'One less of the bichos,' came the coldly satisfied response. 'I think I'd better stay here for a while. Paranoids have been infiltrating. Both Heath and Burkhalter think so. There's some contingent plan I can't read yet; the paranoids are thinking about it only on their own band.'

'Then stay. Keep in touch. What about Burkhalter?'

'What we suspected. He's in love with the paranoid Barbara Pell. But he doesn't know it.'

Both shocked abhorrence and unwilling sympathy were in the answering thought. 'I can't remember anything like this ever happening before. He can read her mind; he knows she's paranoid—'

Hobson smiled. 'The realization of his true feelings would upset him plenty, Jerry. Apparently you picked the wrong man for this job.'

'Not from Burkhalter's record. He's always lived a pretty secluded life, but his character's above reproach. His empathy standing was high. And he taught sociology for six years at New Yale.'

'He taught it, but I think it remained remote. He's known Barbara Pell for six weeks now. He's in love with her.'

'But how – even subconsciously? Baldies instinctively hate and distrust paranoids.'

Hobson reached Sequoia's outskirts and kept going, past

the terraced square where the blocky, insulated power station sat. 'So it's perverse,' he told the other Mute. 'Some men are attracted only to ugly women. You can't argue with a thing like that. Burkhalter's fallen in love with a paranoid, and I hope to heaven he never realizes it. He might commit suicide. Or anything might happen. This is—' His thought moved with slow emphasis. 'This is the most dangerous situation the Baldies have ever faced. Apparently nobody's paid much attention to Selfridge's talk, but the damage has been done. People *have* listened. And non-Baldies have always mistrusted us. If there's a blow-off, we're automatically scapegoats.'

'Like that, Ben?'

'The pogrom may start in Sequoia.'

Once the chess game had started, there was no way to stop it. It was cumulative. The paranoids, the warped twin branch of the parallel telepathic mutation, were not insane; there was a psychoneurotic pathology. They had only one basic delusion. They were the super race. On that foundation they built their edifice of planetary sabotage.

Non-Baldies outnumbered them, and they could not fight the technology that flourished in the days of decentralization. But if the culture of the non-Baldies were weakened, wrecked—

Assassinations, deftly disguised as duels or accidents; secret sabotage in a hundred branches, from engineering to publishing; propaganda, carefully sowed in the proper places – and civilization would have headed for a crack-up, except for one check.

The Baldies, the true, non-paranoid mutation, were fighting for the older race. They had to. They knew, as the blinded paranoids could not, that eventually the non-Baldies would learn of the chess game, and then nothing could stop a world-wide pogrom.

One advantage the paranoids had, for a while – a specialized band on which they could communicate telepathically, a wavelength which could not be tapped. Then a Baldy technician had perfected the scrambler helmets, with a high-frequency modulation that was equally untappable. As long as a Baldy wore such a helmet under his wig, his mind could be read only by another Mute.

So they came to be called, a small, tight group of exterminators, sworn to destroy the paranoids completely – in effect, a police force, working in secret and never doffing the helmets which shut them out from the complete rapport that played so large a part in the psychic life of the Baldy race.

They had willingly given up a great part of their heritage. It was a curious paradox that only by strictly limiting their telepathic power could these few Baldies utilize their weapon against the paranoids. And what they fought for was the time of ultimate unification when the dominant mutation had become so numerically strong that in all the world, there would be no need for mental barriers or psychic embargoes.

Meanwhile the most powerful of the Baldy race, they could never know, except within a limited scope, the subtle gratification of the mental round-robins, when a hundred or a thousand minds would meet and merge into the deep, eternal peace that only telepaths can know.

They, too, were beggars in velvet.

III

Burkhalter said suddenly, 'What's the matter with you, Duke?'

Heath didn't move. 'Nothing.'

'Don't give me that. Your thoughts are on quicksands.'

'Maybe they are,' Heath said. 'The fact is, I need a rest. I live this work, but it does get me down sometimes.'

'Well, take a vacation.'

'Can't. We're too busy. Our reputation's so good we're getting cases from all over. We're one of the first mental sanitoriums to go in for all-out Baldy psychoanalysis. It's been going on, of course, for years but *sub rosa*, more or less. People don't like the idea of Baldies prying into the minds of their relatives. However, since we started to show results—' His eyes lit up. 'Even with psychosomatic illnesses we can help a lot, and mood disorders are our meat. The big question, you know, is *why*. Why they've been putting poison in the patient's food, why they watch him – and so forth. Once that question's answered fully, it usually gives the necessary clues. And the average patient's apt to shut up like a clam when the psychiatrist questions him. But—' Heath's excitement mounted, 'this is the biggest thing in the history of medicine. There've been Baldies since the Blow-up, and only now are the doctors opening their doors to us. Ultimate empathy. A psychotic locks his mind, so he's hard to treat. But *we* have the keys—'

'What are you afraid of?' Burkhalter asked quietly.

Heath stopped short. He examined his fingernails.

'It's not fear,' he said at last. 'It's occupational anxiety. Oh, the devil with that. Four-bit words. It's simpler, really; you can put it in the form of an axiom. You can't touch pitch without getting soiled.'

'I see.'

'Do you, Harry? It's only this, really. My work consists of visiting abnormal minds. Not the way an ordinary psychiatrist does it. I get into those minds. I see and feel their viewpoints. I know all their terrors. The invisible horror that waits in the dark for them isn't just a word to me. I'm sane, and I see through the eyes of a hundred insane men. Keep out of my mind for a minute, Harry.' He turned away. Burkhalter hesitated.

'O.K.,' Heath said, looking around. 'I'm glad you mentioned this, though. Every so often I find myself getting entirely too empathic. Then I either take my copter up, or get in a round-robin. I'll see if I can promote a hook-up tonight. Are you in?'

'Sure,' Burkhalter said. Heath nodded casually and went out. His thought came back.

I'd better not be here when the Hedgehounds come. Unless you—

No, Burkhalter thought, *I'll be all right.*

O.K. Here's a delivery for you.

Burkhalter opened the door in time to admit the grocer's boy, who had parked his trail car outside. He helped put the supplies away, saw that the beer would be sufficiently refrigerated, and pressed a few buttons that would insure a supply of pressure-cooked refreshments. The Hedgehounds were hearty eaters.

After that, he left the door open and relaxed behind his desk, waiting. It was hot in the office; he opened his collar and made the walls transparent. Air conditioning began to cool the room, but the sight of the broad valley below was equally refreshing. Tall pines rippled their branches in the wind.

It was not like New Yale, one of the larger towns, that was intensely specialized in education. Sequoia, with its great hospital and its cellulose industry, was more of a complete, rounded unit. Isolated from the rest of the world except by air and television, it lay clean and attractive, sprawling in white and green and pastel plastics around the swift waters of the river that raced down seaward.

Burkhalter locked his hands behind his neck and yawned. He felt inexplicably fatigued, as he had felt from time to time for several weeks. Not that this work was hard; on the contrary. But reorientation to his new job wouldn't be quite as easy as he had expected. In the beginning he hadn't anticipated these wheels within wheels.

Barbara Pell, for example. She was dangerous. She, more than any of the others, perhaps, was the guiding spirit of the Sequoia paranoids. Not in the sense of planned action, no. But she ignited, like a flame. She is a born leader. And there were uncomfortably many paranoids here now. They had infiltrated – superficially with good reason, on jobs or errands or vacations; but the town was crammed with them, comparatively speaking. The non-telepaths still outnumbered both Baldies and paranoids as they did on a larger scale all over the world—

He remembered his grandfather, Ed Burkhalter. If any Baldy had ever hated the paranoids, Ed Burkhalter had. And presumably with good reason, since one of the first paranoid plots – a purely individual attempt then – had indirectly tried to indoctrinate the mind of Ed's son, Harry Burkhalter's father. Oddly, Burkhalter remembered his grandfather's thin, harsh face more vividly than his father's gentler one.

He yawned again, trying to immerse himself in the calm of the vista beyond the windows. Another world? Perhaps only in deep space could a Baldy ever be completely free from those troubling half-fragments of thoughts that he sensed even now. And without that continual distraction, with one's mind utterly unhampered – he stretched luxuriously, trying to imagine the feeling of his body without gravity and extending that parallel to his mind. But it was impossible.

The Baldies had been born before their time, of course – an artificially hastened mutation caused by radio-activity acting on human genes and chromosomes. Thus their present environment was wrong. Burkhalter toyed idly with the concept of a deep-space race, each individual mind so delicately attuned that even the nearness of any alien personality would interfere with the smooth process of perfect thought. Pleasant, but impractical. It would be a dead end. The telepaths weren't supermen, as the paranoids contended; at best they had only one fatally miraculous sense – fatal, because it had been mingled with common clay. With a genuine superman, telepathy would be merely one sense among a dozen other inconceivable ones.

Whereas Barbara Pell – the name and the face slid into his thoughts again, and the beautiful body, as dangerous and as fascinating as fire – whereas Barbara Pell, for instance, undoubtedly considered herself strictly super, like all the warped telepaths of her kind.

He thought of her bright, narrow gaze, and the red mouth with its sneering smile. He thought of the red curls moving like snakes upon her shoulders, and the red thoughts moving like snakes through her mind. He stopped thinking of her.

He was very tired. The sense of fatigue, all out of proportion to the energy he had expended, swelled, and engulfed him. If the Hedgehound chiefs weren't coming, it would be pleasant to take a copter up. The inclosing walls of the mountains would fall away as the plane lifted into the empty blue, higher and higher, till it hung in space above a blurred featureless landscape, half-erased by drifting clouds. Burkhalter thought of how the ground would look, a misty, dreamy Sime illustration, and, in his daydream, he reached out slowly to touch the controls. The copter slanted down, more and more steeply, till it was flashing suicidally toward a world that spread hypnotically, like a magically expanding carpet.

Someone was coming. Burkhalter blurred his mind instantly and stood up. Beyond the open door was only the empty forest, but now he could hear the faint, rising overtones of a song. The Hedgehounds, being a nation of nomads, sang as they marched, old tunes and ballads of memorable simplicity that had come down unchanged from before the Blow-up, though the original meanings had been forgotten.

> *Green grow the lilacs, all sparkling with dew;*
> *I'm lonely, my darling, since parting from you—*

Ancestors of the Hedgehounds had hummed that song along the borders of Old Mexico, long before war had been anything but distantly romantic. The grandfather of one of the current singers had been a Mexican, drifting up the California coast, dodging the villages and following a lazy wanderlust that led him into the Canadian forests at last. His name had been Ramon Alvarez but his grandson's name was Kit Carson Alvers, and his black beard rippled as he sang.

> *But by our next meeting I'll hope to prove true,*
> *And change the green lilacs for the red, white and blue.*

There were no minstrels among the Hedgehounds – they were all minstrels, which is how folk songs are kept alive. Singing, they came down the path, and fell silent at sight of the consul's house.

Burkhalter watched. It was a chapter of the past come

alive before his eyes. He had read of the Hedgehounds, but not until six weeks ago had he encountered any of the new pioneers. Their bizarre costumes still had power to intrigue him.

Those costumes combined functionalism with decoration. The buckskin shirts, that could blend into a pattern of forest light and shade, were fringed with knotted tassels; Alvers had a coonskin cap, and all three men wore sandals, made of soft, tough kidskin. Sheathed knives were at their belts, hunting knives, plainer and shorter than the misericordias of the townsfolk. And their faces showed a rakehell vigour, a lean, brown independence of spirit that made them brothers. For generations now the Hedgehounds had been wrestling their living from the wilderness and such rude weapons as the bow one of them had slung across his shoulder, and the ethics of duelling had never developed among them. They didn't duel. They killed, when killing seemed necessary – for survival.

Burkhalter came to the threshold. 'Come in,' he said, 'I'm the consul – Harry Burkhalter.'

'You got our message?' asked a tall, Scottish-looking chief with a busy red beard. 'That thing you got rigged up in the woods looked tetchy.'

'The message conveyor? It works, all right.'

'Fair enough. I'm Cobb Mattoon. This here's Kit Carson Alvers, and this un's Umpire Vine.' Vine was clean-shaven, a barrel of a man who looked like a bear, his sharp brown eyes slanting wary glances all around. He gave a taciturn grunt and shook hands with Burkhalter. So did the others. As the Baldy gripped Alvers' palm, he knew that this was the man who intended to kill him.

He made no sign. 'Glad you're here. Sit down and have a drink. What'll you have?'

'Whisky,' Vince grunted. His enormous hands smothered the glass. He grinned at the siphon, shook his head, and gulped a quantity of whisky that made Burkhalter's throat smart in sympathy.

Alvers, too, took whisky; Mattoon drank gin, with lemon. 'You got a smart lot of drinks here,' he said, staring at the bar Burkhalter had swung out. 'I can make out to spell some of the labels, but – what's that?'

'Drambuie. Try it?'

'Sure,' Mattoon said, and his red-haired throat worked. 'Nice stuff. Better than the corn we cook up in the woods.'

'If you walked far, you'll be hungry,' Burkhalter said. He pulled out the oval table, selected covered dishes from the conveyor belt, and let his guests help themselves. They fell to without ceremony.

Alvers looked across the table. 'You one of them Baldies?' he asked suddenly.

Burkhalter nodded. 'Yes, I am. Why?'

Mattoon said, 'So you're one of 'em.' He was frankly staring. 'I never seen a Baldy right close up. Maybe I have at that, but with the wigs you can't tell, of course.'

Burkhalter grinned as he repressed a familiar feeling of sick distaste. He had been stared at before, and for the same reason.

'Do I look like a freak, Mr. Mattoon?'

'How long you been consul?' Mattoon asked.

'Six weeks.'

'O.K.,' the big man said, and his voice was friendly enough, though the tone was harsh. 'You oughta remember there ain't no Mistering with the Hedgehounds. I'm Cobb Mattoon. Cobb to my friends, Mattoon to the rest. Nope, you don't look like no freak. Do people figger you Baldies are all sports?'

'A good many of them,' Burkhalter said.

'One thing,' Mattoon said, picking up a chop bone, 'in the woods, we pay no heed to such things. If a guy's born funny, we don't mock him for that. Not so long as he sticks to the tribe and plays square. We got no Baldies among us, but if we did, I kind of think they might get a better deal than they do here.'

Vine grunted and poured more whisky. Alver's black eyes were fixed steadily on Burkhalter.

'You readin' my mind?' Mattoon demanded. Alvers drew in his breath sharply.

Without looking at him, Burkhalter said, 'No. Baldies don't. It isn't healthy.'

'True enough. Minding your own business is a plenty good rule. I can see how you'd have to play it. Look. This is the first time we come down here, Alvers and Vine and me. You ain't seen us before. We heard rumours about this consulate—' He stumbled over the unfamiliar word. 'Up to now, we traded with Selfridge sometimes, but we didn't have contact with townsfolk. You know why.'

Burkhalter knew. The Hedgehounds had been outcasts, shunning the villages, and sometimes raiding them. They were outlaws.

'But now a new time's coming. We can't live in the towns; we don't want to. But there's room enough for everybody. We still don't see why they set up these con-consulates; still, we'll string along. We got a word.'

Burkhalter knew about that, too. It was the Cody's word, whispered through the Hedgehound tribes – a word they would not disobey.

He said, 'Some of the Hedgehound tribes ought to be wiped out. Not many. You kill them yourselves, whenever you find them—'

'Th' cannibals,' Mattoon said. 'Yeah. We kill them.'

'But they're a minority. The main group of Hedgehounds have no quarrel with the townsfolk. And vice versa. We want to stop the raids.'

'How do you figger on doin' that?'

'If a tribe had a bad winter, it needn't starve. We've methods of making foods. It's a cheap method. We can afford to let you have grub when you're hungry.'

Vine slammed his whisky glass down on the table and snarled something. Mattoon patted the air with a large palm.

'Easy, Umpire. He don't know . . . listen, Burkhalter. The Hedgehounds raid sometimes, sure. They hunt, and they fight for what they get. But they don't beg.'

'I'm talking about barter,' Burkhalter said. 'Fair exchange. We can't set up force shields around every village. And we can't use Eggs on nomads. A lot of raids would be a nuisance, that's all. There haven't been many raids so far; they've been lessening every year. But why should there be any at all? Get rid of the motivation, and the effect's gone too.'

Unconsciously he probed at Alvers' mind. There was a thought there, a sly crooked hungry thought, the avid alertness of a carnivore – and the concept of a hidden weapon. Burkhalter jerked back. He didn't want to know. He had to wait for the Cody to move though the temptation to provoke an open battle with Alvers was dangerously strong. Yet that would only antagonize the other Hedgehounds; they couldn't read Vine's mind as Burkhalter could.

'Barter what?' Vine grunted.

Burkhalter had the answer ready. 'Pelts. There's a demand for them. They're fashionable.' He didn't mention that it was an artificially created fad. 'Furs, for one thing. And—'

'We ain't Red Indians,' Mattoon said. 'Look what happened to them! There ain't nothing we need from townsfolk, except when we're starving. Then – well, maybe we can barter.'

'If the Hedgehounds unified—'

Alvers grinned. 'In the old days,' he said in a high, thin voice, 'the tribes that unified got dusted off with the Eggs. We ain't unifying, brother!'

'He speaks fair, though,' Mattoon said. 'It makes sense. It was our grand-daddies who had a feud with the villages. We've shaken down pretty well. My tribe ain't gone hungry for seven winters now. We migrate, we go where the pickin's are good and we get along.'

'My tribe don't raid,' Vine growled. He poured more whisky.

Mattoon and Alvers had taken only two drinks; Vine kept pouring it down, but his capacity seemed unlimited. Now Alvers said: 'It seems on the level. One thing I don't like. This guy's a Baldy.'

Vince turned his enormous barrel of a torso and regarded Alvers steadily. 'What you got against Baldies?' he demanded.

'We don't know nothing about 'em. I heard stories—'

Vince said something rude. Mattoon laughed.

'You ain't polite, Kit Carson. Burkhalter's playin' host. Don't do throwing words around.'

Alvers shrugged, glanced away, and stretched. He reached into his shirt to scratch himself – and suddenly the thought of murder hit Burkhalter like a stone from a slingshot. It took every ounce of his will-power to remain motionless as Alvers' hand slid back into view, a pistol coming into sight with it.

There was time for the other Hedgehounds to see the weapon, but no time for them to interfere. The death-thought anticipated the bullet. A flare of blinding crimson light blazed through the room. Something, moving like an invisible whirlwind, flashed among them; then, as their eyes adjusted, they stood where they had leaped from their chairs, staring at the figure who confronted them.

He wore a tight-fitting suit of scarlet, with a wide black belt, and an expressionless mask of silver covered his face. A blue-black beard emerged from under it and rippled down his chest. Enormous muscular development showed beneath the skin-tight garments.

He tossed Alvers' pistol into the air and caught it. Then, with a deep, chuckling laugh, he gripped the weapon in both hands and broke the gun into a twisted jumble of warped metal.

'Break a truce, will you?' he said. 'You little pip-squeak. What you need is the livin' daylights whaled outa you, Alvers.'

He stepped forward and smashed the flat of his palm against Alvers' side. The sound of the blow rang through the room. Alvers was lifted into the air and slammed against the further wall. He screamed once, dropped into a huddle, and lay there motionless.

'Git up,' the Cody said. 'You ain't hurt. Mebbe a rib cracked, that's all. If'n I'd smacked your head, I'd have broken your neck clean. Git up!'

Alvers dragged himself upright, his face dead white and sweating. The other two Hedgehounds watched, impassive and alert.

'Deal with you later on. Mattoon. Vine. What you got to do with this?'

'Nuthin',' Mattoon said. 'Nuthin', Cody. You know that.'

The silver mask was impassive. 'Lucky fer you I do. Now listen. What I say goes. Tell Alvers' tribe they'll have to find a new boss. That's all.'

He stepped forward. His arms closed about Alvers, and the Hedgehound yelled in sudden panic. Then the red blaze flared out again. When it had died, both figures were gone.

'Got any more whisky, Burkhalter?' Vine said.

IV

The Cody was in telepathic communication with the Mute, Hobson. Like the other three Codys this one wore the same modulated-frequency helmet as the Mutes; it was impossible for any Baldy or paranoid to tune in on that scrambled, camouflaged wavelength.

It was two hours after sundown.

Alvers is dead, Hobson. Telepathy has no colloquialisms that can be expressed in language-symbols.

Necessary?

Yes. Absolute obedience to the Cody – a curiously mingled four-in-one concept – *is vital. Nobody can be allowed to defy the Cody and get away with it.*

Any repercussions?

None. Mattoon and Vine are agreeable. They got along with Burkhalter. What's wrong with him, Hobson?

The moment the question was asked, the Cody knew the answer. Telepaths have no secrets but subconscious ones – and the Mute helmet can even delve a little into the secret mind.

In love with a paranoid? The Cody was shocked.

He doesn't know it. He mustn't realize it yet. He'd have to reorient; that would take time; we can't afford to have him in the side lines just now. Trouble's bound to pop.

What?

Fred Selfridge. He's drunk. He found out the Hedgehound chief visited Burkhalter today. He's afraid his trading racket is being cut from under him. I've told Burkhalter to stay out of sight.

I'll stay near here, then, in case I'm needed. I won't go home yet. Briefly Hobson caught sight of what home meant to the Cody; a secret valley in the Canadian wilderness, its whereabouts known only to wearers of the helmets, who could never betray it inadvertently. It was there that the technicians among the Baldies sent their specialized products – via the Mutes. Products which had managed to build up a fully equipped headquarters in the heart of the forest, a centralization, it was true, but one whose whereabouts were guarded very thoroughly from the danger of discovery by either friend or enemy. From that valley laboratory in the woods came devices that made the Cody the legendary figure he was among the Hedgehounds – a Paul Bunyan who combined incredible physical prowess with pure magic. Only such a figure could have commanded the respect and obedience of the woods runners.

Is Burkhalter safely hidden, Hobson? Or can I—

He's hidden. There's a round-robin on, but Selfridge can't trace him through that.

O.K. I'll wait.

The Cody broke off. Hobson sent his thought probing out, across the dark miles, to a dozen other Mutes, scattered across the continent from Niagara to Salton. Each one of them was ready for the underground mobilization that might be necessary at any moment now.

It had taken ninety years for the storm to gather; its breaking would be cataclysmic.

Within the circle of the round-robin was quiet, complete peace that only a Baldy can know. Burkhalter let his mind slip into place among the others, briefly touching and recognizing friends as he settled into that telepathic closed circuit. He caught the faintly troubled unrest from Duke Heath's thoughts; then the deep calm of rapport swallowed them both.

At first, on the outer fringes of the psychic pool, there

were ripples and currents of mild disturbance, the casual distresses that are inevitable in any gregarious society, and especially among hypersensitive Baldies. But the purge of the ancient custom of the confessional quickly began to be effective. There can be no barriers between Baldies. The basic unit of the family is far more complete than among non-telepaths, and by extension, the entire Baldy group was bound together with ties no less strong because of their intangible subtlety.

Trust and friendship: these things were certain. There could be no distrust when the tariff wall of language was eliminated. The ancient loneliness of any highly specialized, intelligent organism was mitigated in the only possible way; by a kinship closer even than marriage, and transcending it.

Any minority group as long as it maintains its specialized integrity, is automatically handicapped. It is suspect. Only the Baldies, in all social history, had been able to mingle on equal terms with the majority group and still retain the close bond of kinship. Which was paradoxical, for the Baldies, perhaps, were the only ones who desired racial assimilation. They could afford to, for the telepathic mutation was dominant: the children of Baldy father and non-telepathic mother – or vice versa – are Baldies.

But the reassurance of the round-robins was needed; they were a symbol of the passive battle the Baldies had been fighting for generations. In them the telepaths found complete unity. It did not, and never would, destroy the vital competitive instinct; rather, it encouraged it. There was give and take. And, too, it was religion of the purest kind.

In the beginning, with no senses that non-Baldies can quite understand, you touched the minds of your friends, delicately, sensitively. There was a place for you, and you were welcomed. Slowly, as the peace spread, you approached the centre, that quite indescribable position in space-time that was a synthesis of intelligent, vital minds. Only by analogy can that locus even be suggested.

It is half-sleep. It is like the moment during which consciousness returns sufficiently so that you know you are not awake, and can appreciate the complete calm relaxation of slumber. If you could retain consciousness while you slept – that might be it.

For there was no drugging. The sixth sense is tuned to its highest pitch, and it intermingles with and draws from the other senses. Each Baldy contributes. At first the troubles and disturbances, the emotional unbalances and problems, are cast into the pool, examined, and dissolved in the crystal water of the rapport. Then, cleansed and strengthened, the Baldies approach the centre, where the minds blend into a single symphony. Nuances of colour one member has appreciated, shadowings of sound and light and feeling, each one is a grace note in orchestration. And each note is three-dimensional, for it carries with it the Baldy's personal, individual reaction to the stimulus.

Here a woman remembered the sensuous feel of soft velvet against her palm, with its corresponding mental impact. Here a man gave the crystal-sharp pleasure of solving a difficult mathematical equation, an intellectual counterpoint to the lower-keyed feeling of velvet. Step by step the rapport built up, until there seemed but a single mind, working in perfect cohesion, a harmony without false notes.

Then this single mind began building. It began to think. It was a psychic colloid, in effect, an intellectual giant given strength and sanity by very human emotions and senses and desires.

Then into that pellucid unity crashed a thought-message that for an instant made the minds cling together in a final desperate embrace in which fear and hope and friendliness intermingled. The round robin dissolved. Each Baldy waited now, remembering Hobson's thought that said:

The pogrom's started.

He hadn't broadcast the message directly. The mind of a Mute, wearing his helmet, cannot be read except by another Mute. It was Duke Heath, sitting with Hobson in the moonlit grounds outside the hospital, who had taken the oral warning and conveyed it to the other Baldies. Now his thoughts continued to flash through Sequoia.

Come to the hospital. Avoid non-Baldies. If you're seen, you may be lynched.

In dozens of homes, eyes met in which the terror had leaped instantly to full flower. All over the world, in that moment, something electric sparked with unendurable tension from mind to sensitive mind. No non-Baldy noticed. But, with the speed of thought, the knowledge girdled the planet.

From the thousands of Baldies scattered through the villages, from helicopter and surface car, came a thought of reassurance. *We are one*, it said. *We are with you.*

That – from the Baldies. From the paranoids, fewer in number, came a message of hatred and triumph. *Kill the hairy men!*

But no non-telepath outside Sequoia knew what was happening.

There was an old plastic house near the edge of town where Burkhalter had been hiding. He slipped out of a side door now into the cool quiet of the night. Overhead, a full moon hung yellow. A fan of diffused light reached upward from Redwood Street in the distance, and dimmer paths in the air marked the other avenues. Burkhalter's muscles were rigid. He felt his throat tense with near-panic. Generations of anticipations had built up a violent phobia in every Baldy, and now that day had come—

Barbara Pell came dazzling into his thoughts, and as his mind recalled her, so her mind touched his, wild and fiery, gloating with a triumph his whole being drew back from, while against all judgment something seemed to force him to receive her message.

He's dead, Burkhalter, he's dead! I've killed Fred Selfridge! The word is 'kill,' but in the mind of the paranoid is was not a word or a thought, but a reeking sensation of triumph, wet with blood, a screaming thought which the sane mind reels from.

You fool! Burkhalter shouted at her across the distant streets, his mind catching a little of her wildness so that he could not wholly control it. *You crazy fool, did you start this?*

He was starting out to get you. He was dangerous. His talk would have started the pogrom anyhow – people were beginning to think—

It's got to be stopped!

It will be! Her thought had a terrible confidence. *We've made plans.*

What happened?

Someone saw me kill Selfridge. It's the brother, Ralph, who touched things off – the old lynch law. Listen. Her thought was giddy with triumph.

He heard it then, the belling yell of the mob, far away, but growing louder. The sound of Barbara Pell's mind was fuel to a flame. He caught terror from her, but a perverted terror that lusted after what it feared. The same fury of bloodthirst was in the crowd's yell and in the red flame which was Barbara Pell's mad mind. They were coming near her, nearer—

For a moment Burkhalter was a woman running down a dim street, stumbling, recovering, racing on with a lynch mob baying at her heels.

A man – a Baldy – dashed out into the path of the crowd. He tore off his wig and waved it at them. Then Ralph Selfridge, his thin young face dripping with sweat, shrieked in wordless hatred and turned the tide after this new quarry. The woman ran on into the darkness.

They caught the man. When a Baldy dies, there is a sudden gap in the ether, a dead emptiness, that no telepath will willingly touch with his mind. But before that blankness snapped into being, the Baldy's thought of agony blazed through Sequoia with stunning impact, and a thousand minds reeled for an instant before it.

Kill the hairy men! shrieked Barbara Pell's thoughts, ravenous and mad. This was what the furies were. When a woman's mind lets go, it drops into abysses of sheer savagery that a man's mind never plumbs. The woman from time immemorial has lived closer to the abyss than the male – has had to, for the defence of her brood. The primitive woman cannot afford scruples. Barbara Pell's madness now was the red, running madness of primal force. And it was a fiery thing that ignited something in every mind it touched. Burkhalter felt little flames take hold at the edges of his thoughts and the whole fabric that was his identity shivered and drew back. But he felt in the ether other minds, mad paranoid minds, reach out toward her and cast themselves ecstatically into the holocaust.

Kill them, kill – kill! raved her mind.

Everywhere? Burkhalter wondered, dizzy with the pull he felt from that vortex of exultant hate. *All over the world, tonight? Have the paranoids risen everywhere, or only in Sequoia?*

And then he sensed suddenly the ultimate hatefulness of Barabara Pell. She answered the thought, and in the way she answered he recognized how fully evil the red-haired woman was. If she had lost herself utterly in this flaming intoxication of the mob he would still, he thought, have hated her, but he need not have despised her.

She answered quite coolly, with a part of her mind detached from the ravening fury that took its fire from the howling mob and tossed it like a torch for the other paranoids to ignite their hatred from.

She was an amazing and complex woman, Barbara Pell. She had a strange, inflammatory quality which no woman perhaps, since Jeanne d'Arc had so fully exercised. But she did not give herself up wholly to the fire that had kindled within her at the thought and smell of blood. She was deliberately casting herself into that blood-bath, deliberately wallowing in the frenzy of her madness. And as she wallowed, she could still answer with a coolness more terrible than her ardour.

No, only in Sequoia, said the mind that an instant before had been a blind raving exhortation to murder. *No human must live to tell about it,* she said in thought-shapes that dripped cold venom more burning than the hot bloodlust in her broadcast thoughts. *We hold Sequoia. We've taken over the airfields and the power station. We're armed. Sequoia is isolated from the rest of the world. The pogrom's broken loose here – only here. Like a cancer. It must be stopped here.*

How?

How do you destroy any cancer? Venom bubbled in the thought.

Radium, Burkhalter thought, Radioactivity. The atomic bombs—

Dusting off? he wondered.

A burning coldness of affirmation answered him. *No human must live to tell about it. Towns have been dusted off before – by other towns. Pinewood may get the blame this time – there's been rivalry between it and Sequoia.*

But that's impossible. If the Sequoia tele-audios have gone dead—

We're sending out faked messages. Any copters coming in will be stopped. But we've got to finish it off fast. If one human escapes—

Her thoughts dissolved into inhuman, inarticulate yammering, caught up and echoed avidly by a chorus of other minds.

Burkhalter shut off the contact sharply. He was surprised, a little, to find that he had been moving toward the hospital all during the interchange, circling through the outskirts of Sequoia. Now he heard with his conscious mind the distant yelling that grew loud and faded again almost to silence, and then swelled once more. The mindless beast that ran the streets could be sensed tonight even by a non-telepath.

He moved silently through the dark for a while, sick and shaken as much by his contact with a paranoid mind as by the threat of what had happened and what might still come.

Jeanne d'Arc, he thought. She had it too, that power to inflame the mind. She, too, had heard – 'voices?' Had she perhaps been an unwitting telepath born far before her time? But at least there had been sanity behind the power she exercised. With Barbara Pell—

As her image came into his mind again her thought touched him, urgent, repellently cool and controlled in the midst of all this holocaust she had deliberately stirred up. Evidently something had happened to upset their plans, for—

Burkhalter, she called voicelessly. *Burkhalter, listen. We'll co-operate with you.*

We hadn't intended to, but – where is the Mute, Hobson?

I don't know.

The cache of Eggs has been moved. We can't find the bombs. It'll take hours before another load of Eggs can be flown here from the nearest town. It's on the way. But every second we waste increases the danger of discovery. Find Hobson. He's the only mind we can't touch in Sequoia. We know no one else has hidden the bombs. Get Hobson to tell us where they are. Make him understand, Burkhalter. This isn't a matter affecting only us. If word of this gets out, every telepath in the world is menaced. The cancer must be cut out before it spreads.

Burkhalter felt murderous thought-currents moving toward him. He turned toward a dark house, drifted behind a bush, and waited there till the mob had poured past, their torches blazing. He felt sick and hopeless. What he had seen in the faces of the men was horrible. Had this hatred and fury existed for generations under the surface – this insane mob violence that could burst out against Baldies with so little provocation?

Common sense told him that the provocation had been sufficient. When a telepath killed a non-telepath, it was not duelling – it was murder. The dice were loaded. And for weeks now psychological propaganda had been at work in Sequoia.

The non-Baldies were not simply killing an alien race. They were out to destroy the personal devil. They were convinced by now that the Baldies were potential world conquerors. As yet no one had suggested that the telepaths ate babies, but that was probably coming soon, Burkhalter thought bitterly.

Preview. Decentralization was helping the Baldies, because it made a temporary communication-embargo possible. The synapses that connected Sequoia to the rest of the world were blocked; they could not remain blocked for ever.

He cut through a yard, hurdled a fence, and was among the pines. He felt an impulse to keep going, straight north, into the clean wilderness where this turmoil and fury could be left behind. But, instead, he angled south toward the distant hospital. Luckily he would not have to cross the river; the bridges would undoubtedly be guarded.

There was a new sound, discordant and hysterical. The

barking of dogs. Animals, as a rule, could not receive the telepathic thoughts of humans, but the storm of mental currents raging in Sequoia now had stepped up the frequency – or the power – to a far higher level. And the thoughts of thousands of telepaths, all over the world, were focused on the little village on the Pacific Slope.

Hark, hark! The dogs do bark!
The beggars are coming to town—

But there's another poem, he thought, trying to remember. Another one that fits even better. What is it—

The hopes and fears of all the years—

v

The mindless barking of the dogs was worst. It set the pitch of yapping, mad savagery that washed up around the hospital like the rising waves of a neap tide. And the patients were receptive too; wet packs and hydrotherapy, and, in a few cases, restraining jackets were necessary.

Hobson stared through the one-way window at the village far below. 'They can't get in here,' he said.

Heath, haggard and pale, but with a new light in his eyes, nodded at Burkhalter.

'You're one of the last to arrive. Seven of us were killed. One child. There are ten others still on their way. The rest – safe here.'

'How safe?' Burkhalter asked. He drank the coffee Heath had provided.

'As safe as anywhere. This place was built so irresponsible patients couldn't get out. Those windows are unbreakable. It works both ways. The mob can't get in. Not easily, anyhow. We're fireproof, of course.'

'What about the staff? The non-Baldies, I mean.'

A grey-haired man seated at a near-by desk stopped marking a chart to smile wryly at Burkhalter. The consul recognized him: Dr. Wayland, chief psychiatrist.

Wayland said, 'The medical profession has worked with Baldies for a long time, Harry. Especially the psychologists. If any non-Baldy can understand the telepathic viewpoint, we do. We're non-combatants.'

'The hospital work has to go on,' Heath said. 'Even in the face of this. We did something rather unprecedented, though. We read the minds of every non-Baldy within these walls. Three men on the staff had a pre-conceived dislike of Baldies, and sympathized with the lynchings. We asked them to leave. There's no danger of Fifth Column work here now.'

Hobson said slowly, 'There was another man – Dr. Wilson. He went down to the village and tried to reason with the mob.'

Heath said, 'We got him back here. He's having plasma pumped into him now.'

Burkhalter set down his cup. 'All right. Hobson, you can read my mind. How about it?'

The Mute's round face was impassive. 'We had our plans, too. Sure, I moved the Eggs. The paranoids won't find 'em now.'

'More Eggs are being flown in. Sequoia's going to be dusted off. You can't stop that.'

A buzzer rang; Dr. Wayland listened briefly to a transmitted voice, picked up a few charts and went out. Burkhalter jerked his thumb toward the door.

'What about him? And the rest of the staff? They know, now.'

Heath grimaced. 'They know more than we wanted them to know. Until tonight, no non-telepath has even suspected the existence of the paranoid group. We can't expect Wayland to keep his mouth shut about this. The paranoids *are* a menace to non-Baldies. The trouble is, the average man won't differentiate between paranoids and Baldies. Are those people down there' – he glanced toward the window – 'are they drawing the line?'

'It's a problem,' Hobson admitted. 'Pure logic tells us

that no non-Baldy must survive to talk about this. But is that the answer?'

'I don't see any other way,' Burkhalter said unhappily. He thought suddenly of Barbara Pell and the Mute gave him a sharp glance.

'How do you feel about it, Heath?'

The priest-medic walked to the desk and shuffled case histories. 'You're the boss, Hobson. I don't know. I'm thinking about my patients. Here's Andy Pell. He's got Alzheimer's disease – early senile psychosis. He's screwed up. Can't remember things very well. A nice old guy. He spills food on his shirt, he talks my ear off, and he makes passes at the nurses. He'd be no loss to the world, I suppose. Why draw a line, then? If we're going in for killing, there can't be any exceptions. The non-Baldy staff here can't survive, either.'

'That's the way you feel?'

Heath made a sharp, angry gesture. 'No! It isn't the way I feel! Mass murder would mean cancelling the work of ninety years, since the first Baldy was born. It'd mean putting us on the same level as the paranoids? Baldies don't kill.'

'We kill paranoids.'

'There's a difference. Paranoids are on equal terms with us. And ... oh, I don't know, Hobson. The motive would be the same – to save our race. But somehow one doesn't kill a non-Baldy.'

'Even a lynch mob?'

'They can't help it,' Heath said quietly. 'It's probably casuistry to distinguish between paranoids and non-Baldies but there *is* a difference. It would mean a lot of difference to us. We're not killers.'

Burkhalter's head drooped. The sense of unendurable fatigue was back again. He forced himself to meet Hobson's calm gaze.

'Do you know any other reason?' he asked.

'No,' the Mute said. 'I'm in communication, though. We're trying to figure out a way.'

Heath said, 'Six more got here safely. One was killed. Three are still on their way.'

'The mob hasn't traced us to the hospital yet,' Hobson said. 'Let's see. The paranoids have infiltrated Sequoia in considerable strength, and they're well armed. They've got the airfields and the power station. They're sending out faked tele-audio messages so no suspicion will be aroused outside. They're playing a waiting game; as soon as another cargo of Eggs gets here, the paranoids will beat it out of town and erase Sequoia. And us, of course.'

'Can't we kill the paranoids? You haven't any compunctions about eliminating them, have you, Duke?'

Heath shook his head and smiled; Hobson said, 'That wouldn't help. The problem would still exist. Incidentally, we could intercept the copter flying Eggs here, but that would just mean postponement. A hundred other copters would load Eggs and head for Sequoia; some of them would be bound to get through. Even fifty cargoes of bombs would be too dangerous. You know how the Eggs work.'

Burkhalter knew, all right. One Egg would be quite sufficient to blast Sequoia entirely from the map.

Heath said, 'Justified murder doesn't bother me. But killing non-Baldies – if I had any part in that, the mark of Cain wouldn't be just a symbol. I'd have it on my forehead – or inside my head, rather. Where any Baldy could see it. If we could use propaganda on the mob—'

Burkhalter shook his head. 'There's no time. And even if we did cool off the lynchers, that wouldn't stop word of this from getting around. Have you listened in on the catch-phrases, Duke?'

'The mob?'

'Yeah. They've built up a nice personal devil by now. We never made any secret of our round-robins, and somebody had a bright idea. We're polygamists. Purely mental polygamists, but they're shouting that down in the village now.'

'Well,' Heath said, 'I suppose they're right. The norm

is arbitrary, isn't it – automatically set by the power-group? Baldies *are* variants from that norm.'

'Norms change.'

'Only in crises. It took the Blow-up to bring about decentralization. Besides, what's the true standard of values? What's right for non-Baldies isn't always right for telepaths.'

'There's a basic standard of morals—'

'Semantics.' Heath shuffled his case histories again. 'Somebody once said that insane asylums won't find their true function till ninety per cent of the world is insane. Then the sane group can just retire to the sanitoriums.' He laughed harshly. 'But you can't even find a basic standard in psychoses. There's a lot less schizophrenia since the Blow-up; most d.p. cases come from cities. The more I work with psycho patients, the less I'm willing to accept any arbitrary standards as the real ones. This man' – he picked up a chart – 'he's got a fairly familiar delusion. He contends that when he dies, the world will end. Well – maybe, in this one particular case it's true.'

'You sound like a patient, yourself,' Burkhalter said succinctly.

Hobson raised a hand. 'Heath, I suggest you adminster sedatives to the Baldies here. Including us. Don't you feel the tension?'

The three were silent for a moment, telepathetically listening. Presently Burkhalter was able to sort out individual chords in the discordant thought-melody that was focused on the hospital.

'The patients,' he said. 'Eh?'

Heath scowled and touched a button. 'Fernald? Issue sedatives—' He gave a quick prescription, clicked off the communicator, and rose. 'Too many psychotic patients are sensitive,' he told Hobson. 'We're liable to have a panic on our hands. Did you catch that depressive thought—' He formed a quick mental image. 'I'd better give that man a shot. And I'd better check up on the violent cases, too.' But he waited.

Hobson remained motionless, staring out the window. After a time he nodded.

'That's the last one. We're all here now, all of Us. Nobody's left in Sequoia but paranoids and non-Baldies.'

Burkhalter moved his shoulders uneasily. 'Thought of an answer yet?'

'Even if I had, I couldn't tell you, you know. The paranoids could read your mind.'

True enough. Burkhalter thought of Barbara Pell, somewhere in the village – perhaps barricaded in the power station, or at the airfield. Some confused, indefinable emotion moved within him. He caught Hobson's bright glance.

'There aren't any volunteers among the Baldies,' the Mute said. 'You didn't ask to be involved in this crisis. Neither did I, really. But the moment a Baldy's born, he automatically volunteers for dangerous duty, and stands ready for instant mobilization. It just happened that the crisis occurred in Sequoia.'

'It would have happened somewhere. Sometime.'

'Right. Being a Mute isn't so easy, either. We're shut out. We can never know a complete round-robin. We can communicate fully only with other Mutes. We can never resign.'

Not even to another Baldy could a Mute reveal the existence of the Helmet.

Burkhalter said, 'Our mutation wasn't due for another thousand years, I guess. We jumped the gun.'

'We didn't. But we're paying. The Eggs were the fruit of knowledge, in a way. If man hadn't used atomic power as he did, the telepathic mutations would have had their full period of gestation. They'd never have appeared till the planet was ready for them. Not exactly ready, perhaps,' he qualified, 'but we wouldn't have had quite this mess on our hands.'

'I blame the paranoids,' Burkhalter said. 'And . . . in a way . . . myself.'

'You're not to blame.'

The Baldy grimaced. 'I think I am, Hobson. Who precipitated this crisis?'

'Selfridge—' Hobson was watching.

'Barbara Pell,' Burkhalter said. 'She killed Fred Selfridge. Ever since I came to Sequoia, she's been riding me.'

'So she killed Selfridge to annoy you? That doesn't make sense.'

'It fitted in with the general paranoid plan, I suppose. But it was what she wanted, too. She couldn't touch me when I was consul. But where's the consulate now?'

Hobson's round face was very grave. A Baldy intern came in, offered sedatives and water, and the two silently swallowed the barbiturates. Hobson went to the window and watched the flaring of torches from the village. His voice was muffled.

'They're coming up,' he said. 'Listen.'

The distant shouting grew louder as they stood there in silence. Nearer and louder. Burkhalter moved forward to Hobson's side. The town was a flaming riot of torches now, and a river of light poured up the curved road toward the hospital.

'Can they get in?' someone asked in a hushed voice.

Heath shrugged. 'Sooner or later.'

The intern said, with a touch of hysteria: 'What can we *do?*'

Hobson said. 'They're counting on the weight of numbers, of course. And they've got plenty of that. They aren't armed, I suppose, except for daggers – but then they don't need arms to do what they think they're going to do.'

There was a dead silence in the room for a moment. Then Heath said in a thin voice, 'What they *think*—?'

The Mute nodded toward the window. 'Look.'

There was a small rush toward the glass. Peering over one another's shoulders, the men in the room stared down the slope of the road, seeing the vanguard of the mob so near already that the separate torches were clearly distinguishable, and the foremost of the distorted, shouting faces. Ugly, blind with hatred and the intention to kill.

Hobson said in a detached voice, as if this imminent disaster were already in the past. 'We've got the answer, you see – we know about *this*. But there's another problem I can't solve. Maybe it's the most important one of all.' And he looked at the back of Burkhalter's head. Burkhalter was watching the road. Now he leaned forward suddenly and said.

'Look! There in the woods – what is it? Something moving – people? Listen – what is it?

No one paid any attention beyond the first two or three words he spoke, for all of them saw now. It happened very swiftly. One moment the mob was pouring unchecked up the road, the next a wave of shadowy forms had moved purposefully out of the trees in compact, disciplined order. And above the hoarse shouting of the mob a cry went terribly up, a cry that chilled the blood.

It was the shrill falsetto that had once been the Rebel Yell. Two hundred years ago it echoed over the bloody battlefields of the Civil War. It moved westward with the conquered rebels and became the cowboy yell. It moved and spread with westerners after the Blow-up, the tall, wild men who could not endure the regimentation of the towns. Now it was the Hedgehound yell.

From the window the hospital watchers saw it all, enacted as if on a fire-lit stage below them.

Out of the shadows the men in buckskin came. Firelight flashed on the long blades they carried, on the heads of the arrows they held against the bent bows. Their wild, shrill, terrible yell rose and fell, drowning out the undisciplined screams of the mob.

The buckskin ranks closed in behind the mob, around it. The townsmen began to huddle together a little, until the long loosely organized mob had become a roughly compact circle with the woodsmen surrounding them. There were cries of, 'Kill 'em! Get 'em all!' from the townsmen, and the disorderly shouts rose raggedly through the undulations of the Hedgehound yell, but you could tell after the first two or three minutes who had the upper hand.

Not that there was no fighting. The men at the front of the mob had to do something. They did – or tried to. It was little more than a scuffle as the buckskin forms closed in.

'They're only townsmen, you see,' Hobson said quietly, like a lecturer explaining some movie scene from old newsreel files. 'Did you ever think before how completely the profession of the fighting man has died out since the Blow-up? The only organized fighting men left in the world are out there, now.' He nodded towards the Hedgehound ranks, but nobody saw the motion. They were all watching with the incredulous eagerness of reprieved men as the Hedgehounds competently dealt with the mob which was so rapidly changing into a disorganized rabble now as the nameless, powerful, ugly spirit that had welded it into a mob died mysteriously away among them.

All it took was superior force, superior confidence – the threat of weapons in more accustomed hands. For four generations these had been townsmen whose ancestors never knew what war meant. For four generations the Hedgehounds had lived only because they knew unremitting warfare, against the forest and mankind.

Competently they went about rounding up the mob.

'It doesn't solve anything,' Burkhalter said at last, reluctantly, turning from the window. Then he ceased to speak, and sent his mind out in rapid thoughts so that the non-telepaths might not hear. *Don't we have to keep it all quiet? Do we still have to decide about – killing them all? We've saved our necks, sure – but what about the rest of the world?*

Hobson smiled a grim, thin smile that looked odd on his plump face. He spoke aloud, to everyone in the room.

'Get ready,' he said. 'We're leaving the hospital. All of us. The non-Baldy staff, too.'

Heath, sweating and haggard, caught his breath. 'Wait a minute. I know you're the boss, but – I'm not leaving my patients!'

'We're taking them, too.' Hobson said. Confidence was in his voice, but not in his eyes. He was looking at Burkhalter. The last and most difficult problem was still to be met.

The Cody's thought touched Hobson's mind. *All ready.*

You've got enough Hedgehounds?

Four tribes. They were all near the Fraser Run. The new consulate set-up had drawn 'em from the north. Curiosity.

Report to group.

Scattered across the continent, Mutes listened. *We've cleaned out Sequoia. No deaths. A good many got pretty well beaten up, but they can all travel.* (A thought of wry amusement). *Your townspeople ain't fighters.*

Ready for the march?

Ready. They're all rounded up, men, women and children, in the north valley. Umpire Vine's in charge of that sector.

Start the march. About the paranoids, any trouble there?

No trouble. They haven't figured it all out yet. They're still in the town, sitting tight. We've got to move fast, though. If they try to get out of Sequoia, my men will kill. There was a brief pause. Then – *The march has started.*

Good. Use the blindfolds when necessary.

There are no stars underground, the Cody's thought said grimly.

No non-Baldy must die. Remember, this is a point of honour. Our solution may not be the best one, but—

None will die.

We're evacuating the hospital. Is Mattoon ready?

Ready. Evacuate.

Burkhalter rubbed a welt on his jaw. 'What happened?' he asked thickly, staring around in the rustling darkness of the pines.

A shadow moved among the trees. 'Getting the patients ready for transportation – remember? You were slugged. That violent case—'

'I remember.' Burkhalter felt sheepish. 'I should have watched his mind closer. I couldn't. He wasn't *thinking*—' He shivered slightly. Then he sat up. 'Where are we?'

'Quite a few miles north of Sequoia.'

'My head feels funny.' Burkhalter rearranged his wig. He rose, steadying himself against a tree, and blinked vaguely. After a moment he had reoriented. This must be Mount Nichols, the high peak that rose tall among the mountains guarding Sequoia. Very far away, beyond intervening lower summits, he could see a distant glow of light that was the village.

But beneath him, three hundred feet down, a procession moved through a defile in the mountain wall. They emerged into the moonlight and went swiftly on and were lost in shadow.

There were stretcher-bearers, and motionless, prone figures being carried along; there were men who walked arm in arm; there were tall men in buckskin shirts and fur caps, bows slung across their shoulders, and they were helping, too. The silent procession moved on into the wilderness.

'The Sequoia Baldies,' Hobson said. 'And the non-Baldy staff – and the patients. We couldn't leave them.'

'But—'

'It was the only possible answer for us, Burkhalter. Listen. For twenty years we've been preparing – not for this, but for the pogrom. Up in the woods, in a place only Mutes know about, there's a series of interlocking caves. It's a city now. A city without population. The Codys – there are four of them, really – have been using it as a laboratory and a hideout. There's material there for hydroponics, artificial sunlight, everything a culture needs. The caves aren't big enough to shelter all the Baldies, but they'll hold Sequoia's population.'

Burkhalter stared. 'The non-Baldies?'

'Yes. They'll be segregated, for a while, till they can face truth. They'll be prisoners; we can't get around that fact. It was a choice between killing them and holding them incommunicado. In the caves, they'll adapt. Sequoia was a tight, independent community. Family units won't be broken up. The same social pattern can be followed. Only – it'll be underground, in an artificial culture.'

'Can't the paranoids find them?'

'There are no stars underground. The paranoids may read the minds of the Sequoians, but you can't locate a mind by telepathic triangulation. Only Mutes know the location of the caves, and no paranoid can read a Mute's thoughts. They're on their way now to join us – enough Mutes to take the Sequoians on the last lap. Not even the Hedgehounds will know where they're going.'

'Then the secret will be safe among telepaths – except for the Hedgehounds. What if they talk?'

'They won't. Lots of reasons. For one, they have no communication to speak of with the outside world. For another, they're under an autocracy, really. The Codys know how to enforce their rules. Also, have you thought how the towns would react if they knew Hedgehounds had cleaned out a whole village? To save their own skins the Hedgehounds will keep their mouths shut. Oh, it *may* leak out. With so many individuals involved you never can be absolutely sure. But I think for an extemporaneous plan, it'll work out well enough.' Hobson paused and his mind brushed with the keenness of a quick glance against Burkhalter's mind. 'What's the matter, Burk? Still worried about something?'

'The people, I suppose,' Burkhalter admitted. 'The humans. It doesn't seem exactly fair, you know. I'd hate to be cut off for ever from all contact from the rest of the world. They—'

Hobson thought an explosive epithet. It was much more violent thought than voiced. He said, 'Fair! Of course it isn't fair. You saw that mob coming up the road, Burk – did they have fairness in mind then? If anyone ever deserved punishment that mob does!' His voice grew milder. 'One thing we tend to lose sight of, you see. We grow up with the idea of indulgence toward humans pounded into us to such an extent we almost forget they're responsible people, after all. A pogrom is the most indefensible concerted action a group can be guilty of. It's always an attack by a large majority on a defenceless minority. These people would have killed us all without a qualm, if they could. They're lucky we aren't as vicious as they were. They deserve a lot worse than they're getting, if you ask me. We didn't ask to be put in a spot like this. There's unfairness involved all around, but I think this solution is the best possible under the circumstances.'

They watched the procession below moving through the moonlight. Presently Hobson went on. 'Another angle turned up after we put this thing in motion, too. A mighty good one. By sheer accident we're going to have a wonderful laboratory experiment going on in human relations. It won't be a dead-end community in the caves. Eventually, we think the Baldies and the non-Baldies will intermarry there. The hospital staff are potential goodwill ambassadors. It'll take careful handling, but I think with our facilities for mind reading and the propaganda we can put out adjusted by the readings, things will work out. It may be the basis for the ultimate solution of the whole Baldy-human problem.

'You see, this will be a microcosm of what the whole world ought to be – would have been if the Blow-up hadn't brought us telepaths into being ahead of our normal mutation time. It will be a community of humans dominated by telepaths, controlled by them benevolently. We'll learn how to regulate relations with humans, and there'll be no danger while we learn. It'll be trial and error without punishment for error. A little hard on the humans, perhaps, but no harder than it's been for generations on the Baldy minority all over the world. We might even hope that in a few years' time the experiment may go well enough that even if the news leaked out, the community members would elect to stay put. Well, we'll have to wait and see. It can't be solved any better way that we know of. There *is* no solution, except adjustment between the races. If every Baldy on earth committed voluntary suicide, there'd still be Baldies born. You can't stop it. The Blow-up's responsible for that, not us. We ... wait a minute.'

Hobson turned his head sharply, and in the rustling night silences of the forest, broken only by the subdued noises of the proposition far below, they listened for a sound not meant for ears.

Burkhalter heard nothing, but in a moment Hobson nodded.

'The town's about to go,' he said.

Burkhalter frowned. 'There's another loose end, isn't there? What if they blame Pinewood for dusting Sequoia off?'

'There won't be any proof either way. We've about decided to spread rumours indicating two or three other towns along with Pinewood, enough to confuse the issue. Maybe we'll say the explosion might have come from an accident in the Egg dump. That's happened, you know. Pinewood and the rest will just have to get along under a slight cloud for a while. They'll have an eye kept on them, and if they should show any more signs of aggression . . . but of course, nothing will happen. I think . . . look, Burkhalter! There she goes!'

Far away below them the glow that was Sequoia lay like a lake of light in the mountains' cup. As they watched, it changed. A nova flamed in incandescent splendour, whitening the men's faces and showing the pines in starkly black silhouette.

For an instant the soundless ether was full of a stunning, mindless cry that rocked the brain of every telepath within its range. Then there was that terrible void, that blankness of cessation into which no Baldy cares to look. This time it was a mighty vortex, for a great many telepathic minds perished together in that nova. It was a vortex that made the mind reel perilously near its great, sucking brink. Paranoid they may have been, but they were telepathic too, and their going shook every brain that could perceive the passing.

In Burkhalter's mind a reeling blindness struck. He thought, *Barbara, Barbara* . . .

It was an utterly unguarded cry. He made no effort to hush it from Hobson's perception.

Hobson said, as if he had not heard. 'That's the finish. Two Mutes in copters dropped the Eggs. They're watching now. No survivors. Burkhalter—'

He waited. Slowly Burkhalter pulled himself out of that blind abyss into which the beautiful, terrible, deadly image of Barbara Pell whirled away toward oblivion. Slowly he brought the world back into focus around him.

'Yes?'

'Look. The last of the Sequoians are going by. You and I aren't needed here any more, Burk.'

There was significance in that statement. Burkhalter shook himself mentally and said with painful bewilderment, 'I don't . . . quite get it. Why did you bring me up here? Am I—' He hesitated. 'I'm not going with the others?'

'You can't go with them,' the Mute said quietly. There was a brief silence; a cool wind whispered through the pine needles. The pungent fragrance and freshness of the night washed around the two telepaths. 'Think, Burkhalter,' Hobson said, 'Think.'

'I loved her,' Burkhalter said. 'I know that now.' There was shock and self-revulsion in his mind, but he was too stunned by the realization for much emotion to come through yet.

'You know what that means, Burkhalter? You're not a true Baldy. Not quite.' He was silent for a moment. 'You're a latent paranoid, Burk,' Hobson said.

There was no sound or thought between them for a full minute. Then Burkhalter sat down suddenly on the pine needles that carpeted the forest floor.

'It isn't true,' he said. The trees were reeling around him.

'It is true, Burk.' Hobson's voice and mind were infinitely gentle. 'Think. Would you – could you – have loved a paranoid, and such a paranoid as that, if you were a normal telepath?'

Dumbly Burkhalter shook his head. He knew it was true. Love between telepaths is a far more unerring thing than love between blind and groping humans. A telepath can make no mistake about the quality of the beloved's character. He could not if he wished. No normal Baldy could feel anything but utter revulsion toward the thing that had been Barbara Pell. No *normal* Baldy—

'You should have hated her. You did hate her. But there was something more than hate. It's a paranoid quality, Burk, to feel drawn toward what you despise. If you'd been normal, you'd have loved some normal telepathic woman, someone your equal. But you never did. You had to find a woman you could look down on. Someone you could build up to your ego by despising. No paranoid can admit any other being is his equal. I'm sorry, Burk. I hate to say these things.'

Hobson's voice was like a knife, merciless and merciful, excising diseased tissue. Burkhalter heard him, and trod down the latent hatred which the truth – and he knew the truth of it – brought out in his double mind.

'Your father's mind was warped too, Burk,' Hobson went on. 'He was born too receptive to paranoid indoctrination—'

'They tried their tricks on him when he was a kid' Burkhalter said hoarsely. 'I remember that.'

'We weren't sure at first about what ailed you. The symptoms didn't show till you took on the consulate. Then we began to build up a prognosis, of sorts. You didn't really want that job, Burkhalter. Not subconsciously. Those heavy fatigues were a defence. I caught that daydream of yours today – not the first one you've had. Daydreams concerned with suicide – another symptom, and another means of escape. And Barbara Pell – that was the pay-off. You couldn't let yourself know what your real feelings were, so you projected the opposite emotion – hatred. You believed she was persecuting you, and you let your hatred have full freedom. But it wasn't hatred, Burk.'

'No. It wasn't hatred. She . . . . she was horrible, Hobson! She was horrible!'

'I know.'

Burkhalter's mind boiled with violent emotions, too tangled to sort out. Hatred, intolerable grief, bright flashes of the paranoid world, memory of Barbara Pell's wild mind like a flame in the wind.

'If you're right, Hobson,' he said with difficulty, 'you've got to kill me. I know too much. If I'm really a latent paranoid some day I might betray – Us.'

'Latent,' Hobson said. 'There's a world of difference – if you can be honest with yourself.'

'I'm not safe if I live. I can feel – disease – back in my mind right now. I – hate you, Hobson. I hate you for showing me myself. Some day the hate may spread to all Mutes and all Baldies. How can I trust myself any more?'

'Touch your wig, Burk,' Hobson said.

Bewildered, Burkhalter laid a shaking hand upon his head. He felt nothing unusual. He looked at Hobson in complete confusion.

'Take it off, Burk.'

Burkhalter lifted off the wig. It came hard, the suction caps that held it in place giving way with reluctance. When it was off, Burkhalter was amazed to feel that there was still something on his head. He lifted his free hand and felt with unsteady fingers a fine cap of wires like silk, hugging his skull. He looked up in the moonlight and met Hobson's eyes. He could see the fine wrinkles around them, and the look of kindness and compassion on the Mute's round face. For an instant he forgot even the mystery of the strange cap on his head. He cried voicelessly.

Help me, Hobson! Don't let me hate you!

Instantly into his mind came a firm, strong, compassionate locking of thoughts from many, many minds. It was a communion more intimate and of a different quality than anything he had ever felt before. And it was to the mind as the clasp of many supporting hands would be to the body when the body is weary and in infinite need of support.

You're one of us now, Burkhalter. You wear the Helmet. You are a Mute. No paranoid can ever read your mind.

It was Hobson's thought that spoke to him, but behind it spoke the thoughts of many others, many trained minds from hundreds of other Mutes, all speaking as if in a chorus that echoed and amplified all Hobson said.

But I... I'm a latent—

The hundred of minds blended into a cohesive unit, the psychic colloid of the round-robin, but a different, more intense union, wrought into something new by the caps that filtered all their thoughts. The unit became a single mind, strong and sane and friendly, welcoming the newcomer. He did not find miraculous healing there – he found something better.

Truth. Honesty.

Now the warp in his mind, the paranoid quirk and its symptoms and illogic, became very clear. It was the highest kind of psychoanalysis, which only a Baldy can know.

He thought, *It will take time. The cure will take—*

Hobson was standing behind him. *I'll be with you. Until you can stand alone. And even then – we'll all be with you. You are one of us. No Baldy is ever alone.*

CHAPTER 5

I think I am dying.

I have been lying here for a long time now. Sometimes I am conscious, but not often. I can't move at all.

I meant to cut an artery in my wrist and die, but I can't even do that now, and I don't need to. My fingers won't move. I can't move at all, and I'm not cold any more. The light and the warmth are pulsing and fading, fading a little more each time. I suppose this is dying; I know it is.

There is a helicopter overhead. It will be too late. It is getting larger. But I am sinking faster than it is dropping into this canyon between the peaks. They have found me, but not soon enough.

Life and death are not important.

My thoughts are getting sucked down into a black whirlpool. I shall go down there alone, and that will be the end.

There is one thing, one thought, that I can't stop thinking. It's a queer thought to have when you're dying.

Humpty Dumpty sat on a wall.

That was Jeff Cody's thought, wasn't it?

If I could just think about Jeff Cody, maybe I could—

Much too late now.

Cody and Operation Apocalypse, there in the Caverns ... remembering ... remembering ...

... dying alone ...

HUMPTY DUMPTY

AND God said to Noah, the end of all flesh is come before me; for the earth is filled with violence through them...

Under a stone sky Jeff Cody stood, his hands clasped behind him. He was trying to read the mind of an electronic calculator, and trying to keep his own mind from being read with all the violence in it. He shut down all his barriers around his own desperation, pushing hard upon the one thought he did not dare to face. He held it down, trying to drown it under the surface turmoil of his mind. The calculator had a broad, bland, glassy brow, winking with lights and reflections. Somewhere inside it a thin slice of crystal lay that could wipe human life off the face of the planet. Not Jeff Cody's life, and not the life of his people. But all human, non-telepathic life. The responsibility for the crystal was one man's. Cody's.

Behind him Allenby shifted from one foot to another, his reflection blurring in the shining surface of the calculator's control panel. Cody said without turning:

'But if the Inductor is a failure, then we'll have to—' An image of death and dying formed like a cloud in his thoughts.

He had not said this aloud. Allenby interrupted very quickly, not speaking aloud either, but his thought cutting into Cody's, ending it before the image of destruction could take full shape in Cody's mind.

'No. We've had another set-back. But we'll try again. We'll keep on trying. We may never have to use – that.' His mind sketched in the thin crystal in the calculator, with death for most of the race of man locked in it.

'Call it set-back or call it failure,' Cody said, in the silence of his mind. 'The goal's too high. Nobody knows what makes a man telepathic. Nobody's ever going to induce it with a machine. No Inductor will ever work. You know that.'

'I don't know it,' Allenby's thought said quietly. 'I think it can be done. Jeff, you're under too much pressure.'

Cody laughed shortly. 'Merriam lasted three months in this job,' he said. 'Brewster stood it longest – eight months. This is my sixth month. What's the matter? Afraid I'll resign the way Brewster did?'

'No,' Allenby said. 'But—'

'Okay,' Cody interrupted the thought irritably. 'Forget it.' He felt Allenby's mind touch the edges of his with tentative, uneasy brushing motions. Allenby was a psychologist. And therefore Cody was a little afraid of him. He did not want expert attention brought to bear on him just now. There was something terrifying and yet very tempting down close under the surface of his thoughts, and he did not mean to expose it just yet to anyone. He made an effort of the will and summoned up a shimmer of pleasant images like a smoke-screen to puff in Allenby's face. Pine woods with warm rain blowing through them, a quarter of a mile over their heads above the limestone sky. The quiet and clearness of the empty heavens broken only by the buzz of a helicopter and the soft, continual swish of its vanes. The face of Cody's wife when she was in a good mood and laughing gently.

He felt Allenby's uneasiness tentatively subside. He did not turn as he heard Allenby's feet shift on the floor.

'I'll get back, then,' Allenby said without words. 'I just wanted to see you when I told you that we'd hit another dead end. Is it all right, Jeff?'

'Fine,' Cody said. 'I won't keep you.'

Allenby went out.

Cody listened while the receding footsteps crossed the room beyond. He heard the door close and lock. He was alone now, physically, though all through the cavern an interlacing play of telepathic thoughts moved continually, touching his own and passing. Even Allenby sent back a vague uneasiness as he moved away. So Cody kept the images of pine woods and clear sky and laughing woman playing over the surface of his mind. But his eyes turned side-wise and without moving his head he saw lying on the edge of a work table within reach of his hand the thing he had not dared to admit into his mind till now. Too many other minds were watching.

What he saw was a knife with a heavy, narrow blade and a sharp point, left by some careless workman. What he thought of was the man before him in this job, and the way Brewster had resigned from it after eight months. Brewster had used a revolver. But a knife was good, too. There is a place inside the collar-bone, near the neck, and consciousness goes out like a blown candle in a matter of seconds if you drive the knife in there. If your burden is too much to bear, as Merriam's was, and Brewster's. And Jeff Cody's.

All around him in the air, like an eyeless, invisible staring, uneasy telepathic minds were swinging around toward him. A ripple of panic was running through the cavern. Something, somewhere, was wrong. But Cody had controlled his surface thoughts skilfully. He had not let himself really see the knife, really think clearly of that spot inside the collar-bone, until now.

Now he drew a deep breath and let the wonderful release of the thought flash bright and clear through the cavern. They couldn't stop him. Nobody was near enough. He was free.

'So the Inductor won't work,' he said aloud. 'So you can't induce telepathy in a human mind. But there's one way to stop telepathy!'

He took one long side-wise step and the knife was in his hand. With two fingers he felt for the ridge of his collar-bone, to guide the blade.

'Let the Inductor fail,' he thought. 'Let the pogrom come. Let the race die. Turn loose Apocalypse. It's not my problem now!'

Generations ago, the Blow-up had posed the problem by mutating a sub-species of telepaths. And there had been a time when the Baldies hoped that eugenics could solve that problem. But not any more. Time was too short.

Even though the telepathic function was carried by a dominant gene, there were too few Baldies. Given enough time and enough intermarriage, the world might become peopled entirely by telepaths, but there was not enough time. The only answer was the one which Baldies had been seeking for years now – a mechanical device, an Inductor, which would induce the telepathic power in a non-telepath.

It was theoretically possible. The minds of the greatest scientists on earth lay open to the Baldies. And here in the caves the electronic calculator could solve the problem, given enough data. But this problem it had not completely solved, for there was not enough data, in spite of the treasure of knowledge stolen from hundreds of brilliant, seeking non-Baldy minds.

Still, it was the answer. If every man and woman in the world could become a telepath, simply by wearing a compact mechanical device, the miracle could be worked. The last barriers would go down. The fear and hatred non-telepaths had for Baldies would vanish – not instantly, but it would dissolve little by little in the great sea of interacting minds. The walls, the *difference*, would vanish, and with it the fear that relentlessly forced the coming of the pogrom.

But the Inductor was still a theory. The calculator had not yet solved that problem, if it ever would. Instead, it had given the answer to the basic problem in an unexpected way, coldly mechanical and terribly logical. The problem could be solved, the calculator said. Destroy all non-telepathic humans. The method? It searched its vast memory-library and found—

Operation Apocalypse.

There was a virus which, by means of certain stimuli, could be mutated into a variant which was air-borne and propagated quickly. It destroyed human neural tissue. There was only one kind of human neural tissue it could not harm.

Telepaths were naturally immune to the mutated virus.

No Baldy knew what the virus was, or the method of mutation. Only the calculator knew those things, and the inhuman mind of an electronic calculator cannot be read.

Somewhere in the great machine was a tiny crystal of barium titanate bearing a series of frozen dots of energy in a binary digit code. And that code held the secret of the deadly virus.

If Jeff Cody took three steps forward and sat down in the cushioned operator's chair before the control panel, and if he touched a certain button, a monitor device would examine the electronic pattern of his brain and identify it as surely as fingerprints are identified. Only one man in the world could satisfy the question the monitor would silently ask.

And then a light would begin to glow – somewhere – on the control panel, and under it would be a number, and, seeing that number, Cody could make the calculator reveal its secret. Before Cody, Brewster had carried this crushing burden. And before Brewster, Merriam. And after Cody – someone else would have the unendurable responsibility for deciding whether to say: *The end of all flesh is come before me . . . behold, I will destroy them with the earth.*

The crash of protesting minds burst by sheer force through the shell of defence Cody had put up around his own as he took up the knife. From all over the busy cavern telepaths stopped in their tracks and hurled their strong, urgent thoughts toward the interlocked centre that was Cody.

It was stunning. He had never felt so strong an impact before. He did not mean to falter, but the burden of their protest was almost tangible, almost a thing to stagger under. Even from above-ground he could hear and feel the instant thrust of down-driving thought. A quarter of a mile above this limestone sky, above the rock and the soil with the pine tree roots clenched downwards through it, a hunter in ragged buckskins paused among the trees and sent his own shocked, sympathetic protest dropping toward the cavern. The thought came blurred to Cody by the stone between, and starred with tiny, bright, brainless thoughts of small burrowing things in the soil overhead.

Someone in a helicopter high up in the hot blue sky locked minds with the group underground, faint and far-off but as instant as the man in the nearest cave beyond Cody's locked door.

'*No, no,*' the voices said in his mind. '*You can't! You are all of us. You can't. Jeff, you are all of us!*'

He knew it was true. The way out was like a deep, dark well, and vertigo pulled him toward it, but he knew that he would be killing his whole race, a little, if he killed himself. Only telepaths can experience death and still live. Each time a telepath dies, all the rest within mind's reach feel the blackness close upon an extinguished mind, and feel their own minds extinguish a little in response.

It happened so fast Cody was still feeling with two fingers along the edge of his collarbone, and the knife was not yet firm in his fist, when the single, interlocking cry of anguished protest from a hundred minds speaking as one closed down upon him. He shut his thoughts and was obdurate. He could fight them off long enough. This would only take a second. The door was locked and physical force was the only thing that could stop him.

But he was uneasy even in this urgent press of voices and action. For Allenby's mind was not speaking with the rest. Why?

Now the knife was firm in his hand. Now he spread his two fingers apart a little to make way for it, knowing the place to strike. Had Brewster felt as he felt, when Brewster stood here six months ago and laid down the unbearable burden of decision? Had it been hard to pull the trigger? Or easy, as it was easy to lift the knife and—

A burst of blinding white light exploded in the middle of his brain. It was like a shooting star that crashed and shattered upon the very texture of the mind itself. In the last winking instant of consciousness Cody thought he had already struck the self-destroying blow and that this was what death looked like from within.

Then he knew that the meteor of impact was Allenby's mind striking his a numbing blow. He felt the knife slip from his hands, he felt his knees buckle, and he felt nothing more for a very long, an immeasurable, time.

When he was aware of himself again Allenby was kneeling beside him on the floor, and the calculator looked up above him glassy and reflecting from an unfamiliar angle, a child's eye view seen with a knee-high vision. The door was unlocked and stood open. Everything looked strange.

Allenby said, 'All right, Jeff?'

Cody looked up at him and felt the pent-up and unreleased tension in him boil toward the surface in an outburst of rage so strong that the supporting minds he felt hovering around him drew back as if from fire.

'I'm sorry,' Allenby said. 'I've only done that twice before in my life. I had to do it, Jeff.'

Cody threw aside the hand on his shoulder. Scowling, he drew his feet under him and tried to rise. The room went around him in an unsteady circle.

'Somebody had to be the man,' Allenby said. 'It was the odds, Jeff. It's hard on you and Merriam and Brewster and those others, but—'

Cody made a violent gesture, cutting off the thought.

'All right,' Allenby said. 'But don't kill yourself, Jeff. Kill somebody else. Kill Jasper Horne.'

A little burning shock went through Cody's mind. He stood motionless, not even his mind stirring, letting that strange new thought glow in the centre of it.

Kill Jasper Horne.

Oh, Allenby was a wise man. He was grinning at Cody now, his round, ruddy face tense but beginning to look happy again.

'Feeling better? Action's what you need, Jeff – action, directed activity. All you've been able to do for months is stay put and worry. There are some responsibilities a man can't carry – unless he acts. Well, use your knife on Horne, not yourself.'

A faint flicker of doubt wavered in Cody's mind.

Allenby said, 'Yes, you may fail. He may kill you.'

'He won't,' Cody said aloud, his voice sounding strange to him.

'He could. You'll have to take the chance. Get him if you can. That's what you want to do, but you haven't really known it. You've got to kill someone. Horne's our basic problem now. He's our real enemy. So kill Horne. Not yourself.'

Cody nodded without a word.

'Good. We'll locate him for you. And I'll get you a copter. Will you see Lucy first?'

A little wave of disturbance ran through Cody's mind. Allenby saw it, but he did not let his own mind ripple in response. Quietly the innumerable linking minds of the other telepaths all around them had drawn back, waiting.

'Yes,' Cody said. 'I'll see Lucy first.' He turned toward the door of the cave.

Jasper Horne – and what he represented – was the reason why the Baldies could not let even themselves learn the method of Operation Apocalypse and the nature of the deadly selective virus from the calculator. That secret had to be kept from Jasper Horne and his fellow paranoids. For their approach was: *Why not kill all the humans? Why not, before they kill us? Why not strike first, and save ourselves?*

These were hard questions to answer, and Jasper Horne was very adept at putting it to the test. If you could say the group of paranoid telepaths had any leader, then Horne was that leader. How much the man knew of the Caves was uncertain. He knew they existed, but not where. He knew some of the things that were going on in it, in spite of the frequency-scrambling Mute helmets every Cave Baldy wore. If he knew about the Inductor, he would – if he could – have dropped an Egg on it with the greatest joy in life and watched the smoke-cloud arise. Certainly he knew the Operation Apocalypse had been planned, for he was doing his best to force the Baldies to release the virus that would destroy all non-telepathic human life.

And he knew the way to force this decision. If – when – a total pogrom started, then the virus and the Apocalypse would be loosed upon the world, Then there would be no choice. When your life depends on killing your enemy, you don't hesitate. But when the enemy is your brother....

That was the difference. To the normal Baldies, the race of non-telepathic humans was a close kin. To the paranoids they were hairy sub-men fit only for extermination. So

Jasper Horne worked in every way he knew to force trouble to the surface. To precipitate a pogrom. To make sure the Baldies released the virus and destroyed the hairy men.

And Horne worked in a decentralized post-Blow-up society founded on fear, a fear that had been very real once. Today, no further move seemed possible. The society wavered between re-contraction and further expansion, and each man, each town, was on guard against all others. For how can you trust another when you do not know his thoughts?

American Gun and Sweetwater, Jensen's Crossing and Santaclare and all the rest, clear across the curve of the continent. Men and women in the towns going about their business, rearing their children, tending their gardens and their stores and their factories. Most of them were normal human beings. Yet in every town the Baldies lived too, rearing *their* children, tending *their* stores. Amicably enough for the most part. But not always – not always.

And for weeks now, over most of the nation, had lain a humid, oppressive heat wave, in which aggressions rose steadily higher. Yet, outside of a few knife-duels, no one dared strike the first blow. Other men were armed too, and every town possessed a cache of atomic Eggs, and could strike back with deadly precision.

The time was more than ripe for a pogrom. So far, no mob had formed, no potential lynchers had agreed on a target.

But the Baldies were a minority.

All that was needed was a precipitating factor — and the paranoids were doing their best to provide that.

Cody glanced up at the cavern's grey stone sky and reached with his key for the lock of his wife's apartment door. With the key already in place, he hesitated, not from indecision this time but because he knew what probably waited inside. There was a furrow between his brows, and all the little lines of his face were pulled tense and held that way by the perpetual tension that held every Baldy from the first moment after he entered the caves.

The stone sky held down and bottled in such a complex

maze of thoughts, echoing off the walls and interlacing and interlocking in a babel of confusion. The Cavern of Babel, Cody thought wryly, and turned the key with a gesture of small resolution. Indoors he would exchange one babel for another. The walls would give him a little shelter from the clouds of stale, sullen resentment outside, but there was something inside he liked even less. Yet he knew that he could not leave without seeing Lucy and the baby.

He opened the door. The living-room looked bright enough, with its deep, broad divan-shelf running along three sides, soft, dark mossy green under the shelves of book-spools, coloured cushions scattered, the lights low. An electric fire glowed behind a Gothic inter-weaving of baffles, like a small cathedral on fire from within. Through the broad window in the fourth wall he could see the lights of the Ralphs' living-room next door reflecting on the street, and across the way June and Hugh Barton in their own living-room, having a pre-dinner cocktail before their electric fire. It looked pleasant.

But in here all the clear colours and the glow were clouded by the deep miasma of despair which coloured all Jeff Cody's wife's days, and had for – how long now? The baby was three monds old.

He called, 'Lucy?'

No answer. But a deeper wave of misery beat through the apartment, and after a moment he heard the bed creak in the next room. He heard a sigh. Then Lucy's voice, blurred a little, said, 'Jeff.' There was an instant of silence, and he had already turned toward the kitchen when her voice came again. 'Go into the kitchen and bring me a little more whisky, will you, please?'

'Right away,' he said. The whisky was not going to hurt her much, he thought. Anything that could help her get over the next few months was that much to the good. The next few—? No, the end would come much sooner than that.

'Jeff?' Lucy's voice was querulous.

He took the whisky into the bedroom. She was lying face up across the bed, her reddish curls hanging, her stocking feet against the wall. Marks of dried tears ran down across her cheek toward her ear, but her lashes were not wet now. In the corner the baby slept in a small cocoon of his own incoherent animal-like thoughts. He was dreaming of warmth and enormous all-enveloping softness that stirred slowly, a dream without shape, all texture and temperament. His light-red curls were no more than a down on his well-shaped head.

Cody looked at Lucy. 'How do you feel?' he heard himself asking inanely.

Without moving a muscle she let her eyes roll side-wise so that she was looking at him from under her half-closed lids, a stony, suffering, hating look. An empty water-glass stood on the bed-table within reach of her lax hand. Cody stepped forward, unstopped the bottle and poured a steady amber stream into the glass. Two inches, three. She was not going to say when. He stopped at three and replaced the bottle.

'You don't have to ask how anybody feels,' Lucy said in a dull voice.

'I'm not reading you. Lucy.'

She shrugged against the bedspread. 'You say.'

Looking again at the sleeping baby, Cody did not answer. But Lucy sat up with great suddenness, making the bed groan, startling Cody because the motion had been so spontaneous he had not even caught the anticipation of it in her mind. 'He's not yours. He's mine. All mine, my kind, my race. No—' The thought went on, '—no taint in his blood at all. Not a freak. Not a Baldy. A nice, normal, healthy, perfect baby—' She didn't say it aloud, but she didn't have to. She caught at the thought half-way through, and then deliberately let it go on, knowing she might as well have said it aloud. Then she added in a flat voice, 'And I suppose you didn't read *that*.'

Silently he held out the whisky glass to her.

It had been five years now since the Egg dropped on Sequoia. Five years since the cavern colony saw the last daylight they might ever see. And the people herded from Sequoia to the caves had settled down sullenly, resentful or resigned according to their temperaments. They had every comfort of underground living which their captors could provide. They were as content as skilled psychologists could make them, psychologists who could look into their minds and read their needs almost before the needs took shape. But they were captives.

The intermarriages had started within a few months of the capivity. It was one of the large-scale experiments which could have happened only in the caves under such controlled conditions. Partly it was to demonstrate good intent to the captives, to make them feel less isolated.

No telepath really wants to marry a non-telepath. There are among non-telepaths quite as high a percentage of desirable mates as among Baldies, but to a Baldy, a non-telepathic human is a handicapped person. Like a lovely young girl who has every desirable attribute of mind and body but happens also to be deaf, dumb, and blind. She may communicate in finger-language, but the barrier remains all but insurmountable.

And there is this added factor – around every human who starts out life with the best of heredity and environment, shadows of the prison-house are inevitably, slowly but inexorably closed in by all the problems of living which he fails to solve completely without even realizing it. But not the Baldies. There are always friends to help, there are always minds to lean upon in crises and uncertainties. There is constant check and balance, so that no Baldy suffers from those inward quandaries, those only partly recognized clouds of confusion and bewilderment which fog the happiness of every other human being. In the telepathic mind there are comparatively few unswept chambers cluttered with old doubts and fears. It makes for a clarity of the personality which no non-telepath quite achieves.

A telepath may become psychotic, of course, but only when subjected to such stresses, over a long period of time, as a non-telepath could endure only briefly without breaking. (The paranoid telepaths were in a different class; heredity was an important factor there.)

So marriage between Baldy and non-telepath is, at best,

marriage between an alert, receptive, fully aware being and one murky and confused, handicapped in communication and always, on some level, latently resentful.

But by now almost every marriageable non-telepath in the caverns had been painstakingly courted by and married to a Baldy. They were at the same time, of course, inevitably married to an espionage agent, a willing but not always accepted psychoanalyst, and, most importantly, to the potential parents of other Baldies.

The gene is dominant, which means that the children were almost invariably telepathic. Only when the Baldy spouse possessed one recessive non-telepathic gene as well as one dominant telepathic gene could the child be born a non-telepath.

That was what had happened to Lucy and Jeff Cody....

No human was ever to leave the caves again. No Baldy was to know of the captivity who did not wear the Mute helmet, since if the world ever learned of this captivity, the long-awaited pogrom would touch off automatically. No child of human parents would ever leave, unless it left as an infant in arms, too young to remember or tell the story. But a telepath child was a recruit at birth to the ranks of the captors. The hope had been that in a generation or two the captives could automatically be blended with the Baldies or taken out of the caves at infancy, so that the colony would once more revert to its original state of a population composed only of telepaths.

That had been the original plan, but growing pressures had already made it obsolete.

Lucy wiped her mouth on the back of a lightly tanned hand and held out the emptied glass to Cody. She waited a moment while the whisky burned its way down and spread in a slow, hot coating over the walls of her stomach.

'Take a little,' she said. 'It helps.'

Cody didn't want any, but he tilted a short half-inch into the glass and drank obediently. After a time Lucy gave a short sigh and sat up cross-legged on the bed, shaking the hair back from her eyes.

'I'm sorry,' she said. 'Irrational.'

She laid her hand palm up on the bedspread and Cody closed his own hand over it, smiling unhappily at her.

'I've got an appointment outside,' he said. 'I'll have to leave in a few minutes, Lucy.'

Her look shot wild and unguarded toward the crib in the corner. Her thought, at once blurred and clarified by the release of alcohol, unfurled like a flag. Cody almost winced at the impact of it, but he was even more schooled in discipline than most Baldies, being husband to a non-telepath, and he showed nothing. He only said.

'No, it isn't that. I won't take him until you say so.'

She gave him a sudden startled glance.

'It's too late?'

'No,' Cody said quickly. 'Of course not. He isn't old enough yet to remember – this.'

Lucy moved uneasily.

'I don't want to keep him down here. You know I don't. It's bad enough for me, without knowing my own son wouldn't ever—' She shut off the thought of sunlight, blue air, distances. 'Not just yet,' she said, and pushed her feet over the edge of the bed. She stood up a little unsteadily. She gave the baby one blind glance and then walked stocking-footed toward the kitchen, bracing herself against the wall now and then. Cody reached automatically toward her mind, then drew back and got up to follow her. She was at the kitchen sink splashing water into a glass. She drank thirstily, her eyes unfocused.

'I have to go,' Cody said. 'Don't worry, Lucy.'

'Some – woman,' Lucy said indistinctly over the edge of the glass. 'There's – somebody. I know.'

'Lucy—'

'One of *your* kind,' Lucy said, and dropped the glass in the sink. It rolled in a bright arc, spilling water.

All he could do was look at her helplessly. There was nothing he could say. He couldn't tell her he was on his way to try to kill Jasper Horne. He couldn't tell her about Operation Apocalypse or the Inductor or the position of fearful responsibility he held. He couldn't say, 'If we can perfect the Inductor in time, Lucy, you can go free – you and our child.' Nor could he say, 'I may have to kill you – you and our child and every non-telepath on earth – with Operation Apocalypse.'

No, there was nothing he could say.

She drew a wet hand across her face, pushing back her hair, looking up at him blurrily, and then came on uncertain shoeless feet across the kitchen to lay her cheek on his shoulder and push her arms under his, around his chest.

'I'm sorry,' she said. 'I'm – crazy. It's hard for you too, Jeff.'

'Yes.'

'We'll send the baby away next week,' she promised. 'Then I'll be sane again. I – I *hate* whisky. It's just that—'

'I know.' He smoothed the hair away from her wet face, tried to find words for the complex waves of love, pity, remorse, terror and pain which filled his mind constantly as long as he was with his wife, or thinking of her. It is curious that telepaths are often almost inarticulate when it is necessary to communicate nuances of feeling in words. They never need to use words, among their own kind.

'Be patient with me, Lucy,' he said finally. 'There's trouble coming. There isn't much time, and I may fail. I – I'll come home as quickly as I can.'

'I know you will, dear. I wish I could do – anything.'

He held her.

'I'll bring you something you'll like,' he said. 'A surprise. I don't know what yet, but something nice. And Lucy after – next week – if you mean it, we'll move if you want. Find a new apartment over in Cave Seven. You can order new furniture, and we'll—' He scarcely knew what he was saying. Illusion and reality were too confused.

'We'll think of something, dear,' she said. 'It's all right.'

'I'll go, then,' he said.

She nodded. 'I'll miss you. Hurry back.'

Cody shut the grille of the lift behind him and leaned his head against the steel wall, slumping wearily as he shaped in his mind the code-signal to activate the mechanisms.

A preoccupied mind somewhere responded with another segment of the cipher, and a third (someone going by rapidly, late to dinner) tossed in the necessary remaining symbols. Three mental images had to be projected simultaneously to operate the lift. It was a precaution. Escape exits could be operated by telepaths only.

He pushed a slanting door open into a welter of dripping leaves and the sharp odour of wet pine and rain. A startled rabbit exploded out of the underbrush. Cody shut the camouflaged portal and looked up, squinting against the rain that drove in his face. From somewhere above a voiceless greeting came, a motor hummed and a dark coil rolled smoothly down out of the greyness. Cody set his foot in the stirrup and felt the soft instant upward lift of the basket seat snatching him aloft as he sank into it. The hovering copter received him through a single gaping jaw.

Arn Friedmann did not glance back from the controls. He did not need to. Short, squat, gravely expressionless in face and manner, he leaned his dark-capped head forward to peer through the rain, his mind detaching enough of itself from attention to the business at hand to send a wordless greeting.

For a moment Cody only leaned back and let the cool, untroubled silence of the open sky wash his mind clean. It was like allowing long-taut muscles to relax at last. The cavern was so filled with closed-down resentments, guilts and fears and tensions that after a while even the air became hard to breathe, for a telepath.

Friedmann had something urgent he wanted to convey. Cody felt the touch of it on the outer edges of his awareness, waiting, letting the newcomer breathe clean air a while. Friedmann's mind hovered as the copter had hovered, patient, abiding the signal.

Under them pine woods swept backward, tossing, rain-blurred. Water ran down the panes. The motor hummed pleasantly in the coolness. Lucy. Five years now without sight of rain or trees or sky. A lifetime ahead of her without them, or else a quick death, or – the Inductor.

'We've got to have more time,' Friedmann's thought

came. 'If a pogrom starts now, it'll spread. I think the paranoids are counting on that. They've been filtering into the key towns – the places where riots would be apt to start. Like American Gun. Jasper Horne's there.'

'Since when?' Cody asked.

'Three weeks or so. And he's been working hard. You know how the paranoids do it. Read a mind and drop a loaded word at the right time, to keep the tension building. Probably Horne could start a riot in American Gun any time he liked, by now.'

'Not if he's dead,' Cody's thought said, with grim anticipation. He leaned back, watching the mists scud past, thinking of American Gun. It was a gambling town. That was the speciality, anyway, although there was a famous research laboratory in the town, and a master artisan in plastics lived there. But basically men came to American Gun to gamble.

That's what I'll be doing, Cody thought. He watched sunlight dry the rain-drops on the window beside him.

Friedmann left Cody at the outskirts of American Gun and sent the copter hurrying east. He had an errand of his own in the town of Bleeding Kansas, five hundred miles away. Cody watched the copter lift in a perfectly empty blue sky.

American Gun lay in a great flat half-saucer rimmed by rising hills and cut across and bounded by a broad, slow river. There were a number of distant toothpick figures on the beach, and a variety of boats on the river, transparent plastic canoes and skiffs glinting in the sun. Dark dots against the placid green indicated swimmers. But the wind blowing up from the river was hot.

Cody stood on the lower foothills, looking down over American Gun. A certain calm relaxed him, now that he was moving directly toward a clearly-seen goal. There were in the town perhaps a hundred buildings, few of them large, and none close to the others. Trees flourished, or would have if their leaves had not drooped limply – all but the ones near the river bank. Only children were moving fast. Under a live-oak Cody could see a little party around a spread white rectangle, having a picnic. Against the white cloth he could see the green and red of water-melon.

A small white dog trotted slowly past him, its tongue lolling. It gave him a bored but wary glance. In its mind was a dim image of a frightful, slavering beast somewhat larger than a tiger. With some difficulty Cody identified the Terror as a dachshund whom the small white dog feared.

Somewhat diverted, Cody began to descend the slope toward American Gun. He didn't hurry. The moist, warm air was pleasant against his skin. Unthinking, receptive, for the moment, he let the cross-currents of thought sweep like the sound of a sea through him, while he moved on in half-hypnotic rhythm, focusing on a long Byzantine-style building ahead, and watching it grow larger, step by step.

. . . There was room enough on earth. And surely there were enemies enough besides other men. Man had been fighting a war ever since he stood upright, and there had never been any armistice declared against the oldest enemy of all, the enemy that burned in the hot blue sky, that hid, rod-shaped, toxic and invisible, in the soil, that ebbed now in the river but could rise and flood, the enemy that went on unknowing and unheeding man, whose ancient power always pounded at the dyke man's intelligence had built.

Enemy and friend at once – this gift of the gods. Without it, without the physical and chemical forces which had built this air, this water, this shallow valley of fertile loam, there would have been no life at all. A fairy gift – this planet. Guard it, keep it, watch it – learn to predict and control it – and it will serve you. Forget it while you fight among yourselves, and the burning sun, the flooding waters, the deadly cold, and the fecund micro-organisms will work as they have always worked, in their old pattern, and in that pattern there is no planned place for man. How like a god!

By now Cody was at the little park before the long Byzantine building. Trees were wilting above the brownish lawns. A shallow rectangular pool held goldfish, who gulped hopefully as they swam to the surface and flipped down again. The little minds of the fish lay open to Cody, minds thoughtless as so many bright, tiny, steady flames on little birthday candles, as he walked past the pool.

He did not enter the Byzantine building. He had not intended to, physically. Instead, he turned toward one of the shoulder-high pedestals set in irregular rows along the front of the building and stopped before one that was not in use. A few men and women had their heads bowed over the pedestals, peering into eyepieces. Not many. It was too hot, even here in the shade.

Cody bent over the eyepiece of his pedestal, found a coin in his pocket, and pushed it into the slot. The blackness at which he stared turned into a pattern of bright letters: *Radio-cobalt*. Then a series of number-ranges appeared, one by one. At random Cody pushed the button that indicated his choice. That started the mechanism. He found himself looking into a magnified Wilson cloud-chamber, streaked with flashing trails of sub-atomic activity. Just above the image a counter ticked off the number of electronic collisions. If his guess had been accurate enough, he might win the jackpot, and prove—

Nothing. Nothing at all. But as Cody's mind began to range, he felt the eager, troubled anticipation in the minds around him, and realized that to win, for most of these others, would prove a great deal.

For, basically, those minds held no confidence at all. Over all of them lay the heavy threat that had shadowed the world since the Blow-up and put an irresistible weapon in every hand, a cache of Eggs in every town. Instead of national walls, there was now a wall around each town – and around each individual. Survival still depended on luck – blind chance.

And so the gambling towns, like American Gun, flourished. Here, at the casinos, at the slot-machine, at roulette and craps and chuck-a-luck and faro, men could prove that the blind goddess favoured them, and that they were still safe. The social uncertainty was shifted to the mechanical uncertainty of the fall of dice or the spin of a wheel, and personal responsibility was shifted to the hands of the lady the Greeks called Tuche and the Romans, Fortuna.

Cody felt people moving past him, in and out of the casino. To his sensitive mind the hot air seemed to spark. Perhaps that was because of the steadily mounting tension spreading from no source a human could identify and which no human could ignore. But Cody knew the source. Jasper Horne had not been in American Gun for weeks without a purpose.

Here, if anywhere, the pogrom could be started.

And here, in American Gun, was the force which had driven Cody helplessly into his dilemma, relentlessly forcing him toward the choice that no man could contemplate for too long without seeking some easier answer. Here was the pressure which had forced his hand to the knife, and the knife to his neck. And here, too, was the man who was responsible.

Jasper Horne, Cody thought as the flashing streaks of the cloud-chamber burned before his eyes. His mind polarized toward that goal with a deadly intentness. Allenby, back in the Caves, had been right. To kill Horne, not himself, was the real goal for Cody – because that would risk merely his own life; it would not mean betrayal of his own people by dropping the responsibility he carried for all of them. The paranoids had been the enemy, from the very beginning. Always they had worked to destroy the acceptance of the Baldies by the rest of mankind. They were the ones who had caused the destruction of Sequoia, and the need to keep humans captive in the Caves. Had that not happened, he would probably have never met Lucy, and she would be happier now, and so would he. Now, no matter how hard both of them might try, there could never be any real answer for them, or for their child. There was no way out. No matter what happened, there were wounds that could never heal.

The earth itself was both enemy and friend. But the paranoids were all enemy, and of them all, Jasper Horne was somewhere here in American Gun, within Jeff Cody's reach – a man to be killed, if for no other reason, than because he and his kindred paranoids had made the Baldies killers.

The glittering streaks of light in the cloud-chamber died. The viewer went dark. Cody had won nothing. He slipped another coin into the slot and again watched the electronic bombardment, while his mind ranged and closed in toward his quarry.

Within the Byzantine building a flurry of thoughts whirled like the roulette wheels. This was a gossip centre for American Gun. Here, now and then, he caught images which he identified with Horne. Gradually he tested these thoughts, like directional antenna, until a picture of Horne's habits began to clarify. But other things clarified as well – the mounting pressure of events in the town which no non-telepath connected with the paranoid's presence.

No one in American Gun had shaved for twenty-four hours. Oh, some had – but not many. The Baldies had no need to shave, and, of course, there were humans courageous enough to risk suspicion. In the nearby research laboratories the no-shaving movement had not taken hold. And there were others, but not many, and those with smooth chins often moved in a circle of suspicious glances and left trails of hostile murmurings behind them.

So it might be doubly difficult to kill Horne. Violence could be the move that touched off the pogrom – exactly what Cody had hoped to avoid by eliminating the paranoid. That meant Horne would have to be killed privately, above all, away from any potential mob leaders who might trigger a riot. (There were such men in American Gun; Horne had found them already. They would be the ones to lead the mob when the time came.)

—he's at the Last Chance.

Cody lifted his head, dazzled for an instant by the deep blue shadow and the white sunlight. His mind mapped a picture of American Gun from the data he had already gathered. The Last Chance would be at the north end of town, near the research laboratories. Horne might or might not still be there, but it would be easy to pick up his trail.

Cody skirted the goldfish-pool, past the tiny flickering

flames of the small, drifting minds, and took a path leading northward through the town. His thoughts continued to range. Several times he caught the thoughts of other Baldies. Through them he could have located Horne instantly and accurately, but they did not wear the Mute helmets, and their minds could have been read in turn by the paranoid. And Horne must not be forewarned. Cody reached up to touch the fine-spun skein of filaments hidden beneath his wig. As long as he wore the Mute helmet, Horne could not read his mind.

The crowds began to thicken. Rumours went softly flickering past like heat lightning in the sweltering air, gathering corroborative detail as they went. Someone (Cody's mind heard the whisper) had broken the bank at the Gold Horseshoe last night, walked out with two heavy sacks of credits, and carelessly let his wig blow off in the doorway, revealing a hairless head. Yes, the Baldies were casting off the mask now and grabbing up credits in every way they could, preparing for the zero hour when they would take over the nation...

Cody walked a little faster. Stray thoughts from the Baldies in American Gun whispered to him. *Things are getting out of hand*, the word went silently through the air from mind to mind, from anxious group to group, from Baldies going stoically about their business among the humans and showing impassive faces as their minds touched and clung together on the verge of panic. Today mothers had kept their children home, and the family copters were fuelled and ready.

Above the crowd, Cody saw the flashing sign of the Last Chance ahead. He moved on, his mind searching for the presence of Horne. And in spite of the noiseless tensions straining and wrenching through the hot air, he realized that he felt curiously happy. Everything seemed very easy and simple now, for the first time in many months. *Kill Horne*. That was all; that was enough. *Kill Horne*, his mind said, without any of the doubts and unsureness of the last months and years.

He paused outside the old-fashioned photo-electric doors of the Last Chance, searching for his enemy. The rumours blew past him, fresh as if no voice had ever whispered them before. The whispers spoke of the string of freight-copters grounded with a fuel-leak at the edge of town, the repair man working among the cargo who accidentally broke a slat on a crate of oranges. Inside the liner of oranges were – queer-looking rifles – atomic? Three Eggs carefully packed in foam-rubber? Unconscious humans en route to a secret Baldy vivisection lab?

Then an invisible breath seemed to sweep through the hot, still air.

It was the paranoid aura. As, in grand mal, the epileptic attack is presaged by an indefinable feeling of impending disaster, so the physical approach of a paranoid carries before it the shadowy halo pulsing outward from the distorted mind. Cody had felt this before, but each time he knew afresh the same faint shrinking, as though his contact with the bright, hot, green world around him had thinned and snapped for an instant.

He turned slowly and crossed the street, threading past the uneasy, murmuring groups of unshaved men, past their hostile stares. Ahead was a little restaurant – the Copter Vane Eatery. The aura thickened. Cody stopped outside of the door of the restaurant and reached out telepathically.

The rumours flew past him. A man knew a man who had a Baldy neighbour who lost three fingers in a duel a month ago, and today had three fingers growing as good as new, grafted on in a private Baldy hospital. (But Baldies won't duel – never mind that!) *They* could work miracles in medicine now, but you didn't see them doing it for humans, did you? If they weren't stopped soon, who could tell what might happen next?

Stiff with arrogance, wary with suspicion, the mind of Jasper Horne, within the restuarant, sent out its own murky thoughts too – egotistical, prideful, sensitive, and inflexible. And there was a dim thought stirring in that cloudy mind, like an ember under grey ash, fading and brightening again into half-clarity, which made Cody, at the restaurant's door, pause and stiffen into immobility for fear that the telepathic paranoid might sense his presence.

Horne had not come to American Gun to start a pogrom.
His real motive was far more deadly. It was—
What?

That was what Cody could not see – yet. He had glimpsed the shadow of a thought, and that glimpse had been enough to flash a sharp warning to his mind, a signal of terrible urgency. Horne's real motive lay deeply buried. But it had to be found out. Cody felt quite certain of that.

He stepped aside, leaned against the wall of the building, and glanced idly around, while from under the Mute helmet his mind probed very delicately and sensitively toward Horne.

Gently . . . gently.

The paranoid was sitting alone in a booth near the back of the restaurant. His thoughts were clouded with repression. And he was concentrating on his lunch, not consciously thinking of the thing which had drifted across the surface of his mind for a triumphant instant. Unless this concept was summoned into consciousness, Cody could not read it without deep probing, which Horne would immediately sense.

Yet there was a way. The right cues would summon up the appropriate responses in any mind. But those cues would have to be implanted in Horne's thoughts very delicately, so that they would seem perfectly natural, and his own. Cody looked across the street, beyond the murmuring knots of men, at the Last Chance. Horne had been there half an hour ago. It was a fair cue. He sent the concept *Last Chance* softly into Horne's mind.

And that mind flinched warily, searched, found nothing (the Mute helmet guarded Cody), and then the cue summoned up its responses.

Last Chance gambling but I'm the one who's really gambling with them all of them their lives I can kill them all if in time – the thought-chain broke as videomusic swelled within the restaurant. Horne lifted his fork and began to eat again.

Cody fitted the beat of his thought to the music's beat and sent the message to Horne.

Kill them all kill them all kill them all.

Loose the virus, Horne's response came to the stimulus he

thought was his own. *Pomerance is getting closer every day control the resonance mutate a virus kill them all kill them all KILL THEM ALL!*

Cody braced himself against the red rage that poured out from the paranoid.

Pomerance, he thought. *Pomerance*.

Pomerance in the labs, Horne thought, and formed a sensory image. Not far away – only two blocks away – were the research laboratories of American Gun, and in them was a man named Pomerance, a biochemist, a non-telepath. He was working on a certain experiment which – if it succeeded – would enable the paranoids to develop a virus as deadly and as specialized as the virus of Operation Apocalypse.

And this was the real reason for Horne's presence in American Gun. The pogrom-plan was a cover-up. It was camouflage to deceive the Baldies, while Horne went about his real purpose of telepathically following Pomerance's experiments toward the goal of an Operation Apocalypse brought about by the paranoids themselves.

Pomerance was not aiming at such a goal, of course. He was a biochemist; his aim was to develop a more efficient bacterio-phage – but the method he would need to develop that could also be applied to far deadlier aims.

Gently Cody manipulated the paranoid's mind. He learned a little more. Pomerance might fail – Horne realized that. But in that case, then the pogrom could be set off. It would be better to find and use a human-killing virus, for in a pogrom paranoid lives would be lost too – but there would be a pogrom if no better way offered. Conditions were ripe. Horne had built the tension in American Gun; he had located the potential mob-leaders; he could start the pogrom at any time he desired – and that would be the signal for other paranoids across the nation to do the same. That universal pogrom would force the Baldies to release Operation Apocalypse – so the same end would be achieved. But it would be better to wait a little, just a little, following Pomerance's experiments closely. He seemed to be very near his goal.

Too near, Cody thought, his body swaying a little toward the restaurant's door. He was wasting time. *Kill Horne, kill him now*, he told himself – but hesitated still, because there was something else in the paranoid's mind that puzzled him. Too much confidence was built on that twisted, shaky foundation of paranoid personality. There must be some reason for that surprising lack of anxiety.

Cody probed again with careful cues that brushed the other mind lightly. Yes, there was a reason. There was a bomb hidden in Pomerance's laboratory.

Why?

Horne had that information, and Cody gently extracted it. The biochemist must not be allowed to fall alive into the hands of Baldies. The bomb was triggered to explode whenever Horne summoned to consciousness a certain complex of symbols – the paranoids' mind shifted quickly away from that dangerous equation – and it would also explode if Horne's mind *stopped* thinking.

That is, if Horne died.

Like the pattern of a burglar alarm, an interruption in the flow of current, the radiations emitted constantly by Horne's mind sleeping or waking, would break the circuit and set off the alarm – the bomb that would kill Pomerance. Cody saw the location of that bomb very clearly in Horne's mental image of the laboratory.

So, if he killed Horne, Pomerance would die too. But why was this important to the paranoid?

Cody probed again, and suddenly understood the reason.

Pomerance's research was centred around resonance differential applied to the nucleoproteins that were viruses. But there were other types of nucleoproteins; the telepathic function itself depended on the resonance of nucleoproteins in the human brain. If Pomerance's experiment succeeded, it would mean...

It would mean that telepathy could be induced in a nontelepath!

It was the answer to the problem of the Inductor, the one answer that could solve the universal problem of a world in schism. In the hands of the paranoids, Pomerance's method could destroy all humans. In the hands of the Baldies, it could make all mankind one. It could—

Suddenly Cody knew that Horne had discovered his presence.

Instantly Horne began to build in his mind the equation that would set off the bomb in Pomerance's laboratory. Cody's mind leaped into the future. He could kill Horne before the paranoid had finished, but if he did that, the other's death would trigger the bomb with equal certainty. Pomerance would die – and that must not be allowed to happen. More than lives depended on the biochemist's survival.

There was no way to stop Horne's thoughts except one. Cody's probing into the other's mind had told him a great deal about that proud, inflexible, unsure personality. He now knew more about Horne than the latter himself did. And he had discovered one vital point. Horne was not psychotic; he had not lost touch with reality, but, like many paranoids, he had psychopathological symptoms, and one of these was his strong tendency to what Allenby would have called hypnogogic hallucinations – vivid sensory images occurring in the drowsy state just before sleep. And such hallucinations can easily be produced by hypnosis.

All Cody had to do was to convince Horne that he had momentarily been hallucinated. That, and a little more – a good deal more.

At least, Cody had a good insight into what forms such imagery would take for the paranoid, with his strong delusions of persecution and grandeur. So Cody projected the idea that he, representing the Baldies, had come to Horne to offer a truce, to make a pact with the paranoids against the humans – exactly the kind of vivid wish-fulfilling fantasy Horne must often have experienced. And at the same time he summoned up the mental image of Jasper Horne and let Horne see it.

That action was natural enough, even within the frame of an hallucination. When you communicate with another, you visualize him in your own mind, in many more dimensions than the purely visual ones. Your impression of his emotional patterns, his memories, his thoughts, the complex image of his whole personality as you perceive it, is summoned up as a subjective correlative of the objective man with whom you communicate. The burning brightness of that Luciferean image stood clear between the meeting minds, blazingly sharp and vivid, in a way that the murky mind of the paranoid had never known.

The ancient Greeks knew what the mechanism of identification meant – they told the story of Narcissus. And the lure caught Jasper Horne, who could identify with no other man than himself, or a god made in his own image. His paranoid egotism reflected in that ego-image and was reflected again and so endlessly, while Cody delicately tested and touched the thoughts of the other and watched for the first slackening of consciousness.

At least Horne had paused in his mental building of the concept that would destroy Pomerance. The paranoid hesitated, unsure, his grasp of reality telling him that the Baldies could not, would not send an emissary to capitulate, and that therefore his senses, which had warned him of Cody's presence, had lied. Such panics were not unknown to Horne. So he could accept – tentatively – the suggestion that his senses had tricked him.

Very, very gently, still maintaining that dazzling ego-image of Jasper Horne like a glittering lure on a baited hook, Cody sent quiet cue-thoughts slipping into the hesitant mind. At first they were obviously true thoughts, true, at least, according to the paranoid's system of belief. They were pleasant, reassuring thoughts. Lulled, Horne watched the ego-image which he himself had often summoned up – yet never before so clearly and dazzlingly. Narcissus watched his image in the clear, deep pool of Cody's mind.

So, sitting alone in the restaurant booth, Horne let his wariness relax little by little, and Cody's soft assault moved into a new area. The thoughts Cody sent out now were not quite true, but still not false enough to startle the paranoid, who took them for his own thoughts. *I've had these hallucina-*

tions before. Usually just before going to sleep. I'm having them now. So I must be going to sleep. I am sleepy. My eyelids feel heavy ...

The lulling, monotonous thoughts began to submerge Horne's consciousness. Gradually the hypnosis grew. Narcissus watched Narcissus ...

Sleep, sleep, Cody's mind whispered. *You will not waken until I command you. Sleep deeply – sleep.*

The paranoid slept.

Cody began to run along the street as fast as he could. No other Baldy in American Gun was nearer to the research laboratory than he was, and if Pomerance were to be saved, it was his job alone. And he might easily fail. Jasper Horne was sitting in hypnotic sleep in a crowded restaurant, and at any moment someone might speak to him or shake him back into consciousness. The hypnosis was not deep. It might hold, or it might break at any moment. In spite of Cody's final suggestions to the paranoid, the latter could be awakened quite easily, and by anyone.

Cody ran on. Suppose he got Pomerance out of the lab in time? Could he get back to the restaurant again before Horne wakened?

No, Cody thought, the hypnosis isn't deep enough. It'll be a miracle if Horne stays under more than a few minutes. If I can save Pomerance, that will be miracle enough.

But as soon as Horne realizes what's happened, he won't wait. He'll start the pogrom. It's all ready, here in American Gun; he's planted the dynamite, and all he has to do is touch the detonator. All right. I can't be sure that what I'm doing is right. I think it is. I can't be sure. If I save Pomerance, Horne will probably start the pogrom before I can get back and kill him. But I can't let Pomerance die; he can solve the problem of the Inductor.

Hurry!

He ran toward a group of long, low buildings. He knew the way; he had seen it in Horne's mind. He ran toward one of the buildings, thrust open the door, and was in the laboratory.

A gaunt, grey-haired man in a stained smock turned to

stare at him. It was Pomerance; no telepath can ever be mistaken on a question of identity. It was Pomerance – and as Cody realized that, he also realized that two blocks away, in the Copter Vane Eatery, Jasper Horne had stirred, wakened, and reached out in sudden panic to touch Pomerance's mind.

Instantly Cody was racing down the length of the long laboratory. Beyond Pomerance were floor-length windows opening on hot sunlight, blue sky, and parched brown grass. If they could reach the windows—

It seemed to Cody that he crossed the room in no time at all. No time, and yet another kind of time seemed to draw out endlessly as, in the distant mind of the paranoid, he saw the triggering equation building up that would set off the bomb's mechanism. Now the equation was complete. Now time would stop in one bursting moment of death.

Yet there was time. Cody sent out a wordless call, a summons that rang like a great alarm bell in the minds of every Baldy in American Gun. At the same moment he reached Pomerance and used his own momentum to lift the other man bodily as he plunged toward the windows. Then the floor rose underfoot and the air rushed outward before the first soundless compression wave that moved in front of the explosion.

The window loomed before them, bright, high, patterned with small panes. Cody's shoulder struck, he felt wood and glass shatter without a sound because of the great, white, bursting roar of the explosion, louder than any sound could be.

The blast exploded in a white blindness all around him and beyond shattering glass the void opened up under him.

He was falling with Pomerance through hot, dry outdoor air and darkness, darkness in the full heat of the sun, falling and turning while glass rained down around them and the noise of the explosion went on and on for ever ...

In front of the Copter Vane Eatery two transients scuffled. Jasper Horne, in the crowd, said something under his breath. Another man repeated it, louder. One of the transients flushed darkly. (It was a trigger-phrase as certain to rouse this man's aggressions as the equation that had exploded the bomb.) In a moment a dagger was pulled from its sheath, and a full-fledged duel was in progress in the middle of a noisy circle. The winner was a hairy-faced, hairy-chested man with a partially bald head. His knife-work had been very deft and sure. Too sure, Jasper Horne said in a loud whisper. The whispers flew around the circle. Anybody could win a duel if he could read the other man's mind. If *They* could grow fingers maybe they could grow hair.

Jasper Horne said something, exactly the right something to the potential mob-leader beside him.

The potential mob-leader scowled, swore, and took a step forward. Deftly he tripped the winner from behind as he was sheathing his dagger. The knife flew spinning across the pavement. Three men were on the falling baldhead as he went down. Two of them held him while the third tugged at his tonsure-fringe of hair. It held. The victim bellowed with rage and resisted so strongly that four or five bystanders were sent sprawling. One of them lost his wig ...

This was neither sleep nor waking. It was Limbo. He floated in the womb of non-self, the only real privacy a telepath can ever know, and what he wanted was to stay here for ever and ever. But he was a telepath. He could not, even in the secret fastness of his own mind, pretend what was not true, for his mind lay quite open – at least to wearers of the Mute helmets like his own.

Yet it was hard to waken. It was hard to force himself, of his own volition, to stoop and pick up whatever burdens might be waiting for him, new and old. If his life could be lived as had been the last minute he remembered, without any indecision or unsureness, but with only the certain need for physical action (*is Pomerance alive*, something in his wakening mind asked), then it would be easy indeed to lift himself up out of this warm, grey silence which was so infinitely restful, without even dreams (*but Pomerance?*).

And as always, the thought of another made something in Cody brace and lift itself with weary stubbornness. Instantly he was oriented. He did not need to depend on his own sleep-confused senses alone. All through the Caves, and above them, and in copters in mid-air, was a stirring and a confused sense of urgency and troubled motion, and each mind held one thought under whatever other thoughts might be pre-occupying the upper levels of the mind.

The thought was *pogrom*.

Cody asked one question: *Should I have killed Horne instead of trying to save Pomerance?* But he did not wait for an answer. The decision had been his own, after all. He opened his eyes (knowing in what infirmary bed in what sector of the Caves he lay) and looked up at the round ruddy face of Allenby.

Pomerance?' he asked.

'Alive,' the psychologist answered wordlessly. 'Some of the American Gun Baldies got to you right after the explosion. They had to work fast. Horne had set off the pogrom. But they had a fast copter ready, and gave you and Pomerance first aid en route. That was two days ago.'

'Two days?'

'Pomerance was unconscious for only a few hours. But we kept you under till now – you needed it. However, I guess you'll live, in case you're wondering.'

'How long will any of us live?' Cody's thought whispered.

'Get up and dress,' Allenby ordered. 'There's work to be done. Here's your clothes. How long? I don't know. The pogrom's been spreading for two days. The paranoids had everything very neatly planned. It looks like a total pogrom this time, Jeff. But we've got Pomerance. And I think we've got the Inductor.'

'But Pomerance isn't one of us.'

'He's with us, though. Not all humans are anti-Baldy, thank God. As soon as Pomerance understood the situation, he voluntarily offered to help in any way he could. So come along. We're ready to try the Inductor. I wanted you to be there. Can you manage?'

Cody nodded. He was stiff, and quite weak, and there were a good many aches and pains under the sprayed-on plastic bandages, but it felt fine to stand up and walk. He followed Allenby out into the corridor and along it. The troubled, urgent stirring of innumerable thoughts moved all around him. He remembered Lucy. *Not all humans are anti-Baldy*. And not all Baldies are anti-human, he added, thinking of what had been done to the humans like Lucy who had been condemned to life imprisonment within the Caves.

'She'll be there – in the lab,' Allenby told Cody. 'She offered to be one of the subjects. We've got an Inductor jury-rigged according to Pomerance's theory – at least, we started with his theory and went on from there, every scientist among us. It was quite a job. I hope—' The thought of the pogrom shadowed Allenby's mind briefly and was repressed. Cody thought: *I shall find time, Cassius, I shall find time ...*

'Yes,' the psychologist agreed. 'Later, Jeff. Later. The Inductor is our goal right now. Nothing else. You haven't thought of Jasper Horne since you woke up, have you?'

Cody realized that he had scarcely done so. Now, as he did, he saw the paranoid leader as something remote and depersonalized, a moving figure in a great complex of action, but no longer the emotion-charged target of his hate.

'I guess I don't feel the need to kill him,' Cody agreed. 'He's not really important any more. The worst he could do was start the pogrom, and he's done that. I'd kill him if I had the chance, but for a different reason – now.' He glanced at Allenby. 'Will the Inductor work?' he asked.

'That's what we're going to find out. But it ought to – it ought to,' Allenby said, opening a door in the wall of the corridor. Cody followed the psychologist into one of the caverns which had been made into an experimental laboratory.

There was a great deal going on in the cave, but Cody was not distracted by external sense-impressions; he turned immediately toward where Lucy was standing, the baby in her arms. He went toward her quickly. He reached out to her mind and then checked himself. There was, perhaps, too much he did not want to know, now or ever.

Cody said, 'These bandages don't mean anything. I feel fine.'

'They told me,' Lucy said. 'It was one time I was glad of

telepathy. I knew they could really tell if you were all right – even if you were unconscious.'

He put his arm around her, looking down at the sleeping baby.

Lucy said, 'I couldn't tell a thing by watching you. You might have been – dead. But it was so good to have Allenby and the others able to look into your mind and make sure you were all right. I wanted to do something to help, but there wasn't anything I *could* do. Except . . . this. Allenby told me he needed volunteers for the Inductor experiment. So I volunteered. It's one way I *can* help – and I want to.'

So Lucy knew about the Inductor now. Well, the time and need for secrecy was past. It no longer mattered how much or how little the prisoners in the Caves knew. It no longer mattered, now that the pogrom had begun.

'It's a total pogrom this time, isn't it?' she asked, and he had an irrational second of amazement (*telepathy?*) before he realized that Lucy was merely reacting to cues learned through long familiarity with his behaviour. All married couples have flashes of this kind of pseudo-telepathy, if there is real sympathy between them. And in spite of everything, that sympathy had existed. It was strange to know this now, to be sure of it and to feel elation, when so little time might remain. The pogrom could still destroy everything, in spite of the Inductor.

'Lucy,' he said. 'If we fail – we'll make sure you get safely out of the Caves, back home—'

She looked down at the baby, and then turned away from Cody. He suddenly realized, as men have always done, that even with telepathic power to aid him, he would never really understand a woman's reactions – not even Lucy's.

'Aren't you ready yet?' she asked Allenby.

'I think so,' he said. 'Let somebody hold the baby, Lucy.'

She turned back to Cody, smiled at him, and put the baby in his arms. Then she followed Allenby toward an insulated chair, jury-rigged with a tangle of wires which led to a complicated instrument panel.

The mind of the baby had a little flame in it like the flames

Cody remembered in the goldfish in the pool back in American Gun. But there was a very great difference. He did not know exactly what it was, but he had not felt pity and fear as he watched the glimmering minds of the fish. The mind of his child, his and Lucy's, held a small flame that burned with ridiculous confidence for so small and helpless a creature, and yet each slight stimulus, the rocking movement of his arms, the slight hunger-contractions of the child's stomach, made the fragile flame quiver and blow in a new direction before it swung back to its perseverant burning. So many things would shake that flame, in even the best of all worlds – but, he thought with sudden clarity, in that flame the personality of the child would be forged and made strong.

He looked toward Lucy. She was sitting in the chair now, and electrodes were being attached to her temples and the base of her skull. A man he recognized as Pomerance, gaunt and grey-haired, was hovering over her, getting in the way of the experimenters. In Pomerance's mind, Cody saw, was a slight irritation the man was trying hard to repress. *This application, this connection – I don't understand how it fits the theory. My God, if only I were a telepath! But if the Inductor works, I can be. Now how does this hook-up fit into –* and then the thoughts swung into inductive abstractions as the biochemist tried to puzzle the problem out.

The cave-laboratory was crowded. There were the Mute-scientists, and there were a score of captives from the Caves – all volunteers, Cody realized warmly. In spite of everything, they had wanted to help, as Lucy had wanted to.

Now the test was beginning. Lucy relaxed in the chair, her thoughts nervously considering the pressure of the electrodes. Cody withdrew his mind. He felt nervous too. He scanned the group, found a receptive mind, and recognized Allenby.

'Suppose the Inductor works,' Cody said in silence. 'How will that stop the pogrom?'

'We'll offer telepathy to everybody,' Allenby told him. 'There's a video hook-up all ready to cut in on every screen in every town. I think even a lynch mob will stop to listen if they're offered telepathy.'

'I wonder.'

'Besides, there are plenty of humans on our side, like Pomerance. We've got—' The thought paused.

For something was happening to Lucy's mind. It was like a wave, a flood of something as indefinable as abstract music rising in Lucy's thoughts as the nucleoproteins of her brain altered. *She's becoming a telepath, one of us*, Cody thought.

'Power off,' Allenby said suddenly. He bent forward and removed the electrodes. 'Wait a minute, now, Lucy.' He stopped talking, but his mind spoke urgently in silence.

Move your right hand. Move your right hand.

Not a Baldy looked at Lucy's hands. There must be no unconscious signals.

Lucy did not move. Her mind, opened to Cody, suddenly and appallingly reminded him of Jasper Horne's walled mind. He did not know why, but a little thrill of fear touched him.

Move your right hand.

No response.

Try another command, someone suggested. *Lucy – stand up. Stand up.*

She did not move.

It may take time, a Baldy suggested desperately. *She may need time to learn—*

Maybe, Allenby thought. *But we'd better try another subject.*

'All right, Lucy,' Cody said. 'Come over here with me. We're going to try someone else.'

'Didn't it work?' she asked. She went to him, staring into his eyes as though trying to force *rapport* between mind and mind.

'We can't tell yet,' he said. 'Watch June.'

June Barton was in the chair now, flinching a little as the electrodes were attached.

In Cody's thoughts something moved uneasily – something he had not thought of since he woke. If the Inductor failed, then – it would be his problem again, the same old problem, which he had failed to solve. The dilemma which had sent him out to try to kill Jasper Horne. The responsibility that was too great for any one man to carry after a while. Operation Apocalypse. *The end of all flesh...*

Very quickly he turned his mind from that thought. He reached out mentally with a sense of panic, while his arm tightened about Lucy. (*Would he have to kill her – her and their child? It may not come to that. Don't think about it!*) He searched for a concept intricate enough to drive the obsessive terror from his mind. *The Inductor,* he asked at random. *What's the theory? How does it work?*

Another mind leaped gratefully toward the question. It was Kunashi, the physicist. From beneath Kunashi's Mute helmet came quick clear thoughts that could not quite conceal the anxiety in the man's mind. For Kunashi, too, was married to a non-telepath.

'You remember when we asked the calculator for a solution to our problem?' (The electrodes were being unclamped from June Barton's head now.) 'We gathered all the data we could to feed into the calculator. We read the minds of human scientists everywhere, and coded all the data that could possibly be relevant. Well, some of that data came from Pomerance's mind, more than a year ago. He wasn't very far along with his theory then, but the key concepts had been formulated – the hypothesis involving mutation of nucleoproteins by resonance. The calculator integrated that with other data and came up with the simplest answer – the virus. It didn't have the necessary data to follow the theory along the lines of the Inductor, even though both concepts depend on the same basic – resonance.'

(Someone else was sitting down in the chair. The electrodes were being attached. Cody felt the growing distress and anxiety in every mind.)

Kunashi went on doggedly, 'Pomerance is a biochemist. He was working on a virus – Japanese encephalitis type A – and trying to mutate it into a specialized bacteriophage.' The thought faltered for an instant and picked up again. 'The reproduction of a virus – or a gene – depends on high internal resonance; it's a nucleoprotein. Theoretically, anything can change into anything else, eventually. But the physical probability of such a change depends on the relative resonance measure of the two states – high for the aminoacidprotein chain, for example, and the two states of the benzene ring.'

(Kunashi's wife was sitting down in the chair.)

'The change, the reproduction, also involves high specificity of the chemical substances involved. That's the reason telepaths would be immune to the Operation Apocalypse virus, whatever it is. Now . . . now, specificity can vary not only from species to species, but within the species too. Our immunity is innate. The (*will it work? will it work?*) nucleoprotein of the Operation Apocalypse virus must have a high affinity for certain high-resonance particles in the central nervous system of non-telepaths. Such particles have a great capacity for storing information. So our virus would attack the information centres of the non-telepathic brain.

'That affinity depends on resonance differential – and Pomerance's experiments were aimed at finding a way to alter that differential. Such a method would make it possible to mutate virus-strains with great predictability and control. And it can also be used to induce telepathy. Telepathy depends on high resonance of nucleoproteins in the brain's information centres, and by artificially increasing specificity, the telepathic function can be induced in – in—'

The thought stopped. Kunashi's wife was leaving the experimental chair, and the physicist's mind clouded with doubt, misery, and hopelessness. Cody's thoughts linked with Kunashi's, sending a strong message of wordless warm encouragement – not intellectual hope, he did not have much of that himself – but a deep emotional bridge of understanding and sympathy. It seemed to help a little. It helped Cody, too. He watched Kunashi's wife walk quickly to him, and they linked arms and stood together waiting.

Suddenly Lucy said, 'I want to try again.'

'Do you feel—' Cody began, but immediately knew that there had been no change. Her mind was still walled.

Yet Allenby, across the room, nodded.

'It's worth trying,' he said. 'Let's do it with the power on, this time. The resonance effect should last for several minutes after disconnecting the electrodes, but we won't take any chances.' Cody had taken the baby again, and Lucy was settling herself in the chair. 'Ideally, all these gadgets will be in a small power-pack that will be worn and operating continuously ... All right, Lucy? Power on.'

Again mind after mind tried to touch Lucy's. Again Cody sensed, as he had sensed in the minds of the other subjects too, that strange walled aspect that reminded him of Jasper Horne. But Lucy wasn't paranoid!

Yet her mind did not open. So it was failure – not a mechanical failure, for Pomerance's hypothesis had been verified by everything except the ultimate verification of experimental proof. And yet, without that proof, the pogrom would rage on unchecked, spreading and destroying.

She's not paranoid! Cody thought. The baby stirred in his arms. He reached into the warm, shapeless mind and sensed nothing there that reminded him at all of Jasper Horne.

The baby, Allenby thought suddenly. *Try the baby*.

Questions thrust toward the psychologist. But they were not answered. He did not know the answers. He had a hunch, that was all.

Try the baby.

Allenby turned off the power and removed the electrodes from Lucy's head. The baby was laid gently, in his blankets, on the seat Lucy had vacated. The electrodes were attached carefully. The baby slept.

Power on, Allenby ordered.

His thoughts reached out toward the child.

The child slept on.

... Defeat, the last defeat of all, Cody knew. Telepaths and non-telepaths were ultimately different, after all. That wall could never go down. No armistice could ever be made. The pogrom could not be stopped.

The paranoids had been right. Telepaths could not exist side by side with non-telepaths.

And suddenly in Cody's mind blazed the flash and roar of the exploding bomb, the blinding thunderclap that was to engulf the whole world now—

On the chair, the baby squirmed, opened its eyes and mouth, and screamed.

In the soft, floating mistiness of its mind was the formless shape of fear – the sudden flash and roar and Cody's own memory of falling helplessly through space – the oldest fears of all, the only fears which are inborn.

For the first time in history, telepathy had been induced.

Cody sat alone at the control panel of the electronic calculator. For there was no time at all now. In a moment the emergency telecast would begin, the last appeal to the group of non-telepaths. They would be offered the Inductor – conditionally. For they could not use it. Only their children could.

If they were willing to accept the Inductor and halt the pogrom, the Baldies would know very quickly. The most secret thoughts of men cannot be hidden from telepaths.

But if they would not accept – the Baldies would know that, too, and then Cody would touch a certain button on the panel before him. Then Operation Apocalypse would begin. In six hours the virus would be ready. In a week or two, ninety per cent of the world's population would be dead or dying. The pogrom might go on until the last, but telepaths could hide efficiently, and they would not have to remain hidden long. The decision was man's.

Cody felt Allenby come in behind him.

'What's your guess?' he asked.

'I don't know. It depends on egotism paranoia, in a way. Maybe man has learned to be a social animal; maybe he hasn't. We'll soon find out.'

'Yes. Soon. It's the end now, the end of what started with the Blow-up.'

'No,' Allenby said, 'it started a long time before that. It started when men first began to live in groups and the groups kept expanding. But before there was any final unification, the Blow-up came along. So we had decentralization, and that was the wrong answer. It was ultimate disunity and control by fear. It built up the walls between man and man higher than ever. Aggression is punished very severely now – and in a suspicious, worried, decentralized world there's a tremendous lot of aggression trying to explode. But the conscience represses it – the criminal conscience of a fear-ruled society, built up in every person from childhood. That's why no non-telepathic adult today can let himself receive thoughts – why Lucy and the others couldn't.'

'She'll ... never be able to?'

'Never,' Allenby said quietly. 'It's functional hysteric deafness – telepathic deafness. Non-telepaths don't know what other people are thinking – but they believe they know. And they're afraid of it. They project their own repressed aggressions on to others; unconsciously, they feel that every other being is a potential enemy – and so they don't dare become telepaths. They may want to consciously, but unconsciously there's too much fear.'

'Yet the children—'

'If they're young enough, they can become telepaths, like your baby, Jeff. His super-ego hasn't formed yet. He can learn and learn realistically, with all minds open to him, with no walls locking him in as he grows and learns.'

Cody remembered something an old poet had written. *Something there is that doesn't love a wall.* Too many walls had been built, for too long, walls that kept each man apart from his neighbour. In infancy, perhaps in early childhood, anyone was capable of receiving telepathic thoughts, given the Inductor. In infancy the mind of the child was whole and healthy and complete, able to learn telepathic as well as verbal communication. But soon, fatally soon, as the child grew and learned, the walls were built.

Then man climbed his wall and sat on it like Humpty Dumpty – and somehow, somewhere, in the long process of maturing and learning, the mind was forever spoiled. It was the fall, not only of Humpty Dumpty, but the immemorial fall of man himself. And then—

All the king's horses and all the king's men couldn't put Humpty Dumpty together again.

For Lucy, it was forever too late.

After a little while, Cody said, 'What about the paranoids? They were telepathic as children. What happened to them?'

Allenby shook his head.

'I don't know the answer to that one, Jeff. It may be

an hereditary malfunction. But they don't matter now; they're a minority among telepaths – a very small minority. They've been dangerous only because we were a minority among non-telepaths, and vulnerable to scapegoating. We won't be, if...'

'What about the secret wave-bands?'

'The Inductor can be built to adapt to any wavelength the human brain can transmit. There won't be any more walls at all.'

'If our offer is accepted. If it isn't – if the pogrom goes on – then I still have the responsibility for Operation Apocalypse.'

'Is it your responsibility?' Allenby asked. 'Is it ours, even? The non-telepaths will be making their own choice.'

'The telecast's starting,' Cody said. 'I wonder how many will listen to it.'

The mob that swept through the town of Easterday, secretly led by a paranoid, swirled toward a big house with a wide veranda. The mob sent up a yell at sight of the row of men standing on the veranda waiting. But the paranoid hesitated.

The man beside him did not. He shouted and sprinted forward. There was a sharp crack and dust spurted at his feet.

'They've got guns!' somebody yelled.

'*Get 'em!*'

'*Lynch 'em!*'

The mob surged forward. Again a rifle snapped.

The mob-leader – not the paranoid, but the apparent leader – swore and dropped to the ground, clutching at his leg.

On the veranda a man stepped forward.

'Get out of here,' he said crisply. 'Get going – fast.'

The leader stared in amazement.

'Doc!' he said. 'But you're not a Baldy. What the hell are you doing?'

The doctor swung his rifle slowly back and forth.

'A lot of us here aren't Baldies,' he said, glancing along the

209

row of silent men. Several races were represented, but the mob was not concerned with race just now. The lynchers searched out the men on the porch whom they knew to be Baldies – and found each one flanked by coldly determined non-telepaths, armed and waiting.

There weren't many of them, though – the defenders.

That occurred to the leader. He stood up, testing the flesh wound in his calf. He glanced over his shoulder.

'We can take 'em,' he shouted. 'It's ten to one. Let's go get all of 'em!'

He led the wave.

He died first. On the veranda a runty man with spectacles and a scrubby moustache shivered and lowered his gun for a moment. But he did not move from where he stood in the determined line.

The mob drew back.

There was a long pause.

'How long do you think you can hold us off, Doc?' someone called.

The dead man lay on the open ground between the two groups.

The air quivered with heat. The sun moved imperceptibly westward. The mob coalesced tighter, a compact, murderous mass waiting in the sunlight.

Then a telecast screen within the house lit up, and Allenby's voice began to speak to the world.

The telecast was over.

Baldy minds were busy searching, questioning, seeking their answer in minds that could not conceal their true desires. This was a poll that could not be inaccurate. And within minutes the poll would be finished. The answer would be given. On that answer would depend the lives of all who were not telepaths.

Jeff Cody sat alone before the electronic calculator, waiting the answer.

There could be only one answer a sane man, a sane people, could give. For the Inductor meant, for the first time in human history, a unity based on reality. It opened the gates to the true and greatest adventures, the odyssey into the mysteries of science and art and philosophy. It sounded the trumpet for the last and greatest war against the Ilium of nature itself – the vast, tremendous, unknown universe in which man has struggled and fought and, somehow, survived.

No adult living today could live to see more than the beginning of that vast adventure. But the children would see it.

There could be only one answer a sane person could give. A sane people.

Cody looked at the keyboard before him.

The earth is filled with violence through them.

Yes, there could be another answer. And if that answer were given – *the end of all flesh is come before me.*

I will destroy them with the earth!

Cody's mind leaped ahead. He saw his finger pressing the button on the keyboard, saw Operation Apocalypse flooding like a new deluge across the planet, saw the race of man go down and die beneath that destroying tide, till only telepaths were left alive in all the world, perhaps in all the universe. He remembered the terrible, lonely pang Baldies feel when a Baldy dies.

And he knew that no telepath would be able to close his mind against that apocalyptic murder of all mankind.

There would be the wound which could not heal, which could never heal among a telepathic race whose memories would go on and on, unweakened by transmission down through the generations. A hundred million years might pass, and even then the ancient wound would burn as on the day it had been made.

Operation Apocalypse would destroy the Baldies too. For they would feel that enormous death, feel it with the fatal sensitivity of the telepath, and though physically they might live on, the pain and the guilt would be passed on from generation to crippled generation.

Suddenly Cody moved.

His finger pushed a button. Instantly the guarding monitor began to operate. There was a soft humming that lasted less than a second. Then a light burned bright on the control panel, and under it was a number.

Cody pressed another button. The unerring selectors searched the calculator for the bit of crystal that held the code of Operation Apocalypse. The crystal, with its cipher of frozen dots of energy, was ready.

A thousand minds, sensing Cody's thought, reached toward him, touched him, spoke to him.

He paused for an instant while he learned that man had not yet made his decision.

The voices in his mind became a tumultuous clamour. But the ultimate decision was neither man's nor theirs; the responsibility was his own, and he waited no longer.

He moved his hand quickly forward and felt the cool, smooth plastic of a lever sink with absolute finality beneath his fingers.

On the bit of ferro-electric crystal waiting in the calculator, the cipher-pattern of energy shivered, faded and vanished completely.

Operation Apocalypse was gone.

Still Cody's fingers moved. Memory after memory died within the great machine. Its vast pools of data drained their energy back into the boundless sea of the universe and were lost. Then at last the brain of the calculator was empty. There was no way to re-create the Apocalypse – no way and no time.

Only waiting was left.

He opened his mind. All around him, stretching across the earth, the linked thoughts of the Baldies made a vast, intricate webwork, perhaps the last and mightiest structure man would ever build. They drew him into their midst and made him one with them. There were no barriers at all. They did not judge. They understood, all of them, and he was part of them all in a warm, ultimate unity that was source of enough strength and courage to face whatever decision mankind might make. This might be the last time man would ever bind itself together in this way. The pogrom might go on until the last Baldy died. But until then, no Baldy would live or die alone.

So they waited, together, for the answer that man must give.

CHAPTER 6

The helicopter has landed. Men run toward me. They're strangers. I can't read their thoughts. I can't see them clearly; everything is dim, fading into wavering, shadowy ripples.

Something is being slipped around my neck. Something presses against the back of my head.

An Inductor.

A man kneels beside me. A doctor. He has a hypodermic.

The hypodermic comes second. The Inductor first of all. For none of us should die alone. None of us live alone any more. Either we are Baldies, or else we wear the Inductor that has made all men telepaths.

The Inductor begins to operate.

I meant to ask the doctor if I would live, but now I know that this is not the important thing. I know that, as warmth and life come back into the universe, and I am no longer alone. What is important is that my mind, my self, is no longer cut off and incomplete, it is expanding, joining with my people, with all life, as I rise from this lonely grave in which I have lain and I am—

We are—

We are one. We are man. The long, long war is ended, and the answer has been given. The dream has been cleansed, and the fire on the hearth is guarded.

It will not burn out, now, until the last man dies.

Prices and postage and packing rates shown below were correct at the time of going to press.

FICTION

All prices shown are exclusive of postage and packing

GENERAL FICTION

☐ THE CAIN CONSPIRACY	J. M. Simmel	£1.20
☐ THE AFFAIR OF NINA B	J. M. Simmel	£1.20
☐ HMS BOUNTY	John Maxwell	£1.00
☐ A REAL KILLING	William Keegan	80p
☐ SEARCHING FOR CALEB	Anne Tyler	95p
☐ CELESTIAL NAVIGATION	Anne Tyler	95p
☐ THE ENTREPRENEUR	I. G. Broat	£1.00
☐ THE SOUNDS OF SILENCE	Judith Richards	£1.00
☐ THE BOTTOM LINE	Fletcher Knebel	£1.25
☐ ON THE BRINK	Benjamin Stein with Herbert Stein	95p
☐ CHAINS	Justin Adams	£1.20
☐ RUNNING SCARED	Gregory Mcdonald	85p
☐ V. J. DAY	Alan Fields	95p
☐ THE HEIR	Christopher Keane	£1.00
☐ THE LAREDO ASSIGNMENT (Western)	Matt Chisholm	75p
☐ TY-SHAN BAY	Raoul Templeton Aundrews	95p
☐ A SEA-CHANGE	Lois Gould	80p
☐ THE PLAYERS	Gary Brandner	95p
☐ RIDDLE	Dan Sherman	90p

CRIME/THRILLER

☐ THE TWO FACES OF JANUARY	Patricia Highsmith	95p
☐ THOSE WHO WALK AWAY	Patricia Highsmith	95p
☐ A GAME FOR THE LIVING	Patricia Highsmith	95p
☐ THE BLUNDERER	Patricia Highsmith	95p
☐ THE TREMOR OF FORGERY	Patricia Highsmith	80p
☐ STRAIGHT	Steve Knickmeyer	80p
☐ FIVE PIECES OF JADE	John Ball	85p
☐ IN THE HEAT OF THE NIGHT	John Ball	85p
☐ THE EYES OF BUDDHA	John Ball	85p
☐ THE COOL COTTONTAIL	John Ball	80p
☐ JOHNNY GET YOUR GUN	John Ball	85p
☐ THE PEKING PAY-OFF	Ian Stewart	90p
☐ THE TEN-TOLA BARS	Burton Wohl	90p
☐ FLETCH	Gregory Mcdonald	90p
☐ CONFESS, FLETCH	Gregory Mcdonald	90p
☐ THE TRIPOLI DOCUMENTS	Henry Kane	95p
☐ DEADLY HARVEST	Peter Mallory	85p
☐ THE EXECUTION	Oliver Crawford	90p
☐ FROGS AT THE BOTTOM OF THE WELL	Ken Edgar	90p
☐ TIME BOMB	James D. Atwater	90p

ROMANCE

☐ NIGHTINGALE PARK	Moira Lord	90p
☐ ROYAL FLUSH	Margaret Irwin	£1.20
☐ THE BRIDE	Margaret Irwin	£1.20
☐ THE PROUD SERVANT	Margaret Irwin	£1.25
☐ DAUGHTER OF DESTINY	Stephanie Blake	£1.25
☐ FLOWERS OF FIRE	Stephanie Blake	£1.00
☐ BLAZE OF PASSION	Stephanie Blake	£1.20
☐ LOVE'S SCARLET BANNER	Fiona Harrowe	£1.20
☐ MYSTIC ROSE	Patricia Gallagher	£1.20
☐ CAPTIVE BRIDE	Johanna Lindsey	£1.00
☐ A PIRATE'S LOVE	Johanna Lindsey	£1.20
☐ ROSELYNDE	Roberta Gellis	£1.20
☐ ALINOR	Roberta Gellis	£1.20

SCIENCE FICTION

☐ THE OTHER LOG OF PHILEAS FOGG	Philip José Farmer	80p
☐ GRIMM'S WORLD	Vernor Vinge	75p
☐ A TOUCH OF STRANGE	Theodore Sturgeon	85p
☐ THE SILENT INVADERS	Robert Silverberg	80p
☐ THE SEED OF EARTH	Robert Silverberg	80p
☐ CRITICAL THRESHOLD	Brian Stableford	75p
☐ THE FLORIANS	Brian M. Stableford	80p
☐ FURY	Henry Kuttner	80p
☐ HEALER	F. Paul Wilson	80p
☐ CAGE A MAN	F. M. Busby	75p
☐ JOURNEY	Marta Randall	£1.00

HORROR/OCCULT

☐ POE MUST DIE	Marc Olden	£1.00
☐ ISOBEL	Jane Parkhurst	£1.00
☐ THE HOWLING	Gary Brandner	85p
☐ RETURN OF THE HOWLING	Gary Brandner	85p
☐ SPIDERS	Richard Lewis	80p
☐ RETURN OF THE LIVING DEAD	John Russo	80p
☐ DYING LIGHT	Evan Chandler	85p

FILM/TV TIE IN

☐ WUTHERING HEIGHTS	Emily Brontë	80p
☐ AMERICAN GIGOLO	Timothy Harris	80p

(H13B:4-6:79)

NON-FICTION

☐ KILLING TIME	Sandy Fawkes	90p
☐ THE HAMLYN BOOK OF CROSSWORDS 1		60p
☐ THE HAMLYN BOOK OF CROSSWORDS 2		60p
☐ THE HAMLYN FAMILY GAMES BOOK	Gyles Brandreth	75p
☐ STAR-FILE ANNUAL (Ref)	Dafydd Rees	£1.50
☐ THE OSCAR MOVIES FROM A-Z (Ref)	Roy Pickard	£1.25
☐ THE HAMLYN FAMILY MEDICAL DICTIONARY (Ref)		£2.50
☐ LONELY WARRIOR (War)	Victor Houart	85p
☐ BLACK ANGELS (War)	Rupert Butler	£1.00
☐ THE BEST OF DIAL-A-RECIPE	Audrey Ellis	80p
☐ THE SUNDAY TELEGRAPH PATIO GARDENING BOOK	Robert Pearson	80p
☐ THE COMPLETE TRAVELLER	Joan Bakewell	£1.50
☐ RESTORING OLD JUNK	Michèle Brown	75p
☐ WINE MAKING AT HOME	Francis Pinnegar	80p
☐ FAT IS A FEMINIST ISSUE	Susie Orbach	85p
☐ AMAZING MAZES 1	Michael Lye	75p
☐ GUIDE TO THE CHANNEL ISLANDS	Janice Anderson and Edmund Swinglehurst	90p
☐ THE STRESS FACTOR	Donald Norfolk	90p
☐ WOMAN × TWO	Mary Kenny	90p
☐ THE HAMLYN BOOK OF CROSSWORDS 3		60p

KITCHEN LIBRARY

☐ MIXER AND BLENDER COOKBOOK	Myra Street	80p
☐ HOME BAKED BREADS AND CAKES	Mary Norwak	75p
☐ MARGUERITE PATTEN'S FAMILY COOKBOOK		95p
☐ EASY ICING	Marguerite Patten	85p
☐ HOME MADE COUNTRY WINES		40p
☐ COMPREHENSIVE GUIDE TO DEEP FREEZING		40p
☐ COUNTRY FARE	Doreen Fulleylove	80p

All these books are available at your local bookshop or newsagent, or can be ordered direct from the publisher. Just tick the titles you want and fill in the form below.

NAME..

ADDRESS...

....

Write to Hamlyn Paperbacks Cash Sales, PO Box 11, Falmouth, Cornwall TR10 9EN

Please enclose remittance to the value of the cover price plus:

UK: 22p for the first book plus 10p per copy for each additional book ordered to a maximum charge of 92p.

BFPO and EIRE: 22p for the first book plus 10p per copy for the next 6 books, thereafter 4p per book.

OVERSEAS: 30p for the first book and 10p for each additional book.

Whilst every effort is made to keep prices low it is sometimes necessary to increase cover prices and also postage and packing rates at short notice. Hamlyn Paperbacks reserve the right to show new retail prices on covers which may differ from those previously advertised in the text or elsewhere.

(H14:4-6:79)